ANNA SAYBURN LANE

Death On Fleet Street

A 1920s murder mystery

To Marjorie and Dave Swaddling, my grandparents, proud proprietors of Swaddling Toys and Prams in Catford

Foreword

Murder On Fleet Street is the fifth in a series of 1920s murder mystery adventures featuring assistant private investigator Marjorie Swallow.

A word about spelling: I'm a British author, so I use British spelling and grammar.

You can find out more about the books, get free short stories and a prequel novella when you sign up to my Readers Club newsletter on my website, annasayburnlane.com.

Chapter 1

Miss Beatrice Waddon breezed into the room like the figurehead of a ship, her noble brow and wide blue-grey eyes conveying a tremendous air of forward motion.

I jumped up from my desk to greet her. The young woman was the first proper client to have made an appointment at the detective agency since Christmas, and I was keen to see what new adventure her arrival might bring.

'Good morning. I'm Marjorie Swallow, Mrs Jameson's secretary. Please, take a seat. I'll let Mrs Jameson know you're here.'

Miss Waddon shook my hand with a firm grip. 'I appreciate you fitting me in at short notice, Miss Swallow. The matter is rather urgent.'

She wore a smart walking suit of tobacco-brown French serge, with jet beading at the collar and cuffs, and a rather chic black velvet hat. I felt rumpled by comparison, and pulled down my jacket sleeve to cover an ink splodge on the cuff of my blouse.

I showed her to the comfortable leather armchairs we kept for client consultations, gathered around a low table. The detective agency office was a large first-floor room in my employer's town house in Bedford Square. My electric desk lamp was all that illuminated the dreary morning. Outside the tall windows, London plane trees shook their pollarded fists at the flat pewter sky. I switched on the standard lamp in an attempt to disperse the gloom.

It had been a dismal February, and I was glad of the interruption to my administrative work. We hadn't had a good case for a while, so I had been doing my least-favourite Monday morning task: gathering all our receipts and invoices to record our income and expenditure. My desk was strewn with papers, the typewriter pushed aside.

Mrs Jameson was surprisingly firm about regular book-keeping, although I knew she didn't need the money. 'Taxes,' she said darkly, if I questioned the need to record every penny stamp we used. 'Lead us not into taxation, Marjorie.' With the new Labour government in power since the start of the year, business taxes were expected to rise, and she wished to be prepared.

For the past month and a half, I'd attended to the usual duties of a personal secretary: organising Mrs Jameson's social diary, keeping the accounts in order and replying to her voluminous correspondence. Since news of our more colourful cases had spread, I spent much time declining, politely but firmly, to investigate the whereabouts of lost cats or unmask adulterous spouses for the divorce courts. I'd become so impatient for a new case that I would have welcomed the opportunity to chase felines around, although Mrs Jameson said cats were never lost, but simply decided for themselves when to visit the humans who believed they owned them.

Now I ran to fetch Mrs Jameson from the drawing room, where she was reading *The Times* with a despondent air.

'There you are, Marjorie. Has Miss Waddon arrived? Thank

heavens. I am in severe need of distraction. The newspapers never have anything cheerful to report.'

Like me, Mrs Jameson thrived on a knotty investigation and got fretful between cases. Unlike me, she looked as regal as Queen Mary as she entered the office, in a day dress of bottle-green cashmere with a matching turban.

'Good morning, Miss Waddon. Marjorie, please ring for coffee. Now, how may we be of assistance?'

'You were recommended by my former tutor at Girton College, Professor Power,' Miss Waddon said.

Professor Eileen Power, a historian now working at the London School of Economics, was our neighbour in Bloomsbury, and a good friend of Mrs Jameson. I felt a twinge of envy. How marvellous to have attended a Cambridge college and learned such confidence so young.

Miss Waddon picked up her handbag, snapped it open and withdrew a long, thin piece of paper, which she handed to my employer. 'Please tell me what you think of this.'

Mrs Jameson read quickly, her fine grey eyes scanning the paper. She handed it to me. 'Marjorie?'

It was a newspaper cutting, the ink slightly smudged on the soft paper. The headline read: *An unfortunate accident.*

'Fleet Street was today plunged into mourning by the death of the popular newspaper proprietor Lord Ravensbourne, at the age of fifty-one,' I read. *'The first Baron Ravensbourne is said to have suffered an unfortunate accident. His death, we understand, was instantaneous. He is survived by his second wife, Lady Ravensbourne (formerly Miss Annabel Quick), and his four children.'*

I frowned. 'It doesn't say what the accident was.' I raised my eyes to our visitor, puzzled. 'I didn't know Lord Ravensbourne was dead.'

'He's not,' said Miss Waddon, crisply. 'He's my father. And that notice is dated one week from today.'

I checked. Monday, the twenty-fifth of February, 1924. As Miss Waddon said, a week away. A prickle ran up my neck. A death notice, one week early, of a man who was still very much alive.

'Do you think it's a threat to your father?' I asked.

Miss Waddon rolled her eyes. 'Clearly.' She switched her gaze to my employer. 'I want to know who sent it, and ensure no harm comes to him on that day. Is that within your capabilities?'

Mrs Jameson gave her feline smile. 'Oh, I should think so. We are very resourceful, Miss Waddon. Tell me where and when you came by this notice and let us gather the necessary information.'

Chapter 2

Graham the butler, who was a great friend of mine, arrived with coffee and fragrant madeleines made that morning by our excellent cook. We were a small household, but everything ran smoothly under Graham's steady hand. He gave me a conspiratorial nod and placed the cakes on my side of the table with a smile.

I managed to restrain myself from taking one until Mrs Jameson had done so, but our guest merely sipped her drink. Trying not to make crumbs, I opened my notebook and balanced it on my knee.

Miss Waddon gestured to the cutting. 'That thing was left on my desk on Friday, in the office of the periodical I run with my co-editor, Belinda Ponsett,' she said. 'The *Women's Bugle* – you may have heard of it?'

I certainly had. The *Women's Bugle* was the sort of monthly magazine my father wouldn't have in the house. It advocated for women's rights: the right to vote on equal terms with men, the right to equal pay when doing the same work, and – most controversially – the right of access to birth control methods. I was most impressed to meet its editor.

'You do fine work,' said Mrs Jameson. 'I enjoyed your article about the proposed amendment to the Representation of the

People Act. I discussed it with Lady Astor, who admired it very much. She said she was minded to quote from it in the Parliamentary debate next week.'

Miss Waddon flushed pink with pleasure, and it struck me how young she was, despite her poise, to be editing a magazine. Perhaps twenty-three or twenty-four – a couple of years younger than me. Like me, Miss Waddon was too young to vote – unless the proposed amendment was approved next week, which would extend the franchise to all women over the age of twenty-one. It had been a blow after the War, when votes for women turned out to be only votes for property-owning women over thirty.

'And where is the *Women's Bugle* office?' asked Mrs Jameson.

'We have a room in the *Daily Post* building, just off Fleet Street,' she said. 'We use their presses and printers, when they are not in use. And that's what concerns me. This death notice was printed at the *Daily Post*. My father and I both work in the building.'

The *Daily Post* was the flagship title of Ravensbourne Amalgamated Publications, Lord Ravensbourne's group of newspapers and magazines. Miss Waddon's father must have helped her to launch the *Women's Bugle*, I supposed, although I knew the *Post* had opposed votes for women.

Mrs Jameson took up the paper again. 'Explain to me,' she said. 'This column hasn't been printed in the newspaper itself? I assume someone would have noticed before it got that far. It is not worded as a genuine death notice would be, I take it.'

Miss Waddon shook her head. 'It's a galley proof. They're printed after a column of text has been set, so that the sub-editors can check it before it's made up into a page. Hundreds of galley proofs are produced for each edition of the newspaper, and discarded.'

Goodness. Newspapers seemed to require a whole new language. My shorthand was challenged by all the unfamiliar words.

Mrs Jameson frowned. 'And you know this is from the *Post* and not any other newspaper? A rival, for example, wanting to unsettle your father?'

'I do. This is the headline font used by the *Daily* and *Sunday Post* titles. It's unique to the *Post*. Someone – possibly several people – at the *Post* wrote this, made it up and printed it, then left it on my desk.'

Mrs Jameson took a sip of coffee. 'Who would be involved in making a galley proof? How many people are we talking about here?'

Miss Waddon sighed. 'Well, that's the thing. Usually, you'd have a reporter to write it, a sub-editor to check it and write the headline, a linotype man to set the text and a compositor to make it up and print off a proof using a hand press. Which is rather a lot of people to involve.'

'Four people. And would anyone have the skills to do all of that alone?' Mrs Jameson asked.

'I'm not sure. I wouldn't know how to print it,' said Miss Waddon. 'Father might. And I suppose the printers could have written it themselves.' She finally took a madeleine and chewed thoughtfully. I wondered if I could get away with a second one without Mrs Jameson remarking on it. Then I had a thought.

'Why was it just put on your desk?' I asked. 'Why not send it directly to your father, if he's the target?'

She sighed. 'They did. I went to see him as soon as I found mine on Friday. He'd received one, but he threw it away. He said he'd find out whose prank it was and sack them. But he's not taking it seriously as a threat. That's why I'm here.'

She picked up her cup, her mouth set in determination. 'Someone has to look after his interests.'

'And he also received the death notice at the *Daily Post*? Is he often at the offices there?' asked Mrs Jameson.

Miss Waddon smiled fondly. 'You try to keep him away,' she said. 'Father has a town house in Regent's Park, a country estate in Hertfordshire, and a three-room flat at the top of the *Daily Post* building. Where do you think he spends most of his time? The *Post* is his life – the jewel in his crown.'

'I see.' Mrs Jameson thought for a moment. 'So did he receive the notice on his desk in this private residence on Fleet Street?'

Miss Waddon nodded assent. 'The flat is on the sixth floor of the *Post* building. There's a staircase from the room where he works down to the main offices on the fifth floor, connected by a door which is almost always unlocked. He's in and out of his flat all the time. It's where he works and calls people up to see him. But he spends his days rampaging around the building, terrifying the staff.'

He sounded rather alarming. I'd assumed that proprietors left the day-to-day business of running the newspaper to their editors, but apparently that was not Lord Ravensbourne's style.

Mrs Jameson raised her eyebrows. 'He is an exacting employer, then. Does he have many enemies who might wish him ill?'

'Oh, Mrs Jameson. Where do I even start?'

Miss Waddon set down her coffee cup with a shaking hand, and for the first time I realised she was genuinely afraid.

Chapter 3

Lord Ravensbourne's enemies, according to his daughter, included the Communist Party of Great Britain, the National Society of Operative Printers and Assistants, several rival newspaper proprietors, the Labour government, and most of the staff of the *Daily Post*. I scribbled fast, trying to capture all the names in my notebook.

'My father is not an easy man, Mrs Jameson,' said Miss Waddon, with a glint in her eye that made me wonder if she was an easy woman. 'He doesn't suffer fools gladly. Or at all. And he sees his newspapers as political weapons. The *Post* has been running an anti-socialist campaign since well before the election. Father claims the Labour Party is in league with the communists, which is nonsense, of course. But it hasn't made him friends. Rather a lot of the staff are in favour of giving Mr MacDonald a chance. So am I, for that matter.'

Mrs Jameson's nostrils flared, but she said nothing. I knew she had been shocked by the Labour victory, although I couldn't help being excited by the arrival in power of a new party to represent the working man.

'Then there's the print union, NATSOPA. They operate a closed shop on Fleet Street, so printers who don't belong find it difficult to get work, and employers are held to ransom by their pay demands. My father has been scheming to reduce their power, and there's talk of a strike. Father has sworn to sack them all and replace them with non-union men if it goes ahead.

'Most of his rival proprietors are on friendly terms with each other, or pretend to be, at least. But to Father, all is fair in business and war. He doesn't much care about being on friendly terms. Winning is the important thing.'

She paused for breath and took another of the madeleines. I poured more coffee and wondered where Miss Waddon had bought her hat. It was really rather snappy. My parents ran a draper's store, and my father would sometimes let me order fabric at cost, for my mother to make up in the new styles. I decided to buy some black velvet and see if Mum could fashion something similar.

'As the death notice appears to have originated within the building,' said Mrs Jameson, 'perhaps we should concentrate on the *Daily Post* employees to begin with. Is there anyone within the organisation who has a serious motive to harm Lord Ravensbourne?'

'As you say, he is an exacting employer. He works his staff hard, and sometimes that is resented.' Miss Waddon looked scornful. 'He knows his newspapers, Mrs Jameson. He understands what sells. I believe some of the editorial staff would prefer an ignorant proprietor who only visited to dispense bonhomie at Christmas.'

'Please be as specific as you can with your suspicions.' Mrs Jameson was watching her narrowly.

Miss Waddon hesitated. 'I don't really know,' she said. 'I have asked, of course, if anyone knows who was behind it. But I'm his daughter, Mrs Jameson. Even if people did know, they're not likely to tell me.'

Mrs Jameson gave her feline smile. 'Come, Miss Waddon. You do suspect someone. Otherwise, you would have gone to the police, rather than consulting a private detective.'

She waited for an answer, her expression benign. She was good at waiting. Nine times out of ten, whoever she was interrogating would crack and fill the silence with something they did not originally intend to say. However, in Miss Waddon she seemed to have met her match.

'If I knew who had sent it, I would not be consulting anyone.' Miss Waddon's tone was crisp. 'But if you don't think you can help me, please say so.'

While they talked, an idea had been forming in my head. It was daring, it would get me out of the Bedford Square office, it would give me a chance to use the detective skills I'd learned. It would also be rather thrilling.

I waited for the right pause in the conversation to drop it in.

'How about,' I ventured, 'I go undercover at the *Post* as one of the reporters? The staff might talk more freely to me than to the daughter of the proprietor, Miss Waddon. I could find out what they say when you are not around; see if anyone knows about a prank – or something more serious.'

I'd read about the exploits of girl reporters, doing stunts like travelling around the world in eighty days, and rather fancied myself among their dashing crew. I might even turn out to be good at it. Perhaps I could make it into a whole new career.

My aspirations were crushed before I'd even had time to think of a suitably dramatic nom de plume.

'Father doesn't employ female journalists,' said Miss Waddon. 'He says they're too sentimental to write well, and get their facts wrong.'

'But…' I was outraged.

'You don't have any training as a reporter, Marjorie,' Mrs Jameson reminded me tartly. 'Although it's not a bad idea to have someone on the inside. What about secretaries, Miss Waddon? I assume you have female secretarial staff. Could you find an opening for Marjorie there?'

A secretarial post would be rather a busman's holiday, but it would still be undercover work.

Miss Waddon frowned and shot me a dubious look. 'Actually, I probably could. Miss Pringle, Father's current secretary, has given notice to leave to get married. They never last long – a few months working for my father is usually enough to send a woman running up the aisle. He told me to get our usual agency to send some girls for him to view on Wednesday. If you really think Miss Swallow could be of use?'

Mrs Jameson gave me a warning glance and I bit back my protestations.

'Marjorie has been training as a detective with me for eighteen months now,' she said. 'She is very capable and has worked undercover before. And she already possesses the secretarial skills the role requires.'

Miss Waddon nodded decisively. 'All right, then. I can ensure you are one of the girls interviewed, Miss Swallow, and that the alternatives are not… not to his taste.'

I glanced up quickly, noting her brittle tone. I was quite aware of the liberties some men tried to take with their secretaries. I would be sure to have a nice sharp hat-pin in my handbag on Wednesday, and to practise my jiu-jitsu self-defence skills beforehand.

Mrs Jameson's eyes flashed to me with some anxiety. 'Only do this if you wish to, Marjorie,' she said. 'Remember, undercover work can be dangerous. I would not force you into a difficult situation.'

It was nice of her to be concerned, but I'd had enough of filing receipts. 'I'm perfectly capable of looking after myself, Mrs Jameson. I'm happy to act as Lord Ravensbourne's secretary, if it will help the investigation.'

Miss Waddon rose and shook our hands. 'That's settled, then. Thank you, Miss Swallow. I think it would be best if my father doesn't know about this arrangement. He's all too likely to disagree, or even tell everyone who you are.

'Perhaps we could have a rehearsal before the interview, so I can advise you on how to approach him. Come to my flat.' She passed me her card.

Mrs Jameson nodded her approval. 'In my experience, it's best to stick as closely to the truth as possible when working undercover,' she said. 'I shall write an excellent reference, and you may tell Lord Ravensbourne that you have been working as personal secretary for a professional woman who is returning to America.' She glanced out of the window. 'Which is very tempting when the English weather is like this.'

Chapter 4

'Ouch!' I struggled for a moment longer, twisted my hips and attempted to rise, then banged my hand against the floor in surrender. Frankie, Mrs Jameson's chauffeur, clambered off and sat on the rag rug next to me. She rummaged in her overall pockets for her tobacco and rolled a cigarette.

'You haven't been practising, Marge,' she said. 'You should come back to train at Golden Square. It's like stripping down an engine. You can't just learn to do it once and then forget about it. You need to keep in training. Specially in our line of business.'

I didn't bother to point out that I'd never stripped down an engine in my life. Frankie was right, and I knew it. Since Christmas, I'd been out of sorts and had neglected my jiu-jitsu. It was time to shake myself out of my gloom. A few sessions of being thrown on my back should do the trick. As Frankie said, you never knew when you might need to call on your self-defence skills when working for Mrs Jameson.

'You're not still upset about Freddie, are you?' Frankie lit the narrow cylinder of tobacco and puffed at it, smoke filling the neat little room above the mews where Mrs Jameson's Lagonda was garaged. She flicked the match into the fire.

'Ouch,' I said again. I didn't want to talk about it.

I'd broken off with Freddie Gillespie, a pianist in a jazz band with whom I'd been walking out for some time, at Christmas. I still wasn't sure if I'd done the right thing. I was terribly fond of him, and we had fun together. But then he'd gone and asked me to marry him, which had thrown me into a bit of a panic. Although I was twenty-five and most of my old friends from school were settling down, I didn't feel ready for such a step.

Freddie had been jolly decent about it, but he'd stopped calling on Sunday afternoons. 'I'll keep out of your hair for a bit,' was the way he phrased it. I missed him more than I'd expected. I had to admit, I'd rather anticipated a card for Saint Valentine's Day. Nothing had come, from him or anyone else, and I was perversely disappointed.

Frankie sighed, rumpling her cropped hair with her free hand. 'You need to toughen up, Marge. Plenty more fish in the sea, that's what I always say.'

'I'm not fishing.' I waved her smoke away from my face. 'I'm perfectly happy on my own. I don't want a husband.'

'Who says it has to be a husband?' Frankie grinned piratically. 'Come to Caravanserai with me on Saturday night. Plenty of girls there would be happy to cheer you up.'

I blushed. 'Don't be ridiculous.' Frankie made no apology for preferring girls to men, but that didn't mean I was open to such suggestions. One memorable visit to the Caravanserai club in Soho had been quite enough. I looked at the clock over the mantelpiece. 'I should go. I'm meeting Miss Waddon at three o'clock and I need to change.'

Fortunately, Miss Waddon also lived in Bloomsbury. It would take me just ten minutes to walk to her flat in Gordon Square.

I dashed along the side road from the mews to the Bedford

Square house and up to my rooms in the attic. What would be appropriate for a respectable secretary applying for a new job? My wardrobe had expanded since I began working for Mrs Jameson, who paid generous wages, and I liked to try to keep up with the fashion.

I selected a knitted suit in dark red jersey, with a cream crepe-de-chine blouse that tied in a bow at the neck. Smart, but not too racy. I brushed my hair vigorously, until my chin-length bob shone like a chestnut. I wondered if I should dab on a little lipstick but decided against it. My grey wool coat with red trim and dark red cloche hat completed the ensemble.

Graham handed me an umbrella as I buttoned my boots in the hall.

'Shall I hail a taxi-cab, Marjorie? It's raining cats and dogs,' he said.

'Not to worry, Graham. It's only a short walk.'

Chapter 5

By the time I arrived in Gordon Square, I wished I'd let Graham call that taxi. My boots were squelching, and my coat clung damply around me. A young woman I didn't know opened the front door of number forty-one, and eyed me suspiciously.

'Who are you?' she asked. She held the door half-closed, as if about to slam it in my face.

'Let her in, Belinda. It's the woman I told you about,' said Miss Waddon, appearing at her side. Belinda was short, a little plump, and wore her mousy fair hair tied back with a black ribbon. Her grey twill skirt and waistcoat were plainly cut and did nothing to flatter her figure.

I followed them through the narrow hallway and up the stairs. 'We have the first floor,' said Miss Waddon. 'Excuse the mess.'

The chintzy sitting room was covered in papers piled on the sofa, the armchairs, the occasional tables and even on the floor. The old-fashioned decor – tasselled pink lamp-shades, a stiff brocade sofa and insipid floral watercolours around the walls – suggested that the rooms had come furnished, and the two women hadn't the time to spend on redecoration.

'Belinda, this is Miss Swallow, who will be working for me in

Father's office to get to the bottom of the death notice business. Miss Swallow, this is Miss Ponsett. We share the flat, as well as the editorship of the *Bugle*.' Miss Waddon took a pile of old magazines from an armchair. 'Please, sit down.'

They sat opposite me on the sofa. Miss Waddon stared at me with her head to one side, as if I was a poodle she was judging at Crufts Dog Show.

'It's a pity your hair is bobbed,' was her first observation. 'But so many women wear their hair short these days. Never mind. Your suit is smart, but Father won't like the style. Can you tie a belt around the waist? And don't wear boots. Shoes with heels are best. Make sure your ankles show to advantage.'

'My ankles?' I'd thought the idea was to coach me in what to say to Lord Ravensbourne. This critique of my appearance was unexpected, especially coming from someone who advocated for women's rights.

'Yes, he's rather partial to ankles. And wear some lipstick. Just a little; he thinks he dislikes a woman with a made-up face, but if you don't wear any, he'll complain that you're pasty.'

I considered telling them that I wasn't there to win a beauty contest, but held my tongue. Apparently, Lord Ravensbourne's secretarial appointments were exactly that. And if I wanted this job, I'd have to accept it.

'Now, it's best to warn you. My father will shout at you and criticise your work unfairly. He is likely to make personal remarks you may find distasteful. He has… well, tantrums, I suppose. Some people find him frightening.'

I felt it was time to assert myself.

'Miss Waddon, in the course of my duties for Mrs Jameson, I have worked undercover in a nightclub, confronted black-mailers, escaped from gangsters in a Limehouse opium den, spent a night in a French police cell, and prevented a murderer from escaping on an aeroplane,' I said, calmly. 'I can assure you, I am not easily frightened.'

Miss Ponsett surprised me by bursting into giggles. 'I say, have you really? How marvellous. You should join the suffragettes, you know.' She sounded like the schoolgirl she presumably had been until recently.

I returned her smile. 'I've been training with them. I take jiu-jitsu classes in Golden Square. At least, I used to. I need to get into the habit again.'

'Very good, Miss Swallow.' Miss Waddon's reserve had thawed a little. 'I can see you are a person to be reckoned with. So many of my father's secretaries are unequal to the task that I have taken to interviewing them myself first, to weed out those who won't make it past their first meeting.'

She closed the folder. 'The important thing is not to let him see you rattled. Don't smile too much, or he'll think you're laughing at him. Say what you have to say then stop – don't run on. It irritates him. And don't try to argue about politics, for heaven's sake. He can't bear to hear a woman talking about current affairs.'

I gave her a quizzical look. 'Has Lord Ravensbourne read the *Women's Bugle*, Miss Waddon?'

She laughed for the first time, and Miss Ponsett let rip a peal of giggles.

'He read the first issue,' said Miss Waddon. 'He didn't say a word to me about it. But he dictated a letter to the editor, and had his secretary type it up and post it to me. It said the *Bugle* was a load of dangerous codswallop and he would ban his wife and servants from reading it. The letter didn't mention our relation.'

Or that he was paying its bills, I supposed. 'Did you print his letter?'

'Certainly I did. The other newspapers loved it, and all ran stories in their gossip columns. It was excellent publicity. I suspect that's why he wrote it. He's a canny operator.' The mischief around her eyes softened into affection. Miss Waddon was fond of her father, I realised, even if she knew what a monster he could be.

'Tell me more about Lord Ravensbourne,' I said. 'What was he like when you were young, Miss Waddon? If that isn't too personal a question.'

She leaned back and her gaze went to the mantelpiece, where stood a photograph of a young girl on a big horse, a man in a top hat standing beside them. There was no photograph of her mother.

'He was rather marvellous, actually,' she said. 'He always made life exciting. My brother and I spent a lot of time living with our grandparents in Hertfordshire, because Mother was so often unwell. We didn't see him very regularly, and it was quite dull.

'Then Father would arrive in a big party of people, with motor cars and presents. He taught me to ride – not on a pony suitable for a child, but on his own hunter, sitting up before him on his saddle. Mother begged him not to, but I loved it.'

'Your mother is no longer alive?' I asked. I remembered the newspaper cutting mentioning a second wife.

There was no trace of sentiment in Miss Waddon's clear gaze. 'No. She died ten years ago, of tuberculosis. Unfortunately, my father did not act on the doctors' warnings to take her to Switzerland for the mountain air. Father married again, not long afterwards, to a young woman who had been his secretary. Annabel.'

She flushed slightly. 'That caused a bit of a stir, as you can imagine. Although I am on perfectly friendly terms with Annabel.'

'And your brother?' She hadn't mentioned him before. Then I wondered if I should have asked. If Miss Waddon had an older brother, he might be about the same age as my brother, James, would have been. James, who had been killed in action six years ago, right at the end of the War.

But she merely rolled her eyes. 'Theodore. He's a year younger than me. He was a sickly child, and a bit of a mummy's boy. At least he was too young to fight. I suppose that was lucky.'

I nodded, a sudden ache in my throat. Lucky for some. I dropped my gaze to the handbag on my lap and reached inside for my certificates. 'I suppose you should see these,' I said. 'I do actually know how to take shorthand notes and type at eighty words a minute.'

Miss Waddon raised her eyebrows. 'Then you know more than half the journalists working at the *Post*. Most of them still file their copy written out long-hand. The linotype men have to decipher it, which is why there are so many mistakes to correct. And all the articles we get sent at the *Bugle* are hand-written, too. Belinda is the only one of us who can use a typewriter.'

Miss Ponsett leaned forward, eyes gleaming. 'The typewriter will set us free, Miss Swallow. Every modern woman should learn to type. We have to seize the means of production for ourselves.'

I wasn't sure what she meant. The clattering Olivetti machine I used at Bedford Square didn't feel terribly liberating.

Miss Waddon regarded her with a tolerant smile. 'Belinda is very keen on socialism, Miss Swallow. Or may I call you Marjorie? It seems rather ridiculous to be on formal terms, when we're all the same age, doesn't it?'

'Bloomsbury rules,' said Miss Ponsett, with another giggle. 'We're Belinda and Bea. The two bees.'

Busy bees, I thought, looking around the cluttered room.

Beatrice Waddon rose and shook my hand. 'Welcome to the business, Marjorie. I will arrange the interview for nine o'clock on Wednesday. If you are successful – and you will be – you will be expected to start straight away.'

Chapter 6

I stepped down from the omnibus at Ludgate Circus, the leaden dome of Saint Paul's cathedral looming through the gloom, and turned into Fleet Street, trying to avoid the puddles in my strapped shoes.

At half past eight in the morning, the street of newspapers was teeming: dark-suited men in bowler hats with their heads down against the drizzle, labourers in caps and mufflers carrying boxes on their shoulders, trucks with enormous rolls of paper stacked on the back. And everywhere you looked, boys. Boys darting into the traffic, whistling boys standing on the corner with their hands in their pockets, boys in the peaked caps and bright buttons of the Press Association's messenger corps, boys selling morning newspapers and apples and roast chestnuts, and grimy-faced boys with a hungry look, offering to polish your shoes. It was noisy, busy and lifted my heart. If London was a body, Fleet Street was its jugular.

I dodged through the traffic and crossed to the south side of the street. Tall buildings loomed, many with the names of newspapers picked out in the brickwork or on signs hanging over the pavement: the *Yorkshire Evening Post*, the *Bristol Times and Mirror*, the *Dundee Courier*. Most of the regional papers had a London office in Fleet Street.

The *Daily Post* offices were halfway along, the entrance not the grand facade I'd been expecting, but an anonymous double doorway around the corner in Whitefriars Street, which ran from Fleet Street down to the Thames. Despite the confidence I'd pretended to Beatrice and Belinda, I was a little apprehensive to meet the fearsome Lord Ravensbourne. I pulled back my shoulders, practised my professional smile, and stepped inside.

The building opened up into a cavernous entrance hall full of men greeting each other and shaking the rain from their umbrellas. I approached a large middle-aged man behind a desk, who had shiny buttons down his coat and an air of authority.

'Yes, Miss?'

'I'm here for an interview with Lord Ravensbourne. Where should I go?'

He looked me up and down, not without sympathy. 'New secretary, is it? Well, you'd better go up.' He pointed to the lift cage. A uniformed boy reading a newspaper lounged beside it. 'Go to the fifth floor and ask for Miss Pringle.'

I thanked him.

'Good luck,' he called.

The lift boy lowered his newspaper and stared at me frankly. 'Fifth floor?' He whistled. 'You're replacing the Pringle, then? I hope you're ready for His Lordship.' He gave an unpleasant leer.

I felt in my coat pocket for the hat pin and was tempted to test its sharpness on the impudent boy.

I emerged into a long, low-ceilinged room, half-deserted at a quarter to nine. A few weary-looking men in waistcoats and shirt-sleeves sat around a big table, sifting papers and drinking tea. From their air of dishevelment, they might have been there all night.

'Excuse me,' I asked a young man leaning over the table. 'I'm looking for Miss Pringle. I have an interview.'

He looked around and his face split into a grin. 'I know you!' he exclaimed. Oh, dear. Was my cover going to be blown before I'd even met Lord Ravensbourne? 'Miss Swallow, if I remember rightly. You finally made it to Fleet Street, then? Good for you. How's the shorthand coming along?'

I recognised him now. 'Mr Field, isn't it? How nice to see you again. And I'm glad you've made it, too.'

We'd met a year ago at the inquest into a suspicious death, during one of my earliest cases with Mrs Jameson. Jonathan Field had been a journalist on the *Westminster Gazette*, and I'd pretended to be a would-be newspaper reporter, eager to learn the trade.

He beamed. He was young, in his early twenties, with plastered-down fair hair that sprang up from a cowlick at the crown of his head, and an open, friendly face.

'I only started here a month ago, as a junior reporter. It's another world, working for a daily.' Then his expression changed. 'But are you going to be working as secretary to the Big Man? He's a bit of a handful.'

'Well, I haven't been interviewed yet.' I was pleased to have a friend on the newspaper already. I could pump him for gossip, later. 'I need to find a Miss Pringle.'

'That's me.' A pretty, petite brunette with a harassed air bustled into the room from the lift. She unbuttoned a rabbit-fur jacket, hung it on the rack and smoothed down her lilac knit two-piece. 'Are you Miss Swallow, or Miss Weller? There should be two of you.'

A woman I hadn't noticed before rose from a chair beside the window behind me, and kept on rising. 'I'm Miss Weller.' She was tall, almost six foot, and everything about her was long. Big red hands dangled from her brown jacket cuffs, long feet were encased in flat laced-up Oxfords, her long red nose threatened to let fall a drip.

Miss Pringle glanced at her and sighed. 'You can go first, Miss Weller. I expect Lord Ravensbourne is upstairs in his private office. I'll check he's ready, then take you up for the interview.'

She bustled over to a wide desk that sat, sentinel-like, in front of a green-painted door with a brass handle. Miss Pringle dropped her handbag and gloves on the desk next to the typewriter and telephone, opened the door onto a set of stairs and trotted upwards. This, I supposed, must be the entrance to Lord Ravensbourne's apartment.

Jonathan Field mouthed 'good luck' at me, stirring his tea with a pencil he'd removed from behind his ear. Miss Weller subsided into her chair, and I sat next to her.

'Have you come far?' I asked, politely.

'Penge,' she said, with a sigh. 'The trams are murder south of the river. I had to walk half the way.'

Miss Pringle reappeared and looked at us, biting her lip. 'Come along, Miss Weller. Please wait, Miss Swallow. I don't think it'll be long.'

It wasn't. Poor Miss Weller was back down the stairs inside three minutes. She snatched up her umbrella with indignation. 'Didn't even ask to see my qualifications,' she told me. 'I call that downright rude. You're to go up now. And you're welcome to him.'

I stood, adjusted the belt over my jacket and wished I'd used the time to brush my hair and check my lipstick. I straightened my shoulders and stepped smartly through the door and up the stairs to a landing. Miss Pringle was at the top, hovering nervously.

'Quickly,' she said. 'I'm afraid he's in a bit of a temper. I don't know what the agency was thinking.' She gave me a brief worried smile. 'You should be all right. Don't talk until he does. And speak up. He doesn't like it when people mumble.'

She pushed open the door, and I walked through.

Chapter 7

Lord Ravensbourne sat behind an enormous desk and glared. His pale-blue eyes protruded. His pink scalp shone from under thinning strands of grey hair, plastered to his head with pomade. He sported a small toothbrush moustache, a shiny black waistcoat and a tightly knotted bowtie that must have been quite uncomfortable. His shirt-sleeves were rolled to the elbow.

I met his gaze solemnly, hoping my expression conveyed both capability and a pleasant nature.

'Well, Miss. What would you do if it was eight o'clock at night, the presses were running and Downing Street was on the telephone wanting to talk to me?' he asked.

I considered this unexpected situation. Would I really be fielding calls from the prime minister's office? 'I should ask if the call related to anything we might wish to hold the front page for,' I said. 'And then I should ask Your Lordship if you were at liberty to speak to Mr MacDonald.'

He grunted. 'The day I speak to that weasel is the day the country falls. What do you think of votes for women, eh?'

I remembered Beatrice's warning. 'I'm not particularly interested in politics, Lord Ravensbourne. I leave all that to my father.'

He nodded approval. 'Well, then. Why does my daughter have to make such a song and dance about it, eh? Sit down, Miss. What's your name? The Pringle woman told me, but I can't be expected to remember everything. Tell me about yourself.'

I took the low chair in front of his desk, which meant I had to look up at him like a child. Arranging my skirt over my knees, I thought of what Beatrice had told me. Sure enough, he was staring at my ankles, which stuck out in front of me. I pressed my feet together, the black leather shoes as shiny as I could make them.

'I'm Miss Swallow, Your Lordship. I have been working as personal secretary to an American lady, who plans to return to Boston,' I said. 'I have references, if you would like to see them.' I reached for my handbag.

He waved his hand. 'Give them to the Pringle. Worked for a woman, eh? And a Yank. What was she like? Bit of a harridan, I bet.'

I smiled. 'She was exacting. But I enjoy a challenge.'

He barked a laugh. 'The devil you do. Got a young man, hey?'

'No, Lord Ravensbourne.' Not that it was any of his business.

'That's good. Want to get married?'

I had an unwelcome vision of Freddie's face falling from hope to desolation as I turned him down. 'Not particularly. I want to have a career. Earn my own living.'

'Good. Every time I get a secretary broken in, the bally woman goes off to get married. Even the Pringle. What hours are you used to? Hope you're not expecting a cushy little nine to five job.'

'I work whatever hours are required of me, Lord Ravensbourne. My current employer needs me to be flexible,' I said. I didn't mention that my job had included all-night vigils, working undercover in a nightclub and pre-dawn trips to Covent Garden market. It certainly wasn't nine to five.

Miss Pringle put her head around the door. 'How are you getting…' she began. Lord Ravensbourne threw a glass paperweight at her, and she abruptly withdrew. It hit the wall, making a dent in the plaster. I stared at him, open-mouthed. Was that how he treated all his employees? I was about to remonstrate, when I remembered why I was there.

'Bally woman,' he grumbled. 'Never knows when to leave a chap alone.'

'If you're going to play cricket in the office,' I ventured, 'perhaps you should use a softer ball. My head isn't as resilient as that wall.'

He stared at me for a moment, blue eyes bulging. Had I gone too far?

'Ha! Sense of humour. Rare thing in a woman. The last time I had a secretary who made me laugh, I married her. Right, you'll do. Swallow, isn't it? May Swallow.' He grinned at me. 'There's a thought.'

'Marjorie, Lord Ravensbourne. May is my mother's name.'

He scowled. 'I don't give a damn about your mother, d'you hear?' he roared. 'Get out of here. Go and find some work to do.'

Heart hammering, I grabbed my handbag and dodged out of the door before the man could find a missile to lob after me. Miss Pringle was hovering on the landing.

'Are you all right?' we asked each other simultaneously. Then she gave a quavering laugh and steered me down the stairs.

'Let's have a cuppa. This place runs on tea,' she said. 'I hope he said you've got the job?'

I nodded. 'At least, I think so. He told me I'd do.'

'Thank goodness for that.' Her relief was fervent. 'Today's my last day. He told me I'd have to keep coming in until he got a new girl, but I'm getting married on Saturday.'

I congratulated her. She led the way to a dingy kitchenette where a kettle whistled on a single gas ring. Half a dozen chipped cups and saucers sat in murky grey water in the sink.

Miss Pringle climbed onto a chair, reached into a high cabinet and retrieved a packet of tea, two unused cups and a small brown teapot. 'I keep these up here, so I always have a clean one,' she said. 'None of the journalists ever washes up, as you can see. For goodness sake, don't do it for them.'

She scooped cheap tea from the packet into the teapot. 'Never volunteer to make the tea, unless you want to spend the whole day in here,' she said. 'Just make it for Lord Ravensbourne and yourself, and whoever goes up for conference. Pour some milk into a jug to keep on your desk when you arrive, or it'll all be gone by mid-morning. And keep a jar of sugar locked in your drawer.'

We took our tea and sat at her desk outside the green door to Lord Ravensbourne's flat. She opened a big leather-bound journal.

'Here. This is his diary. If anyone wants to go up and see him, check if they have an appointment. If not, call up on the 'phone and check he wants to see them. Unless it's Miss Waddon, his daughter. She can go straight up. There's a key in my desk, if his door is locked.'

I looked at the diary for the day. Noon: Conference (Maltby, Pyke, Beeching, Cooper). One o'clock: Lunch, Savoy Grill.

Three o'clock: Maltby, Pyke, Beeching. Six o'clock: First edition, Maltby. Eight o'clock: Dinner, Regent's Park.

'What time do you usually go home?' I asked Miss Pringle, eyeing Lord Ravensbourne's evening schedule.

She shot me a quizzical look. 'Had enough already? I try to make sure he leaves for dinner, wherever he's due to eat. Then I go home. But it doesn't always work like that. Tonight, he's supposed to be eating at home in Regent's Park with Lady Ravensbourne. He probably won't go until nine at the earliest, and then he'll come back afterwards to check on the late edition. He likes to sleep here during the week.'

She hesitated, glanced around the office at the men with heads bent over their papers, pencils now scribbling furiously. 'Don't go up to his flat after dinner, Miss Swallow, especially if he's got the brandy out. Not on your own.'

Chapter 8

I didn't need to ask why. Not safe in taxis, as the phrase went.

'It's all right if one of the chaps is there,' said Miss Pringle, plucking nervously at a loose thread on her skirt. 'They're a decent bunch, mostly. Ask Charles Maltby or Henry Beeching to go up with you, if you need to talk to him in the evening.'

A heavy-set man with a pleasant smile stopped on his way to the kitchen. He wore a baggy dark suit and a club tie. 'Did I hear my name taken in vain? It's your last day, isn't it, Mary? Who's your new friend?'

'Henry, this is Marjorie Swallow. She's taking over from me today,' she said. 'Miss Swallow, this is Mr Henry Beeching, the chief sub-editor of the *Daily Post*.'

We shook hands. He gave me a kindly look. 'Anything I can do, Miss Swallow, you let me know. Always happy to help.'

'Could you explain what you do?' I asked. 'Chief sub-editor. I'm having trouble understanding what everything means.' I wasn't sure if his title meant he was the main editor below the top editor, or perhaps editor of a sub-section of the newspaper.

He smiled his understanding. 'Newspapers have a language of their own. You'll soon pick it up. Chief means I'm in charge of this rabble,' he waved his arm to indicate the men hunched around the table. 'These are the sub-editors, or subs. Subs take the rubbish that the reporters write and turn it into the King's English, or something approaching it. Then they write the headlines. Then I look at what they've done and rewrite it all properly.' He twinkled at me. 'Every sub feels a burning need to rewrite whatever anyone else has written. That's the main requirement of the job. That, and avoiding widows and orphans.'

After delivering this incomprehensible statement, he checked his watch. 'Is Charles in yet, Mary? I wanted to have a word before conference. Get our ducks in a row.'

'Here he is,' she said. A lean man in his mid-forties, with thinning grey hair and an old-fashioned suit, emerged from the lift with his watch in his hand.

'Am I late?' he asked. 'Has he asked for m-me yet?' He stammered slightly and his nervous air made me think of *Alice in Wonderland*'s White Rabbit.

'Calm down, Charles. No-one's asked for you,' said Mr Beeching. 'I thought we could look at the flat plan. Here. Meet Miss… Swallow, was it? Mary's replacement. Miss Swallow, this is Charles Maltby, editor of the *Daily Post*.'

I had expected the editor of a national newspaper to be imposing, but Charles Maltby looked like he'd jump a foot in the air if you tapped him on the shoulder.

He gave me a quick nod. 'Good luck, M-miss Swallow.' The number of people wishing me luck had become rather alarming.

'Let's go through the early pages,' said Mr Beeching, pulling out a chair at a big desk under the window. 'Any chance of a cuppa, Mary?' She rolled her eyes at me and set off for the kitchen.

Mr Maltby shuffled through his papers as he laid them down

on the table.

'Where's the flat plan? We've got the contact sheet of photographs from the Spring fashion shows in Paris. I thought the women's page could take that, with the society column opposite and Kiddy Korner down page, here.' He scribbled on a large sheet of paper.

'Oh,' I breathed. 'Could I possibly see the photographs from Paris?' I was very keen on fashion.

'If you like,' said Mr Maltby. He handed me a sheet of photographic paper, which was covered with a grid of images of haughty models posing in splendid gowns. The fabrics were smooth and unpatterned, creating a liquid look. Necklines were plain or embellished with a single tassel hanging from a deep V-neck, and waists had disappeared altogether.

'I like that bias-cut evening frock,' I said. 'It would be very elegant in a heavy bronze crepe de chine.'

The men looked up from their deliberations. 'You sound like you know what you're talking about,' said Mr Beeching. 'Careful, or I'll have you writing the captions. Robertson writes the women's page, and to be honest he doesn't have a clue. About clothes, or about women.'

'I'd love to,' I began, but Miss Pringle broke in.

'You're to go up right away,' she said. 'You too, Miss Swallow. His Lordship rang down. He's decided to have conference early. I'd better try to find Mr Pyke and Mr Cooper. Have you seen them yet today?'

'Reggie's in his office,' said Mr Maltby. 'I haven't seen Cooper. He was going out to meet a contact this morning.' He grabbed an armful of papers. 'We'd better go.'

Chapter 9

Up in his office, Lord Ravensbourne had moved from behind his desk and was instead sitting on it. His feet dangled, and I realised he was actually quite short, despite his fearsome air. No wonder he hadn't taken to the lofty Miss Weller.

'Met the new girl, hey?' He seemed to be back in good temper again. 'May Swallow.' He barked his coarse laugh. 'Ha! May not, eh?'

I coloured, but didn't correct him this time. Let him have his little joke.

'I brought the flat plan, Lord Ravensbourne,' said Mr Maltby. 'I thought you'd like to see what we have p-planned for the early pages.'

'Did you? Then you're as much of a fool as you look, Mer-mer-maltby,' said Lord Ravensbourne. The editor flushed, but said nothing about this mocking of his stammer. I supposed he was used to it. 'Put in the usual muck about dresses and debutantes. Don't forget the insurance feature. I want it nice and big. Find someone who's lost a leg or an eye. Something dramatic. Get them to say how bally grateful they are to the *Post*.'

All the newspapers ran insurance schemes. You had to collect coupons, and they would pay out for accidents, illness or death. My mother collected hers from the *Daily Express*, although I wasn't about to mention that.

'Of course, Lord Ravensbourne.' Mr Maltby scribbled on the paper he was holding awkwardly against his arm. We hadn't been asked to sit down.

'Where's Reggie? I want him to write a leader about the women's voting amendment next week. Women outnumbering men. Votes for flappers. Slippery slope. Infants in perambulators demanding the vote, children thinking they're as good as their parents. Hey?'

'He's on his way,' said Mr Beeching, soothingly. 'Mary went down to his office to find him.' He smiled at me. 'Mr Pyke is the chief leader writer, Miss Swallow. And also Lord Ravensbourne's brother-in-law.'

'Brother of my late wife. We're all one big, happy family.' Lord Ravensbourne grinned. 'Aren't we, Reggie?'

A tall man with sleeked-back dark-blond hair slipped into the room. He had a look of Beatrice Waddon about him, but without her air of confidence. I wondered why Miss Waddon had not mentioned that her uncle worked at the *Post*. His thin lips were set in an expression approaching a sneer, although his words were civil enough.

'Good morning, Arthur. Mary said you wanted to see me.'

'Where the devil have you been?'

Mr Pyke made a pantomime of taking out and checking his pocket watch. His charcoal-grey suit was good, but worn at the cuffs and needed pressing. He was a bachelor, I guessed, and didn't have the money for a valet.

'It's ten o'clock. I've had my breakfast, arrived at the office and started writing today's leader.'

'I haven't told you what to write, yet.'

Mr Pyke's jaw tightened, but he said nothing.

'We talked about it yesterday, Lord Ravensbourne,' said Henry Beeching, his tone calm. 'You suggested that Reg should write about the planned industrial action on the trams.'

'Changed my mind. Votes for flappers, slippery slope. Infants in their cradles. Got it?'

Mr Pyke inclined his head.

'Right, then. What are you still here for? Get on with it.'

Mr Pyke left, closing the door with exaggerated care. If this was how Lord Ravensbourne treated his senior staff, not to mention his relatives, I wasn't surprised that some of them fantasised about his early demise. And the man was the brother of Lord Ravensbourne's late wife. I thought of what Beatrice had told me of her mother's death. Did Mr Pyke resent Lord Ravensbourne for not taking his sister to Switzerland, or for marrying his secretary so soon after her death? Perhaps I'd found my first suspect.

'What's the front page lead?' Lord Ravensbourne turned his attention to Charles Maltby.

The editor swallowed. 'It's very early to decide. We've got a couple of candidates. Mr Cooper – he's the chief reporter, M-miss Swallow – is out meeting one of the union leaders about the transport strike. The plan seems to be to co-ordinate action and bring London to a standstill. That could make a splash.'

'No, it couldn't. No-one outside of London cares about London. You lot are always forgetting that. Think of the man on the promenade at Blackpool, Mer-maltby. What does he care about a tram strike in London? Nothing, that's what.' Lord Ravensbourne opened a silver cigar box and took out an enormous cheroot. He lit it and puffed the foul-smelling smoke at us. 'What else?'

'What about the Legge divorce?' asked the editor. 'We've got an awfully good picture of Rose Legge outside the court. She cross-examined her husband, General Legge, in the case he's bringing against her. Rather juicy stuff. He's accused her of having an affair with the b-butler.'

'Muck,' declared Lord Ravensbourne. 'I won't have muck on the front of the *Daily Post*. Put it on page three.' Suddenly he turned his glare on me. 'You. What do your parents talk about over dinner?'

I was temporarily struck dumb. On my regular Sunday visits to Catford, my mother complained about the new vicar, and my father groused about having been passed over for the allotment committee. I didn't suppose that would make the front page of the *Daily Post*. The last time I'd been home, my mother had been lamenting how the cost of everything was going up.

'Prices,' I said. 'Sugar's gone up by a ha'penny a pound. And coal's up more than a shilling a ton. Petrol's getting awfully expensive, too.' Frankie had needed to come back for more money when she last filled the tank of Mrs Jameson's Lagonda.

Lord Ravensbourne stared at me as if I had two heads. 'Girl's a genius,' he declared. 'Cost of living through the roof. Everything's up since the socialists got in. Coal, sugar, petrol… what else? Why's it happened? Who's to blame? Go on, Maltby. Find out. There's your front page. Get out, all of you.'

We made for the door. 'And get a picture of a decent-looking woman to put on it,' he yelled at our backs. 'Don't care who she is. Make sure you can see her ankles.'

We scrambled down the stairs. Mr Beeching laughed and clapped me on the back.

'I say, well done, Miss Swallow. You're in his good books now.'

Charles Maltby was looking glum. 'I should have thought of that,' he said. 'It's all my wife talks about, prices going up. I'd better get onto one of those university chaps, see if they know why.'

Mr Beeching grinned. 'Just call someone from the Conservative Party. They'll tell you it's Ramsay MacDonald's fault, the Big Man will be happy, and we can all go home.'

'You survived, then?' asked Miss Pringle. She was sewing a white silk flower onto a beaded headband, which she shoved into her desk drawer as we emerged into the main office.

'Just about,' I said. 'Now, I need to take a message to Mr Pyke. Where's his office?'

Chapter 10

Reginald Pyke had a room of his own in the corner of the newsroom on the fourth floor. It was tiny, with no windows, so he either had to keep the door open or work by the light of a green-shaded electric lamp. I learned later that the room had been a broom cupboard, assigned to Mr Pyke as one of Lord Ravensbourne's jokes when he insisted that, as chief leader writer, he should have an office to himself.

The door was open, and he leaned back in his chair with his feet up on a grand mahogany desk, far too big for the space. He stared glumly at the ceiling with a cigarette in hand. The sole of one shoe was almost worn through.

I tapped on the door.

'What is it?' He switched his stare to me. 'Who are you?'

'I'm Miss Swallow. I'm replacing Miss Pringle as Lord Ravensbourne's secretary,' I said. 'Could I have a quick word?'

He took his feet off the desk and sat up, then waved a dispirited hand towards a second upright chair, squeezed into the corner. His wet umbrella was hanging over the back of it. I perched on the edge of the seat, trying not to get dripped on.

'I wanted to make sure you knew what His Lordship meant,' I said. 'He was quite cryptic in the meeting. I'd hate for you to write it all and get it typeset and everything, then find out it wasn't what he wanted after all.'

He stared at me. 'He wants me to write a piece opposing universal women's suffrage,' he said. 'Because of the amendment being proposed in the House next week. He didn't send you down here to tell me that, did he?'

I gulped. 'Well, yes. I mean, no, he didn't. But I wanted to explain all that about votes for flappers and babies. Lord Ravensbourne thinks that extending the franchise to women under thirty could be the start of a slippery slope, and that the age limit will come down from twenty-one so that even children can vote.'

'I know what he thinks. I've worked with him for more than a decade. And you've been here for – what – ten minutes? I'm sure you mean well, Miss Swallow. But I know my job. And you should know yours.'

This wasn't going to plan. I wanted to find out whether he was involved at all in the typesetting of the fake article, and if he knew any of the printers. I gestured to the elegant blue ink copperplate handwriting on the paper in front of him, and tried another tack.

'I could type it up for you, if you like? And take it down to the printers for typesetting. It would save you a journey.'

He sighed and ground out his cigarette in a saucer. 'You really are new, aren't you? I'll write it by hand, like I always do. One of the copy boys will collect it and take it down. None of the editorial staff sets foot on the print floor. It's a grubby business, printing. I'm glad to say I've never had to concern myself with the production side of things.'

That answered one question. Reginald Pyke was unlikely to know how to set type or print off a galley proof.

'Right. I'm sorry, Mr Pyke, I must have got hold of the wrong end of the stick. It's my first day, like you said. I was just trying to help.'

He gave a patronising smile. 'Don't mention it, young lady. I'd like a cup of tea, with two sugars. Make sure you don't spill it into the saucer.'

After I'd made and delivered the tea, I ventured down the back stairs in search of the printers in the basement. I pushed through the doors on the floor below ground level, which vibrated slightly. There was a hum in the air, as if something was alive down there, some monster breathing softly, sleeping but ready to awaken at any moment. My nose twitched at a slightly sweet chemical smell – the inky smell of a freshly printed newspaper.

I opened a final door onto a cavernous hall, light streaming down from windows set high towards the ceiling. Perspiration sprang out on my forehead: the room was much warmer than the rest of the building. Another sharp odour hit my nostrils, like a sizzling iron or a hot oven when you open the door to put a cake in. There was a constant clatter as if a troupe of show-girls were tap-dancing out of time, and men shouted to each other over the noise.

Despite the heat, the men all wore big white aprons over three-piece suits as they leaned over long metal tables, their hands moving like lightning as they picked up and set down letters from the trays in front of them. Behind them sat rows of men at machines connected to tubes and pipes that belched steam. The machines resembled a cross between a typewriter and a church organ. Boys dashed about, carrying piles of papers to the men at the machines and collecting long sheets from others working hand presses. Galley proofs, I thought with a thrill. I inched closer to see how they were made.

Standing beside the hand press with a heavy-looking frame of metal type in his hands was a young man in shirtsleeves and a flat cap. He had an angry red scar across half of his face, the skin puckered and shiny, pulling at one corner of his mouth and giving him a lop-sided look. Beneath his cap, I could see his ear was mostly gone.

Poor devil. I'd seen burn scars like that before, on shell-shocked soldiers at the Maudsley Hospital during the War. I remembered how important it had been to look unflinchingly at the men, and how they dreaded visits from horrified wives and sweethearts. Or, even worse, when the visits stopped.

He was arguing with an older man in a suit and apron, who stood with his hands on his hips.

'It won't be for more than half an hour,' said the young man, his voice raised over the sound of machinery. 'We need a meeting to call a strike ballot. NATSOPA should support the tram workers.'

'For God's sake, Bill. Don't provoke them,' said the older man.

'It's not provocation. It's about defending our jobs. We should all go out at the same time. That'd be an end of this threat of bringing in non-unionised labour. You don't want that any more than I do, Mr Quinn, do you?'

NATSOPA. The printers' union, Beatrice had said, which Lord Ravensbourne was plotting to undermine.

'I'm old enough not to go looking for trouble,' said Mr Quinn. 'And so are you, Bill. Lord R won't have it. You call a strike, and he'll have the lot of us sacked and replaced with journeymen.'

Bill shifted his heavy load and set it down on the press. 'If I had my way, he'd be up against a firing squad. They knew what they were doing in Russia.' He made his hand into a gun shape and mimed firing it at Mr Quinn's head. 'Bullet in the brain. Goodbye, Lord Ravensbourne.'

I gasped. Unfortunately, at that moment Bill looked up and saw me hovering.

'Oi! What's she doing in here?' he yelled.

Dozens of heads turned in my direction. None of them looked pleased to see me. Bill strode over, pushing his damaged face towards mine as if daring me to look away.

'This is the print hall. You're lost. Go back the way you came.'

'I only wanted to have a look around.' I tried a winning smile. 'I've just started work today, and I thought I should see how a newspaper was printed. I'm Lord Ravensbourne's new secretary, Miss Swallow. Could you show me what all these machines do?'

This didn't have the desired effect.

'We don't want his spies down here.' Bill rolled up his sleeves. 'Get out of here. Sling your hook, before you cause an industrial dispute.'

'Leave her alone, Bill.' Mr Quinn came to my rescue. 'She's new, that's all.' He smiled at me kindly. 'It's not safe down here for women, my dear. Lots of moving machinery, hot metal and heavy work. You'd better get back upstairs.'

The union man shook his head. 'His bleeding Lordship sent you, didn't he? Snooping around. You shouldn't stand for it, Mr Quinn. The union won't have it, see? Management shouldn't interfere with the print workers.'

'But if Lord Ravensbourne owns the newspaper, surely he can send anyone he likes down here?' I was used to being accused of snooping. It was part of my job description. 'You can't object to your employer wanting to know what happens in his own business.'

'Can't I?' cried Bill. 'I can call the NATSOPA out on strike. And I will, too, if I see you down here again. Unwarranted interference in union business.'

'Bill, for goodness sake. We don't want a row,' said the older man, Mr Quinn. 'Get back to work. I'm sure this young lady didn't mean anything by it. And she's going now, aren't you?' He put a warning hand on my arm.

Bill shook his head again. 'Just you remember, Miss. Times are changing, all over the world. The bosses may think they're in charge now, but that's what the Romanovs thought.'

There was real hatred in his eyes. I backed towards the door. If the death notice had come from the print floor, then the union man seemed to have the venom necessary to generate it.

Chapter 11

I ran back up the stairs and was quite puffed out by the time I reached the fifth floor.

'Where have you been?' hissed Miss Pringle. 'Lord Ravensbourne wanted you.'

'I'm sorry. I got lost,' I lied. 'Shall I go up now?'

'Too late.' She put the cover over her typewriter. 'He's gone out for lunch. Which means we can go, too. Come on, I'll show you the canteen. It's that or the sausage and mash shop on Fleet Street, and you don't want to think about what they put into those sausages.'

We went back down in the lift to the ground floor and pushed through double doors into a big hall, noisy with chatter and scraping of chairs on the floor. At one end, men lined up before a serving hatch. We picked up metal trays and joined the queue. It reminded me of the hospital, snatching meals between long, exhausting shifts.

'I came out of the lift on the wrong floor and ended up in the print hall,' I told Miss Pringle. 'There was a young man with a scarred face. He shouted at me and told me to get out. He was quite rude.'

'Oh, dear,' she said. 'That's Bill Mead, poor chap. He's leader of the printers' union at the *Post*.' She scanned the room. 'Look, there he is, just sitting down at that table by the window. Plotting something, no doubt. Lord Ravensbourne thinks the printers get paid too much, although I think they earn every penny. He says he's going to break the union, one day.'

Mead was talking urgently, half a dozen men shovelling down food as they listened. I saw Mr Quinn carry his tray past and sit by himself at an empty table.

'That man behind him rescued me. He was nice, but he said it was dangerous to be down there with all the machines,' I said.

'George Quinn. He's the head printer. He's been here longer than anyone, I think, long before Lord Ravensbourne bought the *Post*.'

'I'd love to know what they all do,' I said. 'There was a row of big machines with typewriters attached. And lots of people standing over metal tables.'

'They're the compositors. My fiancé is one,' said Miss Pringle, her voice warm. 'Tom. Look, that's him, on the end table.'

I craned my neck to see a handsome dark-haired man raise a hand and give Miss Pringle a cheery wave.

'He told me all about it,' she said. 'First you've got the linotype machines. The operators hit letter keys like on a typewriter, and the machine uses molten metal to make a line of type. Line of type, linotype. See?

'And then the compositors take the galleys – that's a paragraph of lines of type – and make them up into page cases. They add the headlines by hand, and the pictures. They're the ones standing at the tables. The cases are used to make the pages, which fit onto the rollers of the big rotary presses. Then they feed the paper through to print.'

She grinned. 'You'll know it when the presses start rolling. They make a real racket. Shake the whole building.'

'Goodness.' It was all much more complicated than I'd realised. 'How do they learn to do all that?'

She laughed. 'Well, Tom was apprenticed at fourteen and spent four years learning the trade before he got the job here. He's going to learn how to operate the linotype machines, next. Job for life, that is.'

I considered this. 'So, you couldn't do it unless you'd trained as a printer?'

We reached the top of the queue. 'Heavens, no. It's a highly skilled job, Tom says. Now, meet Mrs Johnson, who runs the canteen. Martha, this is Miss Swallow, who's taking over from me.'

A motherly-looking woman in an apron smiled at me from behind a steaming vat. 'Good luck to you, Miss. Now, what'll it be? The shepherd's pie is nice.'

We took our trays and sat down at an empty table. The pie was surprisingly good, savoury and tasty. Cheered, I tucked in with enthusiasm. Jonathan Field, my reporter friend, came to join us, flattening down his cowlick with the palm of his hand.

'How's it going, Miss Swallow? Finding your feet?'

'Just about,' I said. 'I keep getting lost. It's such a huge building. But Miss Pringle here is looking after me.'

'Only for today,' she reminded me darkly. 'You'll be on your own from tomorrow morning. You'll not have time to go wandering around the building then.'

'Of course. How long till the happy day, Miss Pringle?' He gave her a wink. 'Tom Butcher's a very lucky man.'

'And don't you forget it.' The dark-haired young man

stopped by our table with a grin and squeezed Miss Pringle's shoulder. 'All right, Mary? He's letting you go tonight?'

She returned his smile. 'Yes, thank heavens. Miss Swallow here is replacing me.'

Tom gave me a slightly strange look which I couldn't interpret. 'Is she, now? Best of luck, Miss Swallow. I'll call round tonight, Mary, when my shift's over.' He strolled out of the canteen.

'Why don't I show you the newsroom on the fourth floor, Miss Swallow?' offered Mr Field. 'I could introduce you to the reporters. It won't take long. And it might help you tomorrow when Miss Pringle isn't here.'

She sighed. 'Oh, all right then. But make sure you're back in time for the afternoon conference at three o'clock, Miss Swallow. Lord Ravensbourne likes us to take notes.'

Like the sub-editors, the reporters sat around a big wooden table scattered with half-drunk cups of tea, old newspapers, notebooks, sheets of copy paper, pots of pens and pencils, and rather dangerous-looking metal spikes, on which papers were impaled.

'What are those?'

'The spikes? That's where you put stuff when you've finished with it. Say I'd been using Press Association copy to put together a story about a court case, or copy from one of our regional stringers? When I've finished with the copy, I spike it. Then if there are any questions tomorrow – if someone says a name was spelled wrongly or something – I can find it and show them how it was in the original copy. See? Then the papers get collected up and stored, in case of libel complaints.'

Mr Field introduced me to the five news reporters. Only one, a thin-faced man who was introduced as Mr Cooper, the chief reporter, was battering away at a typewriter. The rest were writing stories long-hand, transcribing laboriously from their shorthand notebooks onto sheets of copy paper.

'The Big Man's too mean to buy more than one typewriter for the whole office,' Mr Field said. 'I'm saving up to buy my own. Every reporter should be able to type, really. It's quicker and you get fewer errors from people misreading your handwriting.'

In the corner of the room, across from Reggie Pyke's empty broom cupboard, was a bigger office, its door standing open. A desk with a telephone sat between two windows, which gave onto grey London skies.

'That's Mr Maltby's office. The editor. He'll be in the Cheshire Cheese, or El Vino's,' said Mr Field confidently. 'The journalists mostly go to the pub at lunchtime. They only use the canteen if they don't have time to get out properly. Except me. I'm saving up, and I like free grub.'

I smiled at him. 'Me too.' I might as well ask about the gossip, while we were on our own. 'Did you hear about the death notice that Lord Ravensbourne got sent?'

He whistled. 'Miss Pringle told you, did she? That was a bad day. I've never seen the Big Man so furious. Mr Maltby's supposed to be finding out who did it.' He laughed. 'He called us all in one by one and asked us solemnly if we knew anything about it. Obviously, we all said no, and that's as far as it's got.'

'And do you know?' I asked.

'If you ask me, it's a printers' prank. That's the sort of thing they do – like putting together funny pages for people who are leaving the company, with made-up stories about them as a joke. I suppose it just got out of hand.'

Interesting. I filed the information away in my head. 'What's through there?' I pointed to the door in the far wall, beyond the editor's office.

He chuckled. 'That's the Hive.'

I looked at him blankly.

'The beehive, where the bees work. Miss Beatrice and Miss Belinda, who produce the *Women's Bugle*. It's a magazine. Miss Beatrice is Lord Ravensbourne's daughter, you know.'

'Oh!' I'd almost forgotten about our clients, in the whirl of all the new names and faces around the newspaper offices. 'I've read the *Bugle*. Can I go and have a look?'

He shrugged. 'If you like. I need to get back to work, though. Don't get stung.'

Chapter 12

I tapped on the door and slipped through, intending to bring Beatrice up to date on my discoveries so far. To my surprise, the only inhabitant of the office was a rather extraordinary-looking young man.

He was dressed in a pale grey suit of impeccable cut, with a lavender cravat pierced by a pearl tie-pin and a mauve rosebud in his lapel. His dark-blond hair was side parted and brushed back from a long aquiline nose. He lounged exquisitely on a sofa, lavender silk socks showing at the ankle, eyes closed.

'I say, Bea. You simply have to help me, or it'll all be over. Vicky says she'll throw me over for Bunter Deverell-Grey unless I can come up with some decent clues for next week.' He drawled the words, not bothering to open his eyes.

'I'm not Miss Waddon,' I said. 'I was looking for her myself.'

He opened his eyes and stared at me. 'Howdy do. Are you any good at clues? Only I'm in a fearful hole and I'm far too indolent to dig myself out of it.'

I couldn't help but laugh – he was too ridiculous. 'I'll help if I can,' I said. 'I'm Marjorie Swallow, Lord Ravensbourne's new secretary.'

'Good Lord. I am sorry to hear that,' he said, sitting up. 'Never mind, I expect you'll find someone to marry soon. Been here long?'

'It's my first day.'

He nodded sympathetically. 'How's the old man treating you? Thrown anything yet?'

'Not at me.'

'Good-oh. Luckily, Pater's a terrible shot. Can't hit a barn door from ten yards.'

'Lord Ravensbourne is your father?' I asked. Now I came to think of it, the young man had the same elegant features and wide blue-grey eyes as his sister, although he displayed none of her energy and purpose. I tried to remember what she'd told me about her brother. Sickly. Scared of horses. This young man didn't resemble the mental image I'd constructed of a frail invalid.

"Fraid so. Theodore's the moniker. Theo to family and Dora to my friends, among whom I hope to number you, Marjorie. Now, come and have a look at this.' He flourished a piece of paper. 'Are you brainy? You look too pretty to be clever. But one can never tell these days.'

He was trying to come up with a list of clues for a scavenger hunt around London, he explained. 'It's a bit of a jape. A whole bunch of us – Taffy Morgan, Bunter Deverell-Grey, Pips Stanley and me – turn up in our jalopies with a girlfriend in tow at Piccadilly Circus. Everyone gets a list of clues, then you hare off around London until you've bagged all the swag. We rendezvous back at the Cafe de Paris and the first one there wins a bottle of Bolly.

'But this week it's my turn to write the clues, and my brain simply isn't up to scratch. I was on a bit of a bender last night, d'you see? Can't think of a clue to save my life. And Vicky – that's my girlfriend; she's Lord Northington's daughter – says she'll team up with Bunter next time if I don't come up with the goods. That's why I came to pick Bea's brains. They're in much better shape than mine. You can see my dilemma, hey?'

I'd heard of these scavenger hunts, which were reported with solemn disapproval in newspapers such as the *Daily Post*. They did sound like fun, but I'd never met any of the bright young things who took part before. I remembered seeing photographs of the beautiful Lady Victoria in the *Illustrated London News*. She always looked terribly glamorous, although I'd read that her family, like so many, were having to sell their country estate.

I couldn't resist getting involved. 'Show me what you've got, then.'

'Right-oh.' He handed me the paper. 'Vicky wrote the first one. Can you guess it?'

'Pluck a feather from a royal bird at St James's,' I read. I thought for a moment. Royalty… Buckingham Palace. There was a big map of London mounted on the wall of the office. Buckingham Palace was opposite St James's Park. There were plenty of birds on the park lake. Swans were all owned by the King, which I supposed made them royal. 'Is it a feather from a swan in St James's Park?' I asked.

'Oh, top hole. That's the sort of thing. I need five like that, then I'm done.'

I gazed at the map. My eyes strayed from Buckingham Palace towards the West End, and Covent Garden market. I glanced again at the mauve rose in Theodore Waddon's buttonhole. I'd only seen mauve roses – which I'd thought rather ugly – for sale in the wholesale flower hall at Covent Garden, from a specialist rose dealer.

'What about flowers?' I asked. 'Pick a purple rose from a

nun's garden? Something like that?'

He looked blank. 'A nun's garden? I don't know any nuns, thank heavens.'

'Nuns live in convents. Covent Garden was once Convent Garden,' I explained. 'And now it has the wholesale flower market. You could get a rose from there, like the mauve one in your buttonhole.'

'Oh, rather!' He looked down at his flower. 'It's jolly, isn't it? My man buys them for me. No idea where he gets them from, but you don't see many chaps wearing 'em.' He gestured at the paper. 'Write it down, then. And let's have a few more.'

I was scanning the map for more ideas when Beatrice came back from her lunch break.

'What are you doing here, Theo? Shouldn't you be at work?' She sat at her desk and began to sort through her papers.

Her brother shuddered. 'I really can't bear the place. It's too monstrous, all that dreadful marble and gilding and portraits of ancient coves glowering down at one. I came here to beg for your assistance. I have clues to write. Miss Swallow has been helping me. She's terribly brainy, you know.'

Beatrice shot me a warning glance. 'I'm sure Miss Swallow has better things to do than help with your ridiculous games, Theo.'

He yawned. 'Well, someone's got to help me. Is Uncle Reggie in? He's good with words. I'll go down and have a chat with him.'

And then, Jonathan Field put his head around the door, looking flustered. 'I say, Miss Swallow! Lord Ravensbourne has sent a messenger down to find you. He seems to be in a bit of a paddy. I think you'd better go up.'

Oh, goodness. I'd lost track of time.

'I'll be right there.' I thrust the paper back at Theodore Waddon. 'Good luck with your clues. I'd better dash.'

'Thank you, Marjorie. Remember, terrible shot. You barely need to duck.'

Lord Ravensbourne roared at me for ten minutes solidly, telling me he didn't pay me to go gadding around the building. When I tried to explain that his son had asked me to help him with something, he turned a dangerous-looking purple. He didn't pay me to nursemaid his bally son, either.

Then he told Miss Pringle to go and ask Theodore why he wasn't at the Foreign Office. Even in my shell-shocked state, I was astonished to hear that the lackadaisical young man had a responsible job at the heart of government. I imagined what my father would say if he knew the international relations of the country were in the hands of a dandy with lavender socks.

My bacon was eventually saved by the arrival of Charles Maltby and the senior editorial team for the second conference of the day. Lord Ravensbourne, suitably warmed up by shouting at me, was on fine form for the roasting he delivered to them. The difficulty was not going to be finding someone with a motive to threaten Lord Ravensbourne. It would be harder to find someone without such motivation.

Chapter 13

Somehow, I made it through my first week without being sacked. Saturday dawned sunny after the week's drizzle. I lay in bed, enjoying the sun shining through my curtains and sighing with relief that I didn't have to go to the *Daily Post* and face Lord Ravensbourne today.

However, Beatrice Waddon was coming to Bedford Square to review our progress, and to make plans about how to protect Lord Ravensbourne on Monday. I'd have to get up in a minute.

A tap on the door, and Jenny the maid came in with a tray. 'I brought you some tea,' she said. 'You looked that peaked when you came in last night.'

She placed the tray on my dressing table. It was heavenly to have someone bring me tea, after becoming tea-maker in general to half the *Daily Post* staff.

'Thank you so much, Jenny. Is Mrs Jameson up yet?'

My employer had drawn up lists of suspects for the death notice and cross-questioned me about everything I'd seen or heard after I got home each night.

'She's at breakfast. There's kidneys and mushrooms, but you'll have to be quick,' reported Jenny. 'She's already eaten the fried bread. Cook kept some back for you in the kitchen, though.'

That was enough to propel me out of my warm bed. Mrs Jameson ate heartily when she was thinking. The tea was brewed to a dark tan, just the way I liked it. I gulped it down, hastily pulled on woollen stockings, a brushed cotton blouse and tweed skirt, and clattered down the stairs to the breakfast room.

'Ah, there you are, Marjorie.' Mrs Jameson looked up from the newspaper she was perusing. Since we'd taken on the case, she'd begun reading the *Daily Post* in place of her usual *Times*. 'Who writes these leaders? They seem to have a very muddled way of thinking. This one blames the rise in the price of sugar on the Labour government's recognition of the Soviet Union.'

I loaded my plate with the remaining kidneys and the fried bread that Graham delivered discreetly to my place. 'That's Mr Pyke. But he has to write whatever Lord Ravensbourne tells him.' I pictured him in his broom cupboard, staring gloomily at the ceiling and smoking as he contemplated a blank page. He was still my top suspect for writing the death notice, even if he hadn't printed it himself.

'Then Lord Ravensbourne has a poor understanding of international affairs.' Mrs Jameson set down the newspaper. 'The price of sugar is a result of low stocks in America.'

'I don't think he's terribly interested in international affairs,' I said. 'He just likes to blame the Labour government for everything. And he's very worried about the communists taking over.'

Mrs Jameson emitted a snort. 'There's no need to make up stories. Mr MacDonald will be out of power within a year.'

After breakfast, we gathered in the detective agency office. Beatrice and Belinda, the two bees, buzzed in shortly after ten o'clock.

'But I can't stay long,' said Belinda. 'I am speaking at the League of Nations Society at Conway Hall at eleven.' She was wearing the purple, gold and green sash of the Women's Social and Political Union. 'We plan to rally outside Parliament on Friday for the suffrage amendment vote. I want to ensure the League of Nations people join us.' Her round face was rosy with importance.

'Frankie can drive you there,' said Mrs Jameson. 'It won't take five minutes. Now, Miss Waddon, let us review Marjorie's progress.'

She stood before the large sheets of paper she'd pinned to a cork board on the wall. 'The printer, William Mead, has both the inclination and the means to have produced and sent the death notice. He has access to the machinery, expertise in its use, and from what Marjorie observed, he harbours violent feelings towards your father.'

'He said he'd like to see him put up against a firing squad,' I said, apologetically. 'Like the Bolsheviks did to the Tsar of Russia and his family.'

'There's no actual proof that's what happened to the children,' Belinda said.

'That's beside the point,' snapped Beatrice. 'Mead says that's what should happen to Father. Which means he's contemplating his death, which means he might have written the death notice.'

'Don't blame him just because he's a socialist,' said Belinda. 'He's very well thought of at the Trades Union Congress. He fought in the War, don't forget, and got that horrible burn for his trouble. I've had several interesting conversations with him about workers' councils, like the ones they are setting up in the Soviet Union.

'Why would he mess around with death notices? He wants a strike. He believes we should hit the capitalist system by withdrawing labour. Not by sending people anonymous messages.'

Beatrice frowned. 'I admit, it doesn't sound like him, somehow. Bill Mead is a man of action, not words.'

'I agree, Miss Waddon,' said Mrs Jameson. 'He has means and motive, but the psychology is wrong.'

She turned to the next name on my list. 'Your uncle Reginald Pyke is treated poorly by Lord Ravensbourne, from what Marjorie has observed. Mr Pyke might harbour resentment towards your father for his sister's death and your father's swift remarriage. And, of course, Mr Pyke's weapons are words. Why did you not mention his name before, Miss Waddon?'

She flushed. 'One doesn't like to implicate family.'

Mrs Jameson sighed. 'Miss Waddon, if you had investigated as many crimes as I have, you would know that family is very often at the root of it. Please, tell me more about Mr Pyke.'

Belinda jumped into the silence. 'I always said it was most likely to be him,' she exclaimed. 'Didn't I?' She pressed on, ignoring her friend's irritated glance. 'Tell them about your grandfather and the newspapers, Bea. They need to know.'

Beatrice sighed, got to her feet and walked to the window. 'Very well,' she said, her tone exasperated. Now we were getting somewhere. I leaned forward, pencil poised over my notebook.

Chapter 14

Beatrice turned to face us, chin raised. 'Before my father was ennobled, when he was plain Arthur Waddon, he established a group of weekly periodicals. *Questions and Answers*, *The Ladies' Companion*, that sort of thing. They did well; made money, and he met and married Mother.

'Then he bought the *Post* newspaper group for a knock-down price from her father. My late grandfather Herbert Pyke, who owned the *Post*, had taken on too much debt and applied to Father for help. Instead, he forced a sale. As I believe I mentioned, Father is not sentimental about business. When he sees an advantage, he takes it.' Her gaze was cool, as if challenging us to disapprove.

'Uncle Reggie had expected to take over the titles from his father in due course. Instead, he became Father's employee, which he found distasteful. But as you know, he's still there, so he can't have objected that strongly.'

Mrs Jameson nodded graciously. 'Thank you, Miss Waddon. That is very helpful. Mr Pyke has a clear motive, then. He is forced to keep his dislike of Lord Ravensbourne under wraps. A faked death notice might be psychologically satisfying. A way of attacking your father, without seeming to do so directly.'

Beatrice re-read the notice, which we had photographed and pinned to the wall. 'I can imagine him writing this,' she admitted. 'The sarcastic line about Fleet Street plunged into mourning, when he knows full well half the street would hang out bunting. But the question remains, how would he have put it into print?'

'He might have asked one of the printers to help,' said Belinda.

I shook my head. 'I don't think so. I asked Mr Pyke if I should type his copy or take it down to the print floor. He was very clear about not knowing anything about the production side of the business, and said he had nothing to do with the printers.'

I stared at the list of potential suspects, while Graham unobtrusively entered and served coffee. Today's offerings from Mrs Smithson were small choux pastry buns filled with whipped cream. My mouth watered.

As I reached for one, I was struck by a thought.

'I don't like to get her in trouble,' I said, slowly. 'But Mary Pringle, my predecessor as Lord Ravensbourne's secretary, left to marry a printer. He'd know how to make the galley proof.' They were to marry today, I remembered; Saturday. 'She said he was training to use the linotype machines. I wonder if he might have been behind it. Miss Pringle could have left it on His Lordship's desk, and yours too, Beatrice. I suppose she might even have written it.'

'What motive might this young couple have?' asked Mrs Jameson.

I hesitated. 'Lord Ravensbourne threw a paperweight at her on my first day,' I said. 'She said it wasn't the first time. And... well, she advised me not to be alone with him in the flat in the evenings.' I glanced apologetically at Beatrice, whose face had frozen into blankness.

Mrs Jameson's eyes slid from me to Beatrice and back. 'You think Lord Ravensbourne might have offered Miss Pringle some insult that her fiancé would resent?' she asked.

'It's possible,' I said, reluctantly. 'I don't like to speak ill of your father, Beatrice. But yes, I think that is a possibility.'

More of a probability. On my second day, Lord Ravensbourne had squeezed my knee while we went through his diary, and had tried to persuade me to join him for a glass of brandy before he left for dinner. I'd told him I'd taken the pledge, which had brought on a tirade about socialists and teetotallers, which he seemed to think were one and the same thing.

Beatrice cleared her throat two or three times. 'Perhaps Miss Pringle misinterpreted Father's meaning. I can see how that might annoy her fiancé. And, given that he works for the *Post*, that would provide both motive and means.'

Mrs Jameson added Mary Pringle to the list. 'Do we know her fiancé's name?'

'Tom Butcher,' said Belinda. 'Mary told me she wasn't sure about being Mrs Butcher, but at least it would stop people calling her the Pringle. She hates that.'

Mrs Jameson added Tom Butcher's name. I glanced at the clock and wondered if they were married yet. I felt a little guilty to have brought Miss Pringle into it, especially on her wedding day, but it was important to consider all possibilities. I remembered how she had left at the end of my first day; all but running out of the door with relief, choosing a moment when Lord Ravensbourne was elsewhere and she would not have to say goodbye. Henry Beeching and Charles Maltby had been the ones to wish her well and present her with a bunch of flowers.

'What about the editor, Charles Maltby?' I suggested. 'Lord Ravensbourne is really foul to him, too.' I glanced apologetically at Beatrice, but she was nodding in agreement, seemingly more comfortable with talking about her father's treatment of the editor than that of his secretary.

'One of the reporters said Mr Maltby had been told to find out who did it, but he didn't make much of an effort to do so. His office is next to yours, Beatrice, and he's in and out of Lord Ravensbourne's office quite often. It would be easy for him to leave the galley proofs on your desks.'

'But he's ever so nice,' objected Belinda, taking a second choux bun. 'I can't imagine him doing such a thing.' She bit into it and the cream escaped onto her sash. 'Bother.' She tried to wipe it off with a napkin.

I wasn't so sure. I felt sorry for Mr Maltby, but he seemed to me to have the beaten-down air of a man who would take any opportunity to hit back, if he thought he could do so without being caught. I remembered how cruelly Lord Ravensbourne had mimicked his stammer and could easily imagine Mr Maltby going along with a scheme to frighten him.

'Miss Waddon?' said my employer. 'You know Mr Maltby well, I take it. What are your thoughts?'

She sipped her coffee, weighing her words. 'It's possible,' she admitted. 'He's an old-school journalist. I know he dislikes my father's domination of editorial decisions. I hadn't thought of him before – he's so meek.'

'But the meek may have had enough of turning the other cheek,' said Mrs Jameson, with a sardonic smile. 'Now, let us consider practical matters. Which of these suspects might actually carry out the threat? What implications do our suspicions have for Lord Ravensbourne's safety on Monday?'

It was, of course, only two days before the date on the death notice.

'Charles Maltby is incapable of murder,' said Beatrice, firmly. Mrs Jameson raised her eyebrows. Her philosophy was that anyone was capable of murder if the circumstances demanded it. 'I know nothing about Tom Butcher, Miss Pringle's fiancé. Reginald Pyke…' she hesitated. 'I can hardly be expected to pronounce on my uncle's propensity for murder. William Mead, on the other hand, has an established reputation for violence. I should say he poses the most immediate threat.'

'It might just have been a prank.' I relayed what Jonathan Field had told me. 'He says it's the sort of thing the printers do as a joke.'

Mrs Jameson shook her head. 'There's malice in that notice,' she said firmly. 'Whoever wrote it wasn't joking.'

'I'm sure it wasn't meant to be taken seriously,' said Belinda Ponsett. 'Newspapermen are known for such things, after all.' She glanced at her wristwatch. 'Crikey! I really must dash. I shall be late for the League of Nations.'

Mrs Jameson rang the bell and asked Graham to have Frankie bring the car around.

Once the flurry of Belinda's departure had died down, she turned to Beatrice. 'Now that you are on your own, Miss Waddon, I would like to ask a question. Do you think it is possible that Miss Ponsett was involved?'

Beatrice hesitated long enough that her answer became clear.

'I really hope not,' she said, frankly. 'I hope that Belinda respects my father, and acts according to our friendship. But they are not on good terms. My father has not been welcoming, and Belinda refuses to tone down her political opinions when we dine with the family. That has caused some unpleasant scenes.'

Mrs Jameson nodded. 'I can imagine,' she said. 'You are friends of long-standing?'

'We met at Cambridge, in the university's Suffrage Society. Belinda was studying law. She was a year above me, and very passionate about the cause.' She smiled and arched her eyebrows. 'She is very passionate about all her causes. I liked her enthusiasm. Before we left, I floated the idea with some of the girls about setting up a periodical to promote the cause of women's rights. Belinda was very keen, even after the others dropped away.' She shrugged. 'So here we are. I wanted a place to live away from my family, and rented rooms in Bloomsbury. She needed somewhere to live, so it was natural to suggest she joined me.'

There was something – a slight edge – that made me wonder whether Beatrice regretted yoking herself to her former college friend in both her professional and domestic life.

'Very natural,' agreed Mrs Jameson. 'Now, perhaps it would be as well to discuss how best we can ensure that – whoever sent that death notice – nobody is in a position to see it come true on Monday.'

Chapter 15

Frankie drove me to Fleet Street before eight o'clock on Monday morning, smart in her chauffeur's uniform and peaked cap. I took her up to the fifth floor, earning some queer looks from the lift boy, then let us into Lord Ravensbourne's flat on the floor above, using the key that Miss Pringle had given me when she left.

Together, we hunted for hazards. Frankie checked the electric lamps, telephone and listening-in radiogram for loose wires or sparks. I looked for heavy weights balanced above the door lintels ready to crush an unwary skull, or sharp objects protruding from Lord Ravensbourne's desk drawers or chair. We found nothing.

A brandy decanter sat on the sideboard next to a box of Lord Ravensbourne's favourite cheroots. I'd brought replacements for these from a specialist tobacconist in Jermyn Street, after Mrs Jameson had remarked – half in jest – that exploding cigars were a favoured device of assassins in adventure films.

'Better check the booze,' Frankie said with a grin, dipping her finger into the brandy decanter and licking it. 'Tastes fine to me. Do you think I should try a bit more, though?'

'Leave it.' I swapped the decanter for an identical one, filled with his usual brand. I even replaced the toiletries in Lord

Ravensbourne's bathroom with fresh ones bought from Taylor of Old Bond Street. I'd read a detective novel where the victim was poisoned by his shaving soap.

I was glad to have Frankie with me, especially when we ventured into Lord Ravensbourne's bedroom. The room carried the fusty smell of sleep, and it felt unpleasantly intimate to strip back his blankets and re-fold his silk pyjamas. We found nothing of note, except for a set of photographs of young women in his bedside cabinet, of the type described by the popular press as 'saucy'. In truth, there was nothing cheerful about their grim display.

'Dirty old sod,' Frankie snorted, flicking through them. 'Blimey, look at that one. You wouldn't think that was possible, would you?'

'Put them back, Frankie.' I shivered. 'You don't have to work with him.'

'This one doesn't look very happy about it.'

I glanced at the picture in her hand and gasped. 'Oh, no. That's awful.'

The girl in the picture stared defiantly at the camera, tears on her cheeks. She had her arms crossed over her torn blouse, which had been ripped half off her body. It was Miss Pringle.

Frankie shot me a quick glance. 'You know that woman?'

'My predecessor.' I took the photograph and slipped it into my handbag. I couldn't bear the thought of him gloating over it. Did Tom Butcher know about this? I put the rest back in the cabinet.

'He hasn't tried anything with you, has he?' Frankie's hands balled into fists.

I shrugged. 'Nothing I can't handle. Hopefully I'll be finished here before anything worse happens.'

I closed the cabinet and glanced at the alarm clock. 'We'd better go. It's half past eight already and we've checked everywhere. You should get out of here before he arrives.'

We descended to the fifth floor and Frankie left me to uncover my typewriter and prepare for the day ahead. I went to the office kitchen and boiled the kettle to make a fresh pot of tea. I had brought tea-leaves, milk and sugar from our kitchen at Bedford Square, and locked them in my desk drawer so they could not be tampered with.

Lord Ravensbourne arrived on the dot of nine, in the company of his daughter. As we'd agreed, Beatrice had stayed at her father's town house in Regent's Park on Sunday night and accompanied him to Fleet Street in the chauffeur-driven Rolls Royce.

His Lordship was in high spirits. 'Well, we survived the drive, hey, Beatrice? No blighter managed to crash an omnibus into the Roller.' He grinned at me, showing all his teeth. 'My daughter's superstitious, Miss Swallow. Thinks I'm due to meet my maker today. She's been treating me like an invalid all morning.'

Beatrice gave me a long-suffering glance. 'I'm only taking sensible precautions, Father. Miss Swallow, I leave him to you.'

She swept off to the *Women's Bugle* office, and I offered my employer his tea. 'Freshly poisoned, eh?' He guffawed. 'Let's see you taste it first, Miss Swallow.'

As requested, I sipped the tea, then passed him the cup and saucer. 'No noxious substances, My Lord.'

Was it possible that Lord Ravensbourne was actually nervous? Perhaps the bluster was his way of hiding it. I supposed it must give a person a jolt, to see their own death announced in black and white.

'Good. I'll be up in my office going through the opposition. Don't let any Bolshevik assassins in, will you?' He disappeared up the stairs with a bundle of newspapers. He always read the opposition, as he called his rival publications, before summoning Charles Maltby to demand to know why the *Post* hadn't got this or that story featured in the *Daily Mirror*.

Mr Maltby and Mr Beeching arrived together, before the general rush that heralded the sub-editors and reporters.

'Is the Big Man in?' asked Mr Beeching, hanging up his wet mackintosh and trilby hat. 'What's his mood?'

I reassured them that he seemed quite cheerful. Just then the green door opened, and Lord Ravensbourne emerged, brandishing a copy of the *Sunday Mirror*, his face puce.

'Why hasn't the *Sunday Post* got anything about this woman throwing herself and her children off Westminster Cathedral tower?' he demanded. The *Mirror* had a photograph of the distinctive red-and-white brick bell-tower of the Catholic cathedral, although thankfully not of the woman and her children who had been killed in the fall.

Henry Beeching took the paper from him and scanned it. 'Eye-witness testimony… sandwich wrappers left by the railings… Thud, thud, thud. That's good, that is. Charles, who was covering the news desk on Saturday? We should have picked that up.'

'N-nicolas Cooper,' said Charles Maltby, a little too eagerly. 'You're right, we should have had it. I'll speak to him.'

'Sack him,' said Lord Ravensbourne. He switched his glare to me. 'My tea's cold.' He disappeared back up the stairs to his lair.

The two men looked at each other ruefully. 'So much for

cheerful,' said Mr Beeching. 'Make us a cup while you're at it, Miss Swallow.'

'It's today, isn't it?' said Mr Maltby. He scratched his wrist, where a patch of red flaky skin had been growing since the previous week. 'The death n-notice. I thought he'd be difficult today. I've been dreading it.'

'You never found the culprit?' asked Mr Beeching, casually.

Mr Maltby shook his head. 'I'd hoped he'd forgotten about it.'

'Will you really sack Cooper? He's not a bad reporter. Ambitious.'

Mr Maltby gave a thin smile. 'Of course not. I'll tell him to keep his head down. We've had an invitation to join the Ministry of Trade on a junket to Italy next week, to see what that Mussolini chap is doing with the factories. I'll send him on that. By the time he's back, the Big Man will have moved on.'

Chapter 16

By mid-morning, Lord Ravensbourne had shouted at most of his senior editorial staff, summoned George Quinn from the print floor to order him to sack William Mead and any other officials of the NATSOPA union, and telephoned Liberal Party headquarters to demand that Mr Asquith explain why his party was propping up the socialists.

He topped it all by stomping into the *Bugle* offices to tell his daughter that her periodical was losing too much money, and he would give her twelve weeks to bring it into profit. Beatrice received this demand with equanimity, perhaps hoping like Mr Maltby that Lord Ravensbourne would have moved on to other crusades in three months' time. Belinda Ponsett, however, gasped and went white. Unwisely, she began to argue.

'You can't pull the rug from under us now,' she said. 'It's too important. The vote for the franchise amendment on Friday… the interview I have scheduled with Mrs Bondfield… she's parliamentary secretary to the Minister for Labour, you know, highly influential…'

Lord Ravensbourne turned the force of his fury on her. 'Shut up, you unnatural woman,' he roared. 'Don't think I can't see what you're up to with my daughter. Corrupting her, filling her head with all this nonsense about women's rights. I want you out of this office and out of that flat I pay for. Find yourself a husband to support you, or go back to your own people. I won't have you living off my daughter.'

'Father, do calm down,' said Beatrice, but there was a bright spot of colour in each cheek and her eyes were glittering. 'I'll put together a new business plan.' She glanced at her friend, who was on the verge of tears. 'Belinda's upset. She works very hard on the *Bugle*. We will make it pay, I promise.'

I hovered by the door. I'd been dogging Lord Ravensbourne's every move, ensuring that nobody was alone with him in the office. I could see it was starting to irritate him and was quite tempted to leave him for any assassin to do their worst while I had a nice cup of coffee in the Lyons across the street.

He threw a look of contempt at Belinda. 'You've got six weeks,' he told her. 'That should be long enough to find yourself somewhere to live.' He leered at her. 'Although I can't see you finding a husband. Who in their right mind would have you?'

He stomped off. I heard Belinda break into a wail, and hesitated.

'Go with him,' urged Beatrice. She looked furious, although I wasn't entirely sure who her anger was aimed at. I shut the door quickly and scuttled after Lord Ravensbourne, checking the office clock. The editorial conference would start in His Lordship's flat in ten minutes. I groaned. If this morning had been any guide, it would be a bloody affair.

And so it proved. Charles Maltby thought he'd covered himself by putting Jonathan Field onto the cathedral tower death story. The reporter had spoken to the woman's poor husband and got hold of the note she'd left, which seemed pretty good going. But Lord Ravensbourne shouted at Mr Maltby instead for neglecting to cover in sufficient detail the drug charges brought against 'Brilliant' Chang, a Chinese man accused of supplying cocaine to a young society beauty.

'I want every word of the court case, verbatim,' said Lord Ravensbourne. 'That Chinaman has been corrupting our young women for years. About time the police got something on him. Reggie, I want a leader on the dope menace. Bring in the Freda Kempton case, and that American flapper who died last year. The ambassador's niece.'

'Daisy Caldwell?' Mr Pyke asked. 'She didn't die of cocaine.'

Which I knew only too well, as Mrs Jameson and I had investigated the case. I had also discovered that mere prejudice fuelled some charges of drug-dealing made against foreigners. But I knew better than to add my tuppence ha'penny.

Lord Ravensbourne slammed his fist on the table. 'Do you have to challenge every single thing I say? Where's the respect? Good God, man.'

There was an awkward silence.

'Of course, Lord Ravensbourne,' said Henry Beeching. 'He'll get onto it right away, won't you, Reg?'

Reginald Pyke dragged himself from his chair and slouched out of Lord Ravensbourne's room. Before the door closed, I saw him crack his knuckles and throw His Lordship a look of absolute loathing.

The meeting ground to its conclusion. Finally, having demoralised everyone except himself, Lord Ravensbourne pulled out his watch.

'One o'clock. I'm meeting Winston at the Savoy Grill. Get out of here, all of you.'

Much as I would have liked to be a fly on the wall for the discussion, I could hardly accompany Lord Ravensbourne to lunch with the rebellious Winston Churchill, who had recently resigned from the Liberal Party in protest at their support of the Labour government. But as the editorial staff departed, Beatrice arrived at the flat, cocooned in a chocolate-brown fur and carrying a crocodile handbag that matched her T-bar pumps.

'Ready, Father? I spoke to Mr Churchill's wife this morning. Clemmie said they would be delighted if I joined you both for luncheon. She's going to come too. I've ordered the Rolls Royce around. Shall we go down?'

They departed, using the lift that went directly from the flat to the street. I heaved a sigh of relief and slumped into a chair. How should I spend the time? I could go to check on Belinda, I supposed, or find Jonathan Field in the canteen to get the latest gossip from the news room.

But I was seized with a desire to get out of the febrile *Daily Post* building and breathe some relatively fresh air. I waited a few minutes, then summoned the lift again and descended to street level.

Chapter 17

The private lift gave onto a small lobby on the ground floor, with a door to the street. I examined it: a bolt (not currently shot) and a lock that opened freely from the inside.

I stepped outside and shut the door, hearing the lock click home behind me. I pulled the door knob: it didn't budge. No-one could enter without the key, unless of course they were handy at picking locks. I wondered if Lord Ravensbourne remembered to bolt it overnight, and suspected he did not.

I was in a narrow alleyway, one of hundreds that squeezed their way around the city, burrowing between old buildings or skirting around courts, barely wide enough for two people to walk abreast. A boy rushed past me, holding a slice of steaming hot pie.

I followed him cautiously around the corner. The alley led to busy Whitefriars Street, which went up to join the flood of traffic in Fleet Street. I stopped at the corner to look for the sign: Hanging Sword Alley. An ominous name for an ominous day.

I retraced my steps, back past the anonymous door that led to Lord Ravensbourne's private apartment. Hanging Sword Alley twisted between and even underneath enormous brick factories, from where I could hear the clatter of linotype machines and the shout of print workers drifting out of the high windows. Even at midday, little light made it into the narrow passage. The smell – a powerful mixture of London fog, printing ink and the tang of hot metal – caught in my throat.

Eventually the alley opened into a small square with a few soot-bedraggled trees, surrounded by dingy red-brick houses that might have been quite respectable at one time, but now slumped in defeat against the factory buildings. All the same, it was a relief to see the sky. A blackened street sign declared the place as Salisbury Square.

I wasn't the only worker taking a break from the *Post*. Several of the sub-editors and reporters were making their way through the square, their faces shiny and voices loud, presumably having fortified themselves in one of the public houses. And in the corner, leaning against a tree that seemed barely able to support its own weight, was Bill Mead, the printer. He was smoking a cigarette and – somewhat to my surprise – talking to Belinda Ponsett. They seemed an incongruous pair. Then I remembered that Belinda knew him through the Trades Union Congress.

I drew closer, hoping to hear what they were talking about, secreting myself in a doorway behind some big wooden crates.

'He's all talk,' said Mead, his voice contemptuous. 'Quinn knows better than to try to move against me. It wouldn't just be the *Post*. The whole of Fleet Street would shut down. Your problem is, you've put yourself in the hands of the toffs. You've got no solidarity, no leverage.'

'Beatrice isn't a toff,' said Belinda, her voice sharper than it had been earlier. 'She's a socialist.'

He laughed, a croak that turned into a cough, and spat on

the ground. 'She's her father's daughter. She's playing at being a rebel, but it won't last. And if you're in her way, you won't last either.'

'You're wrong,' said Belinda, but her tone was uncertain. 'She won't let Lord Ravensbourne throw me out.'

Mead croaked his laugh again. 'I wouldn't put money on it. Better get inside, hadn't you? They'll be back from lunch soon. Lunch at the Savoy, in the Rolls Royce. Didn't invite you, did she?'

Belinda Ponsett trudged across the square and passed uncomfortably close to my hiding place. But she was too sunk in gloom to notice anything outside of her own misery. I waited until she'd gone, then straightened up. Bill Mead was lighting another cigarette, coughing as he puffed at the smoke. I strolled over.

'Are you all right? Can I offer you a throat lozenge?'

He looked up, eyes narrowing in suspicion. 'What do you want?'

I smiled. 'You looked like you were choking, that's all. Mr Mead, isn't it? I'm sorry we got off on the wrong foot last week. It was my first day. I'm Marjorie Swallow.'

He spat again. 'Ravensbourne's secretary.'

'That's right. And you're the leader of the print workers' union, aren't you? Lord Ravensbourne was talking about you this morning,' I said. I smiled again and made to walk on.

'Wait!'

I paused.

'What d'you mean? Talking about me how?'

I turned with feigned surprise. 'He told Mr Quinn that he's to sack you, and anyone else who's an official of the union. Didn't Mr Quinn say?'

He flushed until all of his face matched the dark red scar that ran across it. 'The devil he did.'

'I suppose you see Lord Ravensbourne as your enemy,' I continued. 'But if you didn't keep threatening to strike, he would barely notice you. I've discovered that he likes a powerful enemy. It's best to make him think you have no power, then he mostly leaves you alone.'

He stood up and wheezed out a bitter laugh. 'You have, have you? I don't suppose you've worked in a mine, Miss Swallow? Or fought in a trench? You'd know all about powerful enemies if you had. And the need for solidarity to confront them.'

I looked kindly at him. 'I've worked in a hospital, Mr Mead, with men who fought in the trenches. Including some that had scars like yours. I've changed their dressings and given them morphine and sat with them when they woke up screaming in the night. I know what some men have suffered, all right.'

My thoughts went involuntarily to Freddie, who had been a patient at the Maudsley Hospital when I first met him. His neurasthenia had improved in recent years, but he still suffered relapses at times. I wondered how he was getting on.

Mead paused, took a drag of his cigarette and nodded. 'Fair enough,' he said.

'Shall we walk back together?' I wanted to ensure Bill Mead was not waiting in Hanging Sword Alley for Lord Ravensbourne's return from the Savoy.

We parted in the main lobby on Whitefriars Street, and I was relieved to see him descend to the print floor in the company of several compositors. I took the lift back to my position outside Lord Ravensbourne's office. Ten minutes later, the lift door opened again, and Beatrice arrived, alone.

'Is he upstairs?' she gasped, her face pink with emotion.

Chapter 18

She threw her fur coat on my desk and raced up to his office, reappearing seconds later.

'He's not there. Whatever shall we do?'

'Tell me what's happened, Beatrice. Where did Lord Ravensbourne go?'

'I don't know. He got out of the car, then he was gone.'

She clutched at the desk, and I pulled out a chair for her. She sat down abruptly.

'We had a good lunch with the Churchills, I thought. Winston is to stand in the Abbey by-election as an independent and was full of plans. Father was a bit quiet in the car coming back.

'Then just as we arrived in Whitefriars Street, we saw a group of men brawling outside the entrance. The *Post* doorman rushed out when he saw the car, opened the door and told us to stick close behind while he got us into the building. I did as he said, but when I got inside and turned to look for Father, he'd gone.'

She jumped up again. 'I supposed he must have gone around the back way to his private lift. Only he hasn't, and now I don't know where he is.'

'Who were the men fighting?' I asked. 'Were they from the

Post?'

'Just boys, I think. Although… one of them had a printer's apron on. I don't know if he was one of ours. He could have been from anywhere on Fleet Street. It all happened quite quickly.'

'Call George Quinn,' I said. 'Get him to check where Bill Mead is. He was going down to the print floor when I last saw him, but he might have left again.' I pulled on my hat and coat. 'Wait here in case your father comes back. I'm going to check Hanging Sword Alley.'

I went back down in Lord Ravensbourne's private lift. The alley was deserted, except for a hungry-looking cat which stretched its lean belly along the ground, purring like a machine when it saw me. I ran along the alleyway towards Salisbury Square. A pair of street urchins were the only inhabitants this time, looking as grubby and hungry as the cat.

'You haven't seen a man pass here, have you?' They turned solemn eyes on me and said nothing. I fumbled in my pocket for a sixpence. 'A short man with a dark suit, a fat tummy and a little moustache?' I asked.

The girl grinned and pointed to the far side of the square. 'Down that way,' she said, reaching out her hand for the shiny silver coin. 'Bridey's.'

St Bride's Passage. Another narrow, short alley brought me to a courtyard bounded by a brick wall. I trotted down steps, then up again, and I found myself in a passage beside the St Bride Institute, which advertised apprentice reading rooms, public baths and a swimming pool. No sign of Lord Ravensbourne.

I stopped to catch my breath. Had he been kidnapped and

bundled into the back of a tradesman's van? I looked up at the respectable facade of the Institute. Had a mob of apprentices taken him off to be drowned in the swimming pool?

Above me loomed the tiered spire of St Bride's Church, its white stone gleaming through the darkening afternoon sky. For want of any better ideas, I ascended the stairs to the churchyard and walked quickly around to the west door. 'The journalists' church,' read a proud sign outside.

I stepped in. The interior was elegant, the floor black and white marble in a geometric pattern. The high tunnel-vaulted ceiling soared above. Mellow wooden choir stalls lined the sides of the church, leading to a simple altarpiece. The place radiated calm.

A man stood before the altar, hat clutched in one hand. I recognised his silhouette, and my shoulders dropped with relief. I walked down the south aisle, trying to keep my steps silent, until I drew level with him.

Lord Ravensbourne was glaring at the painting of the crucifixion that hung over the altar, his jaw clenched. To my surprise, I saw his eyelids were puffy and gleamed with moisture. Had he been crying? He took out a big white handkerchief and blew his nose, then turned to me, his blue eyes fierce.

'What do you want?'

'To see that you had not come to any harm,' I said.

He stuffed the handkerchief in his pocket. 'Can't a man get a second of peace? I'm fed up with being nannied.'

'I'm sorry, Lord Ravensbourne. Your daughter is very worried about you.'

'Ha!' He let out a disbelieving snort. 'You believe that, do you?' He turned his bulging eyes on me again.

'Of course she...' I began.

'Well, you're wrong. Beatrice can't wait to step into my shoes,' he said, wiping his face. 'She'll be pleased as punch when I finally kick the bucket.'

'Oh, I'm sure that's not the case...'

'And my wife.' He threw out the words furiously. 'You'd think she'd be grateful. Show some respect. Not a bit of it. I know how much Annabel longs to be my widow.' He glared at me, as if daring me to contradict him. 'But I have no intention of dying to please them, Miss Swallow.'

I said nothing. I might have felt sorry for him, if I didn't have the image of poor Mary Pringle's photograph etched on my mind. Goodness knows what his wife had put up with.

'What do you think of that fellow Churchill, eh?'

I was taken aback by the sudden change of subject. 'Well, he's very popular,' I hedged. 'My parents think he's wonderful.'

He jutted his lower lip like an angry child. 'Exactly. Everyone respects him. Murders the natives with impunity in India, causes untold deaths with his mad venture in the Dardanelles, yells at his staff, gets drunk every night over dinner... and everyone thinks he's a great man. Explain that, can you?'

'I'm not sure I can.' As far as my parents were concerned, Winston Churchill could do no wrong, despite the disasters of his war policy.

'I'm as good as he is, Miss Swallow. But Beatrice and Annabel are embarrassed by me. They think I'm common as muck, although they like spending my money, all right.' He barked a mirthless laugh. 'As for my son... well, you've met him. Idle and useless.

'And the staff might be scared of me, but they don't respect me. They play stupid pranks, contradict me, make jokes behind my back.'

He held me in his gaze for a long minute. 'You're not scared of me, are you, Miss Swallow?'

I was rather surprised to discover that I wasn't. He made me think of a small child, a toddler throwing a tantrum when he didn't get what he wanted.

'No, My Lord.'

He snorted again. 'You should be. Now, what are you doing hanging around in churches? I don't pay you to pray. Walk back to the office with me.' He put on his hat and stomped out into the air.

Chapter 19

I felt as if the day would never end. I was kept busy all afternoon attending Lord Ravensbourne's meetings, typing up letters and reports for him, making endless rounds of tea and trying to soothe wounded feelings, whether of his staff, his daughter or His Lordship.

Beatrice had been furious with her father for slipping away, refusing to accept his explanation that he'd wanted a bit of peace and quiet after all her fussing. In turn, Lord Ravensbourne had refused to go back to Regent's Park for dinner with her that evening, and declared he would eat in his flat. I'd had to collect him a meal on a tray from Mrs Johnson in the canteen, shouting my order over the rumbling of the presses. I chose Irish stew for both of us, reasoning that a murderer would be unwilling to poison the entire workforce with one dish.

Lord Ravensbourne dictated endless letters after dinner. 'If you don't have a home to go to, you might as well make yourself useful.' Then he called for the early editions of every other Fleet Street newspaper. Thankfully, he seemed too absorbed in his work to make any attempts on my person.

At a quarter to midnight, Charles Maltby delivered a damp, freshly printed copy of the final edition of the next morning's

Daily Post, the ink smelling heady and sharp from the press.

'Is the Big M-man still up?' he asked. 'I'd better take it to him.' He gave me a tired smile. 'It's been quite a day, Miss Swallow. Nearly over, hey?'

Mr Maltby took the paper upstairs, and I heard Lord Ravensbourne yell at him about the front page headline, even though I knew he'd approved it himself. He would go through it, line by line, and write notes for me to type up and circulate the next morning.

The editor scurried back down the stairs and pulled on his raincoat. 'God, I need a drink,' he muttered, heading for the lift. I checked the clock: ten to midnight. Not long to go, now.

'Miss Swallow!' Beatrice's voice startled me awake. I'd drifted off for a moment. 'I thought I'd better come back and check on Father, as he won't go home tonight. Is he still working?'

'I believe so.' We went up the stairs together and tapped on the door. Silence for a moment, and my heart jumped into my mouth. What had happened while I dozed?

Then came his voice, irascible as ever. 'Who is it?'

We pushed through the door. Lord Ravensbourne sat at his big mahogany desk, which was covered in newspaper pages and the scraps of paper on which he wrote his notes. He was wreathed in pungent smoke, a fat cheroot balanced on a crystal ashtray.

He capped his fountain pen and took a sip of brandy. 'What do you want?'

'You should go to bed, Father. It's midnight,' said his daughter, dropping a kiss on the top of his head.

He looked up at the clock, a triumphant grin on his face. 'Midnight, hey! Satisfied, Bea? It was all a lot of nonsense.'

She smiled. 'I'm glad.' She crossed to the window and opened it. 'Listen.'

Above the clanking of the press, I heard the bells: twelve clear chimes from the journalists' church, and beyond them the fainter clamour of the hundreds of bells in the hundreds of churches across the city. I felt a surge of relief. February the 25th was over, and Lord Ravensbourne remained very much alive.

'I'll be off home, then,' I said, smothering a yawn. 'Goodnight, Lord Ravensbourne.'

'Goodnight, Father. Don't sit up too late.'

Beatrice and I walked back through the almost-empty offices. Only the night shift men remained at their desks, yawning and smoking as they monitored the news wires. The printing press roared louder as we descended to the lobby in the lift, the whole building vibrating.

Outside, chill fingers of brown fog crept into the alleys and swirled across the pavements. Beatrice pulled up the collar of her mink, and I wrapped my scarf tightly around my neck over my woollen coat. One day I'd have a fur, I vowed.

'We can share a taxi-cab back to Bloomsbury,' Beatrice said. 'Thank you for today, Marjorie. I know it hasn't been easy. But we've accomplished what we set out to do. We kept Father safe.'

The taxi set me down and I stumbled through the door at Bedford Square, kicked off my shoes and climbed the weary stairs. My bed was occupied by Sooty, our cat, and her three purring kittens. Too tired to care, I flung my clothes onto a chair, squeezed under the covers, curled up around the cats and fell fast asleep.

Chapter 20

I dreamed that I was trapped beneath one of the enormous cylinders of the printing press, unable to move as it ground through the great rolls of newsprint, whirring endlessly on. I woke to find Sooty had moved onto my chest and was purring loudly in her sleep.

'Get off,' I mumbled, pushing her aside. The kittens were arrayed around my legs. I really should enforce Mrs Jameson's rule that the cats stay below stairs, rather than having the run of the house. But they did add warmth on a chilly morning, like a heavy fur throw over the bed.

I rubbed my eyes and lit the lamp. A quarter to eight by the alarm clock. Bother. I'd forgotten to set it for half past seven, and I really wanted a bath before breakfast. Perhaps it wouldn't matter if I was a little late today.

I heaved myself up, scattering felines, and ran the taps in the bathroom. I felt thankful as always that Mrs Jameson had insisted on having the whole house re-plumbed and an enormous boiler installed for hot water before she moved in. She was accustomed to American luxuries and had no intention of living without hot running water in London, whatever the cost.

The bath revived me, although I was still tired from my long day and late night. I donned my knit suit and went downstairs for breakfast.

Mrs Jameson was drinking coffee and reading the *Daily Post*'s account of the trial of 'Brilliant' Chang for possession of cocaine. 'Very flimsy evidence,' she pronounced. 'It sounds to me like a classic police plant.'

I bolted down a boiled egg and buttered toast. I'd not had a chance to read the story yet, but my eyes had been opened about police practices over the past year. It was entirely possible, if shocking, that Mrs Jameson was right.

'Everything went according to plan yesterday, I take it?' she asked. 'Lord Ravensbourne survived to terrorise Fleet Street another day.'

I nodded. 'Just about. There was one odd thing, though.' I told her about how he'd gone missing, and I'd found him alone in St Bride's Church.

'I didn't think he had any feelings at all, but he seemed really upset. He wanted to know why everyone loves Winston Churchill, while they can't bear him.'

Mrs Jameson set down the newspaper with a sardonic smile. 'Even brutes get sentimental, Marjorie. Mr Churchill has charm, and so can get away with anything. Lord Ravensbourne has none, and will have to console himself with power and riches.'

Before leaving the house, I found an extra scarf and wrapped it around my mouth and nose. Acrid yellow fog had settled across the city, muffling sound, stinging my eyes and penetrating into the lungs. The omnibus from Holborn was crowded with people coughing and sneezing. I sat upstairs, hoping to avoid catching their germs, although the cold bit harder in the open air.

I alighted at Aldwych, deciding that a brisk walk would warm me better than another five minutes on the top of the 'bus. Lawyers and journalists jostled on the pavement outside the Royal Courts of Justice, and clerks hastened into the banks. The bells of St Dunstan in the West church began to chime the half hour, and I hurried on. Lord Ravensbourne would have something to say about my arrival after nine o'clock.

How much longer would I be a part of the street of newspapers? I liked the bustle and the camaraderie; I'd miss it, when the case came to an end. I had protected Lord Ravensbourne from harm, I had identified several suspects for the death notice, but I had not yet found proof of who was responsible. I needed to get George Quinn on my side, I decided. The head printer would know which of the linotype operators might have had the opportunity to set the column of text. And that was the key. Once we knew that, the rest would become clear.

I darted into the building, smiling at the doorman and ignoring the impertinent lift boy as the machinery creaked me up to the fifth floor. Half a dozen men sat around the subs table, heads bent over their copy. Henry Beeching looked up as I flung my hat and coat onto the rack.

'You're late today, Marjorie. Make us a cuppa, there's a good girl. I'm parched.'

'Has he been asking for me?' I uncovered my typewriter and took the box of tea and sugar jar from my desk drawer.

Mr Beeching straightened and frowned, scratching his nose with his pencil. 'Come to think of it, I haven't seen him yet this morning.'

That was unusual. I felt a prickle of unease.

'Maybe I'll just run up and check on him. Put the kettle on, Mr Beeching. I'll make the tea in a minute.'

I ascended to the landing and tapped on the door to Lord Ravensbourne's apartment. No answer. I turned the handle. As usual, it was unlocked. I opened the door and walked in.

Lord Ravensbourne was sitting in his chair facing me. The desk was as it had been last night, heaped with newspapers. The desk lamp glowed. An empty brandy glass was by his clenched hand; a half-smoked cheroot had gone out in the ashtray. Everything was exactly as it had been at midnight. Except for the bullet hole in the centre of Lord Ravensbourne's forehead.

I stared at the small round hole, automatically noting the splatter on the wall behind and the glassy sheen of the man's eyes. His face was rigid, lips drawn back slightly from his teeth. A thin trickle of blood had dried as it ran down his forehead and beside his nose, soaking into his small moustache. I could smell it now, the butcher's shop taint behind the fragrant scent of cigar smoke. My stomach heaved.

For form's sake, I forced myself to his side and laid a finger against his neck. Stone cold, and there was no pulse from the carotid artery. Lord Ravensbourne was very dead indeed.

Chapter 21

Heart hammering, I walked carefully back to the door, trying not to touch anything, and forced myself to scan the room. Mrs Jameson had taught me to be methodical, to notice everything and record it as soon as I could. Aside from the obvious, what had changed since I had left the room last night?

The low chairs were in place before the desk, lined up like school children called to see the headmaster. The brandy decanter was on the sideboard as usual. The level didn't look to have changed much, and the other brandy glasses had not been moved.

On the desk, the glass paperweight held down a stack of scribbled notes, probably criticisms of the day's newspaper which I would have been expected to type up and circulate. Lord Ravensbourne's fountain pen was capped and lay on the blotter. I could not see a gun.

The window, which Beatrice had opened to let in the sound of the bells, was closed. Had the killer closed it, to muffle the sound of the shot? Or Lord Ravensbourne might have closed it himself, to keep out the chill.

There was only one cheroot in the ashtray. He'd been smoking when I last saw him, and he wasn't in the habit of emptying his ashtray himself. I frowned. Did that mean he had been killed shortly after we left? I could check how many had been taken from the new box. Several of the newspapers heaped on his desk had slipped to the floor. Had they been there last night? I wasn't sure; I'd been so tired when Beatrice and I left.

An image of Beatrice flashed into my mind: dropping a goodnight kiss on her father's head. She'd be here by ten o'clock and might come up to the office to say good morning. I would need to lock the door and call the police before she arrived. My heart quailed at the thought of her grief. Would she blame me for not preventing his death?

When I felt sure I had captured as much of the room in my memory as possible, I slipped out and ran down the stairs to my desk.

'Kettle's boiled,' said Mr Beeching. 'I say, are you all right? You've gone very pale.'

'Shan't be a moment.' I took the key to Lord Ravensbourne's office from my drawer, ran back up and locked it. When I returned, I lifted the telephone receiver on my desk and asked the operator to put me through to the nearest police station.

'City of London Police,' said a male voice, thick with a head cold.

I spoke quietly, giving as few details as possible. The switchboard operators at the *Post* were the nexus of all gossip and I knew this would be around the offices in seconds.

'Please send a police officer and a doctor to the *Daily Post* on Whitefriars Street,' I said. 'Ask for Miss Swallow on the fifth floor. A man has been found dead.'

I replaced the receiver.

Mr Beeching was listening, eyes wide. 'The Big Man? Dead?'

I gave a brief nod. 'The police are on their way. But keep it quiet. Miss Waddon should be told first.'

'Of course.' He glanced at the team of sub-editors, who had all stopped work as soon as I'd asked for the police station. 'Get back to it, you lot.' He steered me into the kitchen and sat me down, then for once, he made the tea.

'It won't stay quiet for long in this place, you know. You'd better tell me what's happened. It must have been a shock for you. Most girls would have fainted.'

I sipped my tea. 'I'm all right. I saw worse when I was at the hospital during the War.' I wasn't going to tell anyone exactly what I'd seen in Lord Ravensbourne's office, even nice Henry Beeching. I knew enough to keep the facts of the crime scene to myself.

'Was it…' he looked around, then shut the kitchen door. 'Was it natural? Heart attack or apoplexy or something?'

Charles Maltby burst into the room. 'What's happened? The switchboard says someone's died and the police have been called.'

'It's the Big Man,' said Mr Beeching. 'Marjorie found him.'

Mr Maltby seized the back of the nearest chair, the colour draining from his face. He swayed, and for a moment I feared he would faint.

'Sit down, Charles.' Mr Beeching helped him into the wooden chair. He slumped forward, propping his head in his hands.

'Lord Ravensbourne? He's d-dead? Really dead?'

'I'm afraid so,' I said. 'But we should keep it quiet, if possible. Miss Waddon… she should be the first to be told.'

He looked up at me, raw fear in his eyes. 'But it was a lot of n-nonsense. Lord Ravensbourne said so himself. This is… it's horrible. Like a nightmare.'

Mr Beeching looked puzzled, then his brow cleared. 'Oh! You mean the death notice. I say, that's a thing, isn't it? Puts rather a grim look on it. Did it happen last night, or this morning, d'you think?'

'Beatrice Waddon and I left after midnight last night,' I said. 'He was perfectly well then. It happened today.'

Someone had waited, I thought with a shudder. Someone who knew all about the death notice, and who wanted Lord Ravensbourne to take precautions against attack – until midnight. Until the editorial offices were almost empty and the presses were running, making such a noise that you wouldn't hear a gunshot. Until Beatrice and I had left and hailed a taxi-cab home. Had they been there, waiting in the shadows by Hanging Sword Alley, watching us leave?

'Then… then it wasn't anything to do with the death notice,' said Mr Maltby, looking somewhat cheered. 'Not if it happened today.'

He sat up straight and rubbed his face. 'How did he die? I need to get the reporters onto it right away. We can pull all his cuttings out of the library and put together a double page spread of his life. I'd better go down to the newsroom. Someone will need to get a statement from the family. I don't suppose you could ask M-miss Waddon when she comes in, Miss Swallow?'

I rose. 'I think you should leave Miss Waddon alone. She won't have even heard about it yet.' I was rather shocked by his coldness, but I supposed that was his job. 'I'd better go and wait for the police.'

'Of course.' He had the grace to look abashed. 'How did he die, anyway? You haven't said. Natural causes?'

I sighed. 'We'll know soon enough. I hope the police will

bring a doctor with them.'

Chapter 22

The police did bring a doctor, a small timid-looking man with a big moustache and a black bag. He looked almost comical beside the sergeant, a clean-shaven man of some six foot in height, with shiny brass buttons down the front of his tunic and a helmet that made him look even taller.

'I'm looking for a Miss Swallow,' the policeman announced to the room at large. 'I'm Sergeant Voles.' The fifth floor had filled up with reporters, messenger boys and anyone else who'd heard the news, all asking each other what had happened. I hurried through the throng.

'That's me. Come this way, please.'

Quickly I led the sergeant and the doctor up the stairs to the landing, then unlocked the door.

'I found him at nine-forty, when I arrived for work,' I said. 'I checked for a pulse, but I didn't touch anything else. The door was unlocked, and I went at once for the key to lock it, before I telephoned the police station. No-one else has been in here, and I haven't told anyone what I saw. Only that Lord Ravensbourne was dead.'

Sergeant Voles gave me a suspicious look. 'You're very cool about it, Miss. Come across a lot of corpses, do you?'

I thought it best not to answer that. 'It seemed like the right thing to do. Aren't you going in?'

He harrumphed and swung open the door to the scene that I'd already impressed on my memory. I took the opportunity to scribble down shorthand notes to aid my recollection.

The little doctor bustled across and carried out the usual checks with surprising diligence, before pronouncing life extinct and recording the time.

'How long?' asked Sergeant Voles.

The man put his head to one side, considering. He tried to move Lord Ravensbourne's arm, then slipped a thermometer into his armpit. He waited a moment, then checked it.

'Full rigor mortis, eighty-four degrees Fahrenheit. I'd say eight to twelve hours since death. It was a cold night; the body would have cooled quickly.'

'I saw him at midnight,' I interrupted. 'So, he couldn't have died more than ten hours ago. He was sitting right there, smoking a cigar and drinking from that glass of brandy. I'd say someone shot him soon after I left.'

Sergeant Voles turned slowly towards me. 'What are you doing?' he asked, eyeing my notebook with suspicion. 'You shouldn't still be here. Get down those stairs, Miss. Keep away from this office. We will be interviewing you and all the rest in due course, when the inspector arrives.'

'But I thought it would be helpful if I…'

'It would be helpful if you left this to the professionals. Go and make us a cup of tea, there's a good girl. And you'd better give me the details of the next of kin.'

* * *

'What's happened? Where's Father?'

I heard Beatrice's penetrating voice before I reached the bottom of the stairs. Oh, goodness. I hurried into the sub-editors' room and pushed through the crowd.

The chatter had stilled. Beatrice and Belinda stood in the middle of the room, wearing their coats. Henry Beeching reached them before me and put an arm around Beatrice's shoulder.

'Come with me, Miss Waddon.'

Together we got the two women to the kitchen and Henry slammed the door shut against the gawpers. He looked to me to impart the news.

'I'm so sorry, Miss Waddon. Your father is dead.' I put a hand on her arm.

'No!' She pushed me violently, and I staggered into the kitchen table. 'You're lying.'

I braced myself against the table and took a deep breath. 'I'm afraid not. I found his body myself. The police are there now.'

'Oh, Bea. How dreadful.' Miss Ponsett tried to comfort her, but was also shoved away.

'Get off me. Leave me alone.' Beatrice stared wildly from one to the other of us. 'Where is he? I want to see him.'

'He's in his office,' I began. She immediately went for the door. Mr Beeching stood in her way.

'Wait, Miss Waddon. The police are up there with him, and the doctor.'

'The doctor?' She turned to me. 'Then you're wrong, aren't you? He's still alive. He's hurt. Let me through, Henry.' She tugged ineffectually at his arm.

'What did you see, Miss Swallow?' asked Belinda. 'Are you completely sure he's dead?' She looked rather green.

'I'm afraid so. There wasn't any doubt.' I went to Beatrice

again. 'Sit down for a moment. I'll tell the policeman you're here. I'm sure he will come to talk to you straight away. I'm so sorry you had to find out like this.'

She shook me off. 'You stay here. I'm going to talk to the police myself.' She wrenched the door open, pushing Mr Beeching aside. Belinda went to follow, but Beatrice slammed the door in our faces.

'Oh, heavens.' Belinda stared at the closed door. 'Whatever shall we do now?'

It was all getting a bit out of hand. I decided to do what I always did when things got too much for me: call Mrs Jameson.

'I think we should telephone that friend of Miss Waddon you mentioned last week, Miss Ponsett,' I said, mindful that it would be best if Henry Beeching didn't know about the undercover investigation. 'Mrs Iris Jameson, wasn't it? She's had experience of this sort of thing, hasn't she? She'll know what to do.'

The girl stared at me, then nodded vigorously as the penny dropped. 'Oh, yes. Good idea.'

Mr Beeching looked surprised, but asked nothing about this mysterious friend. I decided to enlist his help.

'Can you help me get a bit of quiet out there, Mr Beeching? We need everyone to calm down.'

Outside, reporters and sub-editors milled around Beatrice, brandishing notebooks and asking eagerly if she had anything to say. Mute, she pushed her way over to the stairs to her father's apartment, her face white and set, and disappeared through the door.

Mr Beeching raised his voice. 'Right! Everyone who is not a sub-editor on this newspaper, get out of here. Now. Behave like civilised adults for once. I know it's difficult. And if I hear that a single one of you has tipped off the opposition, you'll be out on your backside with my boot print on it. This is still Lord Ravensbourne's newspaper. We've a duty to him, d'you hear?'

The room began to clear. I pretended not to see Jonathan Field gesticulating to me to tell him what had happened.

Mr Beeching addressed himself to the sub-editors. 'You lot. You can make yourselves scarce, too. Go down to the canteen. Tell Mrs Johnson to make you bacon sandwiches and stay there until I send word you can come back up again.' The subs rose from their table and headed for the lift, looking considerably more cheerful than the reporters.

Soon, Mr Beeching, Belinda Ponsett and I were the only people left. Belinda sat dolefully at the foot of the stairs to Lord Ravensbourne's apartment, like a dog waiting for her master's return.

My employer received the news of Lord Ravensbourne's death in silence. Mindful of the switchboard, I gave no details. I didn't need to. Mrs Jameson always considered sudden deaths to be suspicious, until proven otherwise.

After a moment, she said: 'I will be there presently. Is Miss Waddon with you?'

'She's talking to the police,' I said. 'She's very upset, of course. Miss Ponsett is here, and Mr Beeching, the chief sub-editor.'

'Tell Miss Ponsett to take Miss Waddon to the *Bugle* office and wait for me there. Have the police interviewed you yet?'

'No. There's just a sergeant and the doctor. An inspector is on his way.'

'City of London Police, I suppose.' She tutted. 'How annoying. Scotland Yard is so much easier to deal with.'

As I replaced the receiver, Beatrice walked unsteadily down the stairs, her imperious face pale as marble.

'Bea!' Miss Ponsett scrambled to her feet. 'Come and sit down. Let me get you a cup of tea.'

Beatrice looked at her as if she wasn't sure who she was.

'Perhaps it would be an idea to go to your own office,' I said. 'You can shut out all the reporters and everyone. Mrs Jameson is on her way.'

Beatrice looked at me blankly. 'What for?' she asked. 'We've failed. Father is dead.'

Chapter 23

We'd barely arrived in the *Bugle* office when a boy, out of breath, came to fetch me.

'The policeman wants to talk to you, Miss,' he said, eyes round. 'Did you really see his body, Miss? Was it very bad?'

I hurried back up. The doctor was gone, and Sergeant Voles had been joined by another policeman, this one not in uniform. But he too was unusually tall, and strode long-legged around the sub-editors' table, his mackintosh flapping. Otherwise, the room was empty; Henry Beeching had accompanied us down to the *Bugle*, then disappeared into Charles Maltby's office.

The inspector paused in his pacing as I came through from the lift. He had a long face with deep-set, intelligent eyes. His dark hair was swept back from his high forehead. I was reminded irresistibly of Sherlock Holmes.

'Are you the secretary?'

I decided it would complicate matters to explain my undercover role. I'd play along, at least until I could consult with Mrs Jameson.

'That's right, sir. Marjorie Swallow.'

'You found the body this morning, hey?'

'I did.'

He gestured to one of the vacated chairs. 'Sit down, then, Miss Swallow. I'm Detective Inspector Carfax. You'd better tell me all about it.'

He folded himself into my chair and propped his elbows on my desk. Sergeant Voles perched on a chair nearby with a notebook, recording what I said. I ran through my late departure the previous night with Beatrice, and how I'd been the first person to go up to Lord Ravensbourne's office that morning.

'As far as you know.'

I nodded agreement. 'And I found him sitting there, with the wound in his head. I checked to see if he was still alive, then locked the door and called the police. The doctor said the death had taken place eight to twelve hours previously, so he must have been shot between midnight and about half-past one.'

He nodded thoughtfully. 'Very good. Miss Swallow, were you in the habit of staying at the newspaper until midnight? Why were you so late in leaving yesterday?'

I hesitated. But the police needed to know.

'Miss Waddon was very anxious. She received a printed notice announcing her father's death, a week ago. It was dated yesterday, so she was worried that something would happen to him. She suggested that either she or I should stay with him all day and not leave until midnight had passed. Lord Ravensbourne was in the habit of sleeping in his rooms here during the week. We thought… she thought he would be safe after the day was over.'

Inspector Carfax's dark, bushy eyebrows had shot up his forehead. 'A death notice? May I see it?'

'Miss Waddon has it. She's in her offices on the fourth floor.

She is naturally very distressed.'

'Naturally.' He pressed his fingertips together. 'And when you left at midnight, Miss Swallow, Lord Ravensbourne was quite alone? Who was still in the building?'

'There was nobody in his flat with him when Miss Waddon and I left,' I said. 'There were a few people downstairs in the newsroom. A night editor, a sub and a reporter in case of late-breaking news. Mr Maltby, the editor, will be able to tell you their names.

'Lots of the printers work overnight, of course. I didn't see them, because the print floor is in the basement. The presses start running at eight o'clock and the last run is usually about four in the morning. And there are vans going up and down Whitefriars Street all night, to load the newspapers. There are people in the building around the clock.'

'How come no-one heard the shot, then?' Sergeant Voles interrupted. Inspector Carfax looked around in irritation.

'Perhaps someone did,' I pointed out. 'You haven't asked them all yet. But the noise of the press might have masked it. It's very loud, especially in the basement.' I thought back. 'And it was foggy, of course. The fog always muffles sound, don't you think?' I remembered the faint sound of the bells striking midnight.

'Thank you, Sergeant.' The inspector made the words into a mild rebuke. 'You can leave the questions to me.' He observed me through narrowed eyes. 'How did you get on with Lord Ravensbourne, Miss Swallow? And what about the rest of the staff? Harmonious workplace?'

'I've been working here less than a week. Lord Ravensbourne is a demanding employer, with a short temper. But I got on with him tolerably well, I think.'

'Less than a week? What happened to his last secretary?'

I'd been thinking about Mary Pringle, presumably now Mary Butcher. And about Tom Butcher, her printer husband. She'd said Tom had taken a week off work, and they were going to spend it moving into and furnishing the rooms they'd rented in Kennington, near the cricket ground. What had she told him about Lord Ravensbourne, during their first two days as man and wife? The photograph of her was still in my handbag. It might be needed as evidence, I supposed.

'She left to get married.' I decided to keep my speculation to myself for the time being. 'I started on Wednesday.'

'Hmm. Could you run through his engagements yesterday? It would be helpful to know who he met during the course of the day.'

I got out the big diary and talked him through the various conferences, meetings and lunch engagements. I told him about the panic when Beatrice had lost him after their lunch with the Churchills, and I'd found him alone in St Bride's Church.

'He said he just wanted to be on his own for a few moments,' I said. 'But...' I chewed my lip, thinking of the strange episode. 'Something had upset him.'

The beetle eyebrows made another leap.

'Thinking about it now, I wonder if he had met someone in the church. And that's what had upset him so much.'

Inspector Carfax nodded thoughtfully. 'Very perceptive, Miss Swallow. Now, tell me about the family. I know there's a daughter. What about the rest of them? I need to get someone over to break the news, before it gets out.'

Chapter 24

I was finally released, with a request to send up Charles Maltby with a list of the editorial staff who were working overnight. The editor's office was crowded with people and thick with smoke.

'Me? Why do the police want m-me, for heaven's sake?' asked Mr Maltby, spilling his tea. 'Blast. It's gone all over my trousers.' He dabbed at the wet patch with his handkerchief.

'Calm down, Charles,' said Mr Beeching. 'They just need to know who was here last night. What time did you leave, anyway?'

'About m-midnight, I suppose, after taking up the late edition. I went to the Press Club for a stiff whisky. Didn't I, Reggie? We played billiards till about one.'

'We did,' said Mr Pyke, lounging in the corner against a filing cabinet. The demise of his brother-in-law didn't seem to have cheered him up particularly. 'Two games. We won one each.'

So that was two alibis to investigate. Of all the men working on the editorial staff, Mr Maltby and Mr Pyke had the strongest dislike for Lord Ravensbourne. And they'd been together during the most critical time period from midnight until one, providing each other with an alibi. Was that why Charles Maltby was so jumpy?

I left them to it and hurried over to the *Bugle*. To my enormous relief, Mrs Jameson had arrived and was taking charge.

Beatrice huddled in an armchair, her fur coat wrapped around her. Belinda Ponsett was busy sourcing the things Mrs Jameson wanted: large sheets of paper to pin to the office wall, an office telephone directory, a list of all the staff employed at the *Daily Post*. Mrs Jameson herself was speaking into the telephone, and waved at me to keep quiet.

'Please accept my sincere condolences, Lady Ravensbourne, to your whole family. I expect a representative from the police will be with you before long, to explain what is known so far. I'm sure Miss Waddon will visit as soon as she is recovered from the shock. It might be best for you all to be together.'

She replaced the receiver softly. 'Ah, Marjorie, there you are. What have you told the police? And, more importantly, what have they told you?'

I looked uncertainly at Beatrice, wondering how much she knew.

'The police told me,' she said, toneless. 'Someone shot him, didn't they?' She looked up at me, eyes wet. 'Somebody was waiting for us to leave. And they shot him point-blank, through the head.'

A phrase jarred in my mind. 'Bullet in the brain.' The printer Bill Mead, making a gun of his hand, aiming it at George Quinn. I'd intended to talk to Quinn today, to find out who knew how to operate the linotype machines and galley presses and might have had a chance to use them unsupervised. Perhaps I should begin by finding out whether Bill Mead had been working the previous night.

'I agree,' I told Beatrice. 'The doctor said he had been dead for between eight and twelve hours. We left at midnight, and I got here at nine-forty, so it must have been between midnight and a little after half past one. But Lord Ravensbourne looked as if he hadn't moved since we left him. His brandy glass was still on the desk, one cheroot in the ashtray. I think whoever did this was waiting, like you say.'

I turned to Mrs Jameson. 'I told the police about the death notice. But not that I'm working for you. They think I'm just Lord Ravensbourne's secretary. Inspector Carfax says he wants to see the death notice, Beatrice.'

She nodded and gestured towards her desk. 'It's in there somewhere. You can take it to him if you want.'

'Carfax,' said Mrs Jameson, narrowing her eyes. 'That name's familiar.'

Belinda came back with the items Mrs Jameson had requested, and a pot of freshly made coffee. The smell seemed to have a reviving effect on Beatrice.

'I should go to Regent's Park,' she said. 'See Annabel and the children. We'll need to start to think about the funeral. And someone should tell my brother.'

'The police wanted his address,' I remembered. 'I said I'd ask you. Do you want to go there now? Or I could telephone him for you.'

She sipped her coffee and stared into space. 'I don't know. I suppose so. He has a set of rooms at Albany, off Piccadilly. He's probably still asleep.' She set her coffee down. 'I can't take it in. It doesn't seem real.'

'You should rest,' said Mrs Jameson. 'It's been a horrible shock. Why don't you let Miss Ponsett take you home, or to Regent's Park?'

Beatrice gave a queer sort of shudder. She closed her eyes

and seemed to shrink away from her friend. 'I'll go alone,' she said.

'I'll call a taxi-cab,' said Belinda, hovering anxiously with Beatrice's coat. 'Let me look after you, Bea. You shouldn't be on your own.'

She rose and took the coat. 'I want to go alone.'

'Miss Waddon?' Mrs Jameson rose too and looked her squarely in the face. 'I feel that we have let you down. I should have realised that the danger was not over with the close of the day. I should very much like to continue to investigate and help the police to discover who murdered your father.'

Beatrice returned her gaze, her face rigid. She pulled on her coat. 'Do as you please,' she said. She crossed to the office door and turned. 'Whoever did this thing should hang. I hope that they will,' she added, shutting the door behind her.

Belinda Ponsett collapsed onto the sofa. 'I don't think she should be alone,' she repeated. 'Whatever shall I do?'

Mrs Jameson regarded her for a moment. 'If we are to catch this killer,' she said, 'we shall need your help, Miss Ponsett. Why don't you begin by confirming what time Miss Waddon arrived home last night, and your own movements between midnight and nine-forty this morning?'

Chapter 25

'My movements?' Belinda looked shocked.

Mrs Jameson watched her unblinkingly. 'I shall need to know the movements of everyone connected with Lord Ravensbourne,' she said. 'Including you and Miss Waddon. So why don't we start with you?'

'You can't think I had anything to do with this? I was at home in Gordon Square. Where else would I be?' Belinda's voice became shrill.

I thought with unease of Lord Ravensbourne's threats to her the day before, his ultimatum that Beatrice had three months to bring the *Women's Bugle* into profit, and Belinda had six weeks to find herself somewhere else to live. Her livelihood, her passion and her home, all threatened in one blow. If anyone had good reason to wish Lord Ravensbourne dead, it was Belinda Ponsett.

'What time did you arrive home? You didn't stay until midnight, I take it?' asked Mrs Jameson.

'We left the office at about half past eight. I prepared a late supper; cold cuts from Sunday. We read for a while. I'm to interview Mrs Bondfield, the MP, this week, so I was swotting up about her work with the Trades Union movement.'

I smiled despite the seriousness of the situation. Belinda

was such a schoolgirl.

'It was late, after half past eleven, when Beatrice decided to take a taxi-cab back to Fleet Street. She wanted to be sure her father was all right. I offered to go with her, but she saw I was tired, so I went to bed and was already asleep when she came home.

'It must have been well after midnight when she got back, I think. I woke for a moment – she put her head around the door to say goodnight – then dropped off again.'

'And did you leave the house before you and Miss Waddon came to the office this morning?'

'Of course not.' Belinda's voice was sharp. Why was she so vehement? She might have gone for an early walk, or to buy groceries, quite innocently. 'We walked here together after breakfast.'

'Then you have nothing to worry about, Miss Ponsett, do you?' Mrs Jameson smiled blandly. 'Why don't you return to Gordon Square and wait for Miss Waddon? I shall stay here with Marjorie so we can continue our investigations with the staff of the *Daily Post*. If anyone asks about me, I shall say I am a friend of Miss Waddon and will be working at the *Bugle* until Beatrice is able to take up the reins again.'

After some demurring, Belinda left us alone. I slumped into a chair. 'Oh, Mrs Jameson. Poor Beatrice. I feel so badly for her.'

She gazed at me, her steady grey eyes hooded. 'She came to me for help, and I failed her,' she admitted. 'However, the next best thing we can do is find the culprit. Talk me through what you saw in Lord Ravensbourne's office this morning.'

I did so, trying not to omit any detail that might be useful.

'Did you check the notes on his desk, under the paperweight?' she asked immediately.

I cursed myself for a fool. 'I'll see if the police will let me take them,' I said. 'They're probably about last night's edition of the newspaper, but I should have thought of that.'

'Indeed.' Mrs Jameson looked severe. 'Now, tell me what you thought of Miss Ponsett.'

I hesitated. 'She seemed rather anxious when you questioned her. And she had a terrible row with Lord Ravensbourne yesterday,' I said. 'He told her she'd have to move out of Gordon Square, that he wasn't having her living off Beatrice.' I remembered something else. 'And she was talking to the printer, Bill Mead, in the lunch hour. They seemed quite pally, which I suppose means they could have worked together on the death notice. They both had good reasons to want him dead.'

Mrs Jameson nodded. 'I should like to speak to Mr Mead. Can you find out if he's in the building? I'm sure the police will want to talk to him too. Let's see if we can find him first.'

I slipped out of the *Bugle* office and onto the stairwell. I didn't want to bump into anyone in the lift who might ask why I was going to the print floor. Then, as I reached the ground floor, I checked my watch. It was just past eleven o'clock and I knew the printers liked their grub. I diverted into the big hall and scanned the long tables for familiar faces.

The sub-editors were there, making the most of their banishment from the fifth floor. I could see several of the printers, sitting together playing cards and eating bacon sandwiches. Bill Mead was not among them. The salty smell made me suddenly hungry. It had been a while since my breakfast egg. Then I saw George Quinn, the head printer, carry a mug of tea over to a table under the window.

I dashed to the counter. 'Two bacon sandwiches, please.'

Mrs Johnson served them up, the grease soaking into the doorsteps of bread. 'What's all this about His Lordship? Is it true you found his body?' She leaned confidentially over the counter.

'I'm afraid so. I'll tell you about it later. I need to have a quick word with Mr Quinn.'

I carried my tray over to his empty table, where he'd spread out the *Racing Post* and was circling the names of horses with a pencil.

'Hello, Mr Quinn. Mrs Johnson thought I asked for two sandwiches, so I have one spare. Would you like it?'

He looked at me suspiciously, but the tasty smell got the better of him. 'That's very kind, Miss Swallow. Thank you.'

I sat down opposite him. 'It'll be a busy day for you, I expect,' I said brightly.

He grunted. 'This afternoon certainly will be. They'll run a spoof for the first edition, then we'll have to make up the front and the first five pages again from scratch.'

'A spoof?' I was puzzled. 'What do you mean?'

He grinned, his mouth full of sandwich, and chewed. 'So as the other newspapers can't rip it off. If we have the real story about His Lordship on the first edition, every newspaper in Fleet Street will have it by their final. This way, the regions get the spoof, but by the time the London final goes, it's too late for the rest to catch up.'

I nodded solemnly. I wasn't quite sure why everything at the *Daily Post* had to be about beating the competition, but I'd been there long enough to realise how seriously that was taken.

'I expect you'll be calling everyone in, then,' I said. 'What about Mr Mead? He's not really going to call a strike, is he? That wouldn't seem right, in the circumstances.'

Mr Quinn finished the sandwich and delicately extracted a piece of rind from his back teeth with his fingers. I averted my eyes from the operation.

'He can't call a strike if he's not blooming here, can he? He disappeared halfway through his shift last night, and he's not been back in this morning,' said Mr Quinn. 'Good riddance, except that I'm one man down. If you see him, tell him he's late.'

'That is a nuisance,' I agreed. 'When did he disappear last night?'

He shrugged. 'About eleven. Maybe later.' He picked up his newspaper, then looked at me sharply again. 'Don't you go making anything of it, Miss Swallow. I know what he said, but he's just a hot-head, see? I don't want you getting him in trouble, with the police crawling all over the building.'

'Of course.' I thought again. 'How about Tom Butcher, Miss Pringle's fiancé? Weren't they getting married on Saturday?'

He sighed. 'He's got the week off, hasn't he? Left on Friday night. We'll need to get some journeymen in, I suppose. No rest for the wicked, Miss Swallow.'

I picked up the tray and took our plates back to the servery, mind whirring.

Back upstairs, I passed on the new information to Mrs Jameson, and showed her the photograph of Miss Pringle. She looked at it for a long moment, her lips pressed together, then shook her head and sighed.

'Thank you, Marjorie. Put that away, now. I hope we will not need to show it to anyone else.'

She wrote Bill Mead's name on the timeline she had begun

to construct on a large sheet of paper. I added Charles Maltby and Reginald Pyke, who said they'd been in the Press Club together from midnight until one o'clock. If the fatal shot had been fired soon after Beatrice and I left – and if their alibi stood up to investigation – they would be in the clear. But, of course, we didn't have a precise time of death. From our previous investigations, I'd learned how much could hang on that.

'The more obvious suspects seem to be resolving into teams of two,' Mrs Jameson observed. 'Miss Ponsett and Mr Mead were conversing yesterday. Miss Pringle and Mr Butcher are now man and wife. Mr Maltby and Mr Pyke played billiards together. They all had ample reason to dislike Lord Ravensbourne. Were Mr Maltby and Mr Pyke friends, would you say?'

'I think it was more that they commiserated with each other,' I said. 'Misery likes company. And nobody seems to go home. The journalists all hang around in the office half the night, or go drinking in the pub together. I wonder what their wives make of it.'

The pub, I'd learned, had an almost sacred place in the life of the newspaper. The *Post*'s favoured pub was the rambling Old Cheshire Cheese, just across the road. The more senior editors went to El Vino's, the wine bar that had a strict rule against women, or the Press Club after hours. Not that I'd ever tried to go along; the pubs were notoriously rowdy places, and I wasn't sure Lord Ravensbourne's secretary would be welcome.

'I'll go up to the fifth floor and see if I can get those papers from Lord Ravensbourne's office.' I was still annoyed with myself for not thinking of them at the time. I didn't have much hope the police would allow it, but it never hurt to try.

Chapter 26

The lift doors opened onto Sergeant Voles, who stood foursquare across the entrance to the subs' room. Behind him, I could see Inspector Carfax grilling Charles Maltby.

'What do you want?' demanded the sergeant.

'I was hoping you could let me pick up some papers from Lord Ravensbourne's office,' I said. 'We need to go through his notes on yesterday's paper. It's very important.'

The man sniggered. 'Not any more, it isn't. No-one goes into that office until we've finished with it, see? Crime scene.'

I'd expected this. 'Of course,' I said. 'But…' I tried to force a blush into my cheeks. 'There might be a letter of mine in there. I think I dropped it, when I found the body. Nothing to do with work. It was from my young man. I wouldn't want it to confuse the investigation.'

He sighed. 'This is the trouble with women in the workplace,' he said. 'Unprofessional. You can't leave your private life at home, can you?'

I tried to look penitent. 'I'm sorry. Also,' I reached into my handbag, 'Inspector Carfax said he wanted to see this.' I brandished the galley proof of the death notice.

'What's going on, Voles?' called Inspector Carfax. 'I'm finished with this one. Let the girl through.'

Charles Maltby hurried across the room, more white rabbity than ever. Sweat stood out on his forehead. 'I'm late for conference,' he muttered, then stopped and stared at the proof in my hand, his face wan. 'What are you d-doing with that?' he asked, through pale lips. 'How did you get hold of it?'

I looked with feigned surprise at the paper. He obviously knew what it was. 'Miss Waddon had it in her desk. She said to take it to Inspector Carfax. Haven't you seen it before? I thought Lord Ravensbourne told you to find out who made it. You never found out, did you?'

'Of course not,' he muttered. He looked fearfully at the inspector, who was watching our exchange with interest. 'Listen, M-miss Swallow. Can you come and join us in conference when you're finished? We'll need your help.' He hurried away.

'What a very nervous man,' said Inspector Carfax, cheerfully. He patted the chair next to him. 'You're not nervous, are you, Miss Swallow? A very cool customer. Sit here and show me this death notice.'

He scanned it and whistled. 'Quite the turn of phrase. Will Fleet Street really be plunged into mourning, d'you think?'

I thought it prudent not to answer that. 'I'm afraid I may have dropped a private letter in the office when I found Lord Ravensbourne this morning,' I said. 'Can I go and look for it?'

He laughed heartily. 'Can you go and rifle around the papers in a crime scene? Oh, of course. Be my guest, Miss Swallow. I'm sure you'll report anything interesting to the police, before you give it to Iris Jameson.'

I froze. He knew Mrs Jameson. Which meant he knew I was working for her, undercover.

'Did she send you here with that excuse? Surely she doesn't

think I'll fall for it.' Inspector Carfax leaned back and lit up a pipe, throwing me a sardonic glance as he puffed it alight. 'I trained with the Metropolitan Police, you know. I'm quite well up on all Mrs Jameson's tricks, and I know how she twists Scotland Yard around her little finger. Did Beatrice Waddon call you in today, or were you investigating the death notice? Oh, but you said you started last week. So it was this, of course.' He shook the paper at me. 'Any progress? Or were you planning to keep your discoveries to yourself?'

I was dismayed. Scotland Yard had a healthy respect for Mrs Jameson. But I didn't like the way Inspector Carfax spoke about her tricks, and I worried he would reveal my cover to the other newspaper staff.

The lift doors opened. 'Let me through, Sergeant Voles,' said Mrs Jameson, her clear voice cutting through the room. 'Good morning, Inspector Carfax. I thought it was time we compared notes. It's been a few years since you left the Metropolitan Police, hasn't it? I'd almost forgotten your name.'

She stalked past the sergeant as if he wasn't there; quite a feat given his solid dimensions.

Inspector Carfax rose politely. 'Mrs Jameson. So kind of you to drop by on your way out of the building. Can I order you a taxi-cab?'

Mrs Jameson pulled out a chair and took a seat next to him. 'Miss Waddon, who I believe will be the new proprietor of Ravensbourne Amalgamated Publications, has asked me to investigate her father's murder. We can work together, Inspector Carfax, which would be productive and useful, or we can work separately, which would involve tedious duplication of effort.'

She turned on the inspector her social smile, bland and

impenetrable. 'Which will it be, Inspector?'

He sighed. 'This is a City of London Police investigation. Trained police officers are methodically examining Lord Ravensbourne's office. Trained police officers are methodically interviewing witnesses and suspects.' He eyed me. 'Some of whom will need to be re-interviewed, as they were not candid in their first interview. I will not have you muddying the waters with the exercise of your feminine intuition, however well intended. This is my jurisdiction.'

She held his gaze a moment longer. 'I feared that would be your decision. Well, Inspector Carfax, we shall have to work separately. That's a pity.'

He leaned over and tapped his pipe on her gloved hand, which grasped her Malacca walking cane. I winced. Few people got away with taking such liberties with Mrs Jameson.

'You will leave this office. Or I will ensure every member of staff here knows about your assistant's duplicity.'

That would be a disaster for our investigation. I started forward, but Mrs Jameson shook her head at me. 'I will not get in your way. I shall confine myself to the *Women's Bugle* offices.'

'You will not attempt to interview witnesses or suspects,' he said, sternly. 'Or interfere with the crime scene.'

She smiled again. 'Of course not, Inspector Carfax. I leave that entirely to you.' She rose. 'Come, Marjorie. Let us see whether our feminine intuition can come up with the answers before the methodical investigations of the trained police officers.'

I had expected her to be furious, but to my surprise Mrs Jameson hooted with laughter as we descended to the *Bugle* offices in the lift.

'What an ass that man is,' she said. 'Feminine intuition, indeed. Do you know what that is, Marjorie?'

I'd certainly never heard Mrs Jameson use the term before. She was meticulous about following methods and investigating thoroughly.

'Men call it feminine intuition when we can tell by the way a man addresses us that he is dangerous. They think we are performing some magic trick, when we have trained ourselves to be observant for our own safety.

'A woman notices when she is being followed down the street, because she has been followed before, with distressing consequences. A man is oblivious, because he doesn't expect it. That's why policemen need training,' she concluded, her tone a little sad. 'Women detectives are trained from birth. It is only a matter of directing that observation.'

She produced from her sleeve a small pile of scrappy paper. 'This is what you were hoping to find, I think, Marjorie. The inspector had it on the desk next to his teacup. Let us see what it tells us.'

Chapter 27

As expected, the notes were observations about the previous day's newspaper. My first task most mornings was to gather these notes together, type them into a bulletin and circulate it to the editor and chief sub-editor.

'Tommy rot! Sack whoever wrote this headline,' read one, pinned to a seemingly innocuous article about the forthcoming tram strike. 'Call the Foreign Office,' read another. And then an ungallant note attached to a picture of Queen Mary opening a cottage hospital in Croydon: 'Ghastly photograph. No-one wants to look at that old trout.'

'I'd better go through them.' I sighed. 'I'll see if there's anything out of the ordinary.'

I'd barely begun when my labours were interrupted.

'I say! This is a turn-up. Poor old Pater. Where's my sister got to?'

Theodore Waddon – the new Lord Ravensbourne, I supposed – lounged into the room. Perhaps he had not had time to change into mourning clothes. His pale grey suit was set off with a shimmering peacock-blue silk waistcoat, yellow leather gloves and a yellow rose in the buttonhole. He did not look like a man whose father had just died.

I scrambled to my feet and smoothed down my skirt. 'I'm

so very sorry, Mr Waddon. Please accept my condolences.'

'Very kind, m'dear. Marjorie, isn't it? And you're to call me Dora, remember?' He flung himself onto the pink sofa, dislodging piles of papers. 'What a morning I've had. The police banged on my door at the crack of noon. I thought they were after me for last night's escapade.'

Mrs Jameson rose, her hand outstretched. 'Mr Waddon? Or is it Lord Ravensbourne now? I am Mrs Jameson, a friend of your sister Beatrice. She has asked me to oversee the operations of the *Bugle* while she is indisposed.'

He sat up and shook her fingers. 'How d'you do. Call me Dora; everyone does. You're another of the monstrous regiment, hey? How's Bea? I expect she's awfully cut up. She was devilish fond of the old man.'

Mrs Jameson perched on an upright chair next to him. 'Miss Waddon is naturally very upset. She has gone to see Lady Ravensbourne at Regent's Park. May I ask what you meant by last night's escapade?'

Theodore chuckled. 'Well, only if you promise not to tell the rozzers. We had a bit of an altercation with one of the guard chappies at Buckingham Palace. The clues were all about animals, see? And where else are you going to find hair from a bear, outside of London Zoo?'

Mrs Jameson stared at him in confusion.

It wasn't often I had the advantage of her. 'Another scavenger hunt?' I asked. 'Did you try to get a bearskin from one of the guards?' I passed him a cup of coffee, feeling pleased with myself.

He yawned, showing a very pink tongue like a cat. 'Well, we only wanted a snippet. Unfortunately, the chap was unwilling to play along. He and Taffy got into something of a tussle, and of course I couldn't leave old Taff in the soup. Then another couple of guards joined in. I had to biff one of them and scarper across the park. Fortunately, Vicky can drive like a demon when she has to. She scooped us up on the other side and we were in Kensington before you could say tally-ho!'

'What time was all this going on?' I asked. Theodore's indifference to his father's fate was a chilling contrast to his sister's distress.

'Oh, Lordy. I don't know. Midnight, maybe later? You'd have to ask Vicky. We didn't get back to Albany till six this morning.' He sat up and took a sip of coffee. 'Awfully good brew, this. I feel almost human.'

Mrs Jameson was watching him closely. 'You don't seem particularly upset by your father's death, Mr Waddon.'

He gave her a cool look. 'The thing is, he never saw the point of me. We didn't have much in common, as I'm sure you can imagine. Pater wanted me to have some ghastly career, and I wanted to enjoy myself.'

'With the allowance he gave you?'

He chuckled. 'Of course. As far as it went, and it always did seem to go. Mrs Jameson, my father wanted to act the aristocrat. What could be more aristocratic than having a son who rattles around town with the idle rich? You'd think he'd be grateful to me for burnishing the family image.'

She nodded. 'I do see that, yes. You have debts, then?'

'Of course I have debts. I owe Bunter three hundred quid from our last game of poker; my tailor says his family will be thrown onto the street unless I pay for this very fine waistcoat; and I have to climb out of the window at White's to avoid paying my bar bill.'

He stretched and settled a cushion more comfortably under

his head. 'All of my creditors will be rejoicing tonight, in the reasonable yet forlorn expectation that I shall pay them when my inheritance comes through. I hope to God that Pater has left the company to Bea, though. She's the only one with any brains. I should have to sell it, and no doubt I'd get royally ripped off.'

'Do you know the terms of your father's will, Mr Waddon?'

He closed his eyes. 'Well, he kept threatening to cut me off without a bean. I don't think he ever got around to it, though. Bea would know. I think the general idea was to divide it between us – me, Bea, and that secretary he married. I expect my sister will pay my debts if she gets my share of the loot, so everyone will be happy in the end.'

He opened his eyes again. 'I say. Good news for Bea's *Bugle*, isn't it? She'll be able to chuck as much money as she wants at it now. And that dreary female she runs it with.' His lip curled with disdain.

'Miss Ponsett?' asked Mrs Jameson. 'You don't approve of her?'

He hunted in his pockets for a cigarette lighter. 'It's probably the only point on which Pater and I agreed. All that earnestness is irredeemably vulgar. I can't imagine what Bea sees in her. Neither use nor ornament, as my charwoman says.'

He puffed a cigar alight, the smoke billowing through the room. 'I say, d'you think Ponsett did it? Stormed in with a pistol and shot the blighter dead, like something out of an American movie?'

Mrs Jameson gave a thin smile. 'I'm sure the police will consider all possibilities. You might want to think about your own alibi, Mr Waddon, as you are likely to be a beneficiary of the will.'

He roared with laughter. 'I say, do you really think so? Well, I was with Vicky, of course. Lady Victoria, daughter of the Earl of Northington, that is. Let's see. We were at a cocktail party at seven, then had dinner at the Criterion around nine. There was a terribly good jazz band and we had a bit of a caper on the dance floor. Then we assembled for the scavenger hunt at eleven, and spent the rest of the night tearing round London picking up trophies. You can ask Vicky, if you like. I smuggled her into my rooms this morning. She was jolly annoyed to be woken by that policeman, I can tell you.'

A messenger boy rushed in. 'Miss Swallow, Mr Maltby says can you come to his office? They want you to join the editorial conference.'

I rose and gathered my pencil and notebook.

The boy twisted his cap in his hands, his face bursting with curiosity. 'Miss, everyone's saying you found him with a knife sticking out of his back. Is it true?'

Theodore let out a snort of laughter. 'That does sound like a suitable end for my father. Stabbed in the back by a colleague. But it was nothing so romantic, young man. The police say he was shot through the head.'

'Really?' The boy's eyes became huge, and he disappeared, no doubt to spread the word about the means of death far and wide. So much for keeping it quiet.

'I'd better join the conference,' I said. 'I wonder if the news will have reached them before I get there.'

'Ten to one it has.' Theodore yawned. 'Impossible to keep a secret around here. Marjorie, I'm counting on you to make sure my raid on Buckingham Palace doesn't make the front page. I don't want to end up in clink for biffing that guard.' He checked his watch. 'Breakfast time. If anyone wants me,

I shall be reviving myself in the champagne bar at the Savoy.'
He heaved himself off the sofa.

Chapter 28

Theodore won his bet. When I walked into Charles Maltby's office, barely a minute later, the atmosphere was febrile. You could hardly see across the room for blue tobacco smoke. Six or seven men were shouting over each other.

They quietened as I walked in and turned their eyes on me like a pack of wolves sighting a stray sheep.

'Is it true, Miss Swallow?' asked the editor, his tone eager. 'Was he really shot dead?'

I sighed. Mr Maltby was still a suspect. 'I'm not supposed to say anything. The police asked me to keep it quiet. But as Mr Waddon's let the cat out of the bag, yes. Lord Ravensbourne was shot through the forehead.'

A clamour of questions followed.

'Hush, now. The lassie can't answer you all at once,' said Henry Beeching. 'Marjorie, tell us what you saw. The police have put out a statement, saying that a man's been found dead in the *Daily Post* offices, and they have launched an inquiry. Next of kin informed and so on. But they haven't named him or said how he died. We'll have this as an exclusive. Now, what have you got for us?'

I stood by the door, unsure how much to say. 'Just that. I went up to the office when I arrived – you were there, Mr

Beeching – and saw he was dead, with a bullet wound in his head. Then I went out, locked the door and called the police.'

The chief reporter Nicolas Cooper, a thin sallow man with a face that made me think of a weasel, looked up from his shorthand notebook. 'Was there a lot of blood? Did you scream or faint?'

'No,' I said, firmly. 'I worked in a hospital during the War. I've seen bullet wounds before.'

He looked disappointed. 'What did he look like? Surprised, angry, sad? Was there evidence of a fight – chairs knocked over, that sort of thing? Come on, Miss Swallow. You need to give me something to work with.'

'He was sitting in his chair at the desk. I checked he was dead, then I left the room.' I didn't want to give anything more away.

He sighed and capped his pen. 'Would you say that it came as a great shock, and you were upset and horrified by the dreadful scene of carnage?'

'Well, obviously it was a shock. It was very upsetting,' I conceded.

'Because you liked Lord Ravensbourne?'

I thought it best to be politic. 'He was perfectly pleasant to me.'

He nodded and began to scribble again in his notebook. 'That'll do, then. Don't speak to any of the others, will you?'

'I'd never speak to another newspaper…' I began.

He looked up, a secretive grin on his narrow face. 'Any of the other reporters.'

'All right, then, Cooper,' said Mr Maltby. 'Go and write that up, with the police statement and a quote from the family. Ask Dora Waddon – he'll give you something. And send a reporter around to Regent's Park with flowers and our condolences, to see if they can get anything out of Lady Ravensbourne.'

Charles Maltby banged his pipe out into a tin ashtray. Now that he was in charge of his newspaper, he seemed to be rather enjoying himself. His stammer had almost gone, I noticed.

Nicolas Cooper left the office.

'Reggie, how are you getting on? What angle are you taking with the leader?'

Reginald Pyke waved his cigarette in the air. 'Horrible crime, gun menace, government must act. Deep sadness, giant among men, revered on Fleet Street. All right? Or do you think I should go with good riddance, horrible tyrant, reap what you sow?'

The men chuckled. They all seemed a lot happier without the spectre of Lord Ravensbourne's tantrums hanging over them.

'A bit soon,' said Charles Maltby. 'Wait until after the funeral. Revenge is a dish best served cold, Reg.'

Much as I'd disliked Lord Ravensbourne, their callousness shocked me.

'Remember that Miss Waddon is very upset,' I ventured. 'She's in mourning, even if you aren't. And the chances are, she'll be your boss before long, if Lord Ravensbourne has left her the company.'

The chuckles died away to a thoughtful silence.

'Can't see a woman taking over,' said Reginald Pyke. 'Not even Beatrice. It's one thing to have them fussing around with their ladies' magazine. But running a daily newspaper is man's work.'

My hackles rose. 'Miss Ponsett would disagree,' I said. 'She thinks women can do any job. Including editor of a national newspaper.'

The men stared at me, aghast.

'Miss Waddon wouldn't put Belinda Ponsett in charge,' said Charles Maltby. It sounded more like a plea than a statement. 'That would be madness.'

I smiled, enjoying their discomfort. 'Who knows? I expect Miss Waddon will want to make some changes. You might need to prepare a fresh leader about the suffrage bill on Friday, Mr Pyke. I believe she has quite a different view from her father.'

'She's got a point, Reg,' said Mr Beeching. 'Time for a Damascene conversion to the cause of votes for women.'

The door flew open and George Quinn stamped in, forehead shining with sweat and apron covered in black smudges.

'I need someone to sign off on half a dozen journeymen,' he announced. 'I'm three men down, and if you're going to put through the spoof at six o'clock then the final before midnight, we need to double up. Bill Mead still hasn't come in, Tom Butcher's on his blooming honeymoon, and Alf Corker's got the 'flu.'

'Just call in whoever you need,' said Mr Maltby, exasperated. 'Good grief, Quinn. We can't be counting the pennies at a time like this. Manage your own business. Or do you want me to tie on an apron and operate the linotype machine myself?'

'Could you?' asked Henry Beeching, with a laugh. 'Might come in handy to have another string to your bow, if Belinda Ponsett gets your job.'

'Very funny. I came up through the regions,' said Mr Maltby, with a grin. 'I can do any job on this paper. We didn't have print unions at the *Somerset Chronicle* in the 1890s. I was the first to learn linotype when the machines finally arrived.

Should have stuck with that – I'd be earning more than I am in this job. Right, you lot. You all know what you're doing. Get onto it.'

So, Charles Maltby knew how to operate the linotype machine. That meant he could have been the source of the death notice without help from the printers, I realised. Did that also put him in the frame for murder?

The meeting began to break up, men heading off to their departments to carry out the editor's instructions. 'Lunch in El Vino's?' asked Henry Beeching, looking at his watch. 'It's half past one.'

Mr Maltby grabbed his raincoat. 'You know, I think I will. Coming, Reggie? We can raise a glass to the Big Man. And to the future of the *Post* without him.'

I stood meekly by the door as they all filed out to the lift. Charles Maltby, like Lord Ravensbourne, never locked his office. This was my opportunity to search for evidence. Their voices died away and I turned back to the empty room.

The editor's desk was littered with papers – galley proofs of the 'spoof' front page lead, in which the former foreign secretary Lord Curzon called for Mr Gandhi's arrest over trouble in India; photographs of society beauties on their wedding day for the front page; copy from news wires and court cases all mixed up. Mr Maltby needed secretarial assistance much more urgently than Lord Ravensbourne had. I began to sort through, putting them into order.

'What are you doing?'

I jumped, but it was only Jonathan Field, the junior reporter, peering around the door. His fair hair sprang up from his head, as if he'd been hanging upside down or – more probably – running his hands through it.

'Mr Maltby needs a secretary,' I said. 'His desk is a complete mess. I'm sorting out his correspondence.'

He seemed to accept that. 'I suppose you'll be looking for a new job, now that Lord Ravensbourne's dead.'

'I suppose so.' I hoped he'd go away and leave me to my search.

'Or will you go back to your real job with renowned detective Mrs Iris Jameson?' he asked, sitting in one of the vacated chairs and grinning at me, hands clasped behind his head. Oh dear. Perhaps the police had not been discreet after all.

Chapter 29

'How did you know?' I whispered, glancing at the door. I stepped across the room to shut it.

'Come for a drink and I'll tell you. The reporters are all celebrating in the Cheshire Cheese. I'm stuck in the library going through the cuttings. I've got to put together a load of tedious guff about His Lordship's glorious career. Why don't you tell me what you saw in Lord Ravensbourne's office, so I can write about that? And I'll keep your little secret. Is that a deal?'

I hesitated. 'I can't go out. I need to find something, while they're all out for lunch. Please, Jonathan. I'll tell you what I can. But you have to help me. How did you know about Mrs Jameson?'

He laughed. 'Not difficult, was it? I saw her go into the *Bugle* offices this morning, and recognised her from the inquest into Daisy Caldwell's death. She was with the American ambassador, wasn't she? I thought it was too much of a coincidence that both of you had been at the inquest into one suspicious death, then she suddenly reappeared after Lord Ravensbourne snuffed it. So, I dug into the cuttings in the library and found a whole load of articles about her investigations. Some of which mention her assistant, Miss

Marjorie Swallow.'

I sighed. I'd have to start using a false name. Fame and undercover operations did not go together.

'That makes you the best reporter in the building, then,' I said. 'None of the others have noticed they have a pair of private detectives working under their noses. They just see a secretary as someone to make the tea.'

He looked pleased at the compliment. 'Talking of tea…'

'No. I've got a job to do.' I looked despairingly at the piles of paper. 'Listen, I'll tell you what I'm doing, if you help me. Two heads are better than one, and this is going to take me ages.'

I explained about the death notice that had been sent to Lord Ravensbourne, and how I'd gone undercover in an attempt to find out who produced it.

'Mr Maltby had plenty of motive, and he knows how to use the linotype machine,' I said. 'He was boasting about it in conference. I'm looking for anything that would link him to the galley proof.'

Jonathan whistled. 'You think the editor bumped off Lord Ravensbourne? I wouldn't have thought he had the nerve.'

I shrugged. 'I don't know about the murder. But I'd like to find out if he sent that death notice.'

'Have you been through the spike? Maltby's old school. Ten to one he spikes everything he's touched. And anything more than a week old will be on the spike packets in the cupboard.'

'Thank you,' I breathed. 'That's brilliant.'

We worked together. I checked through everything on the spike on Charles Maltby's desk, while Jonathan heaved big envelopes of paper out of the cupboard. I glanced at the clock. The editor and his cronies had been gone for three quarters of an hour. Their lunch break was usually at least an hour, but with such a busy day, perhaps they'd be back early.

'Nothing here,' I said, trying to rearrange the papers on the spike to disguise my rummaging. 'How are you getting on?'

'Look at this.' The reporter's voice was full of suppressed excitement. He sat on the floor, surrounded by envelopes and paper. I crouched next to him.

'This envelope is from two weeks ago,' he said. 'There's a galley proof of the death notice. And this sheet of paper. That's Maltby's handwriting on the headline – you can see it on all the other notes he's written. But he uses black ink, and that's not the only writing.'

I read the words on the sheet of foolscap paper. Words written in blue ink, with elegant copperplate handwriting.

'Fleet Street was today plunged into mourning as the death was announced of the popular newspaper proprietor Lord Ravensbourne,' Jonathan read aloud. 'What a lot of rot.'

'It's Reginald Pyke's writing,' I said. 'They must have composed it together. Charles Maltby wrote the headline about an unfortunate accident. Then Mr Pyke took over.' I grinned at Jonathan. 'We did it! We found who sent the death notice. I'd better tell Mrs Jameson.'

A loud harrumph sounded from the doorway. We both started up guiltily, the papers spread around us. We'd been too absorbed to notice the door opening.

'Well, well. Someone's been busy. I thought you were going to leave the investigations to me, Miss Swallow.'

Inspector Carfax strolled over and plucked the paper from my hand.

'How interesting. I expect you were about to hand this piece of evidence straight to the City of London Police, weren't you?'

I scrambled to my feet. 'You wouldn't have found it at all if I hadn't gone looking for it,' I pointed out.

'And you wouldn't have found it if I hadn't helped,' said Jonathan, who'd pulled his notebook out of his jacket pocket. 'Jonathan Field, reporter with the *Daily Post*. Can you tell me how this new piece of evidence affects the inquiry into Lord Ravensbourne's death, sir?'

Inspector Carfax let out a low chuckle and pushed Jonathan's notebook away.

'You print a word of this, and I'll have you in a cell for obstructing the course of justice and contempt of court,' he said.

I expected Jonathan to quail at the threat, but he shook his head confidently. 'I found it and you've got it, so I haven't obstructed anything. And no-one's been charged, so it isn't contempt of court. You'll have to get an injunction if you want to keep it quiet,' he said.

The inspector was looking as if he was about to explode with annoyance, when the door opened again.

'What on earth is going on?' asked Charles Maltby, hanging his hat on the stand. 'What are you doing in here, Field?' He saw the paper in Inspector Carfax's hand and took a step back, dismay written across his face.

'You bloody idiot, Charles,' said Reginald Pyke, who'd followed him in. 'You should have burnt it.' He gazed in horror at Inspector Carfax and turned suddenly, running straight into the barrel chest of Sergeant Voles.

Inspector Carfax beamed, a big smile across his saturnine face. 'Well, this is tremendously convenient,' he said. 'Saves me the bother of having to come to you. Arrest them both, Sergeant, on suspicion of conspiracy to murder. We'll continue the conversation at the police station, shall we?'

Outside Mr Maltby's room, Mrs Jameson stood at the door of the *Bugle* office, watching impassively. The reporters, straggling back from their jolly lunch at the Cheshire Cheese, stared with their jaws hanging open, and the legions of boys seemed to multiply before our eyes as Charles Maltby and Reginald Pyke were handcuffed and led through the office to the lift.

The second the lift doors closed, chaos erupted. All the reporters asked each other what was happening. The boys set off in a mass, like chattering starlings, to carry the news to every corner of the building.

Nicolas Cooper, the chief reporter, had arrived just in time to see his editor being frog-marched out of the building. He began shouting contradictory instructions for people to variously shut up, tell him what had happened, get back to their desks and gather for a news meeting.

'In here,' I said to Jonathan. 'Quickly, before he sees you.'

We slipped into the *Bugle* office and shut the door.

'Well?' asked Mrs Jameson. 'Who is your friend, Marjorie?'

I made quick introductions. 'Jonathan recognised us from the Daisy Caldwell case,' I explained. 'But he's going to keep quiet about it for now.'

'Scout's honour, Mrs Jameson,' said Jonathan. 'I just want to know what's happening. Like everyone else. This could make my name on the *Post*.'

'Hmm.' Mrs Jameson eyed him suspiciously.

'He found the first draft of the death notice in Charles Maltby's office,' I added quickly. 'It was a co-production. Mr Pyke and Mr Maltby wrote it together.' I explained how Mr Maltby had boasted at the editorial meeting about being able to do any job on the paper, and I had decided to search his office while he was out for lunch.

'Good work.' Mrs Jameson nodded her approval. 'But I suppose Inspector Carfax will now proceed to make a mountain out of a molehill. Conspiracy to a rather childish prank is not the same as conspiracy to murder.'

I looked at our timeline. Mr Pyke and Mr Maltby said they had been together at the Press Club from around midnight until one, which included the likely time of Lord Ravensbourne's death. Would their alibis stand up? And where did they go afterwards?

'But if they wrote the death notice, surely it isn't a coincidence that Lord Ravensbourne was shot on that same day,' said Jonathan. 'They must be the murderers. Or one of them must. I can't see the editor with a gun in his hand, but Mr Pyke…' He grinned. 'I wouldn't like to meet him in a bad mood down Hanging Sword Alley on a dark night.'

Mrs Jameson tapped the timeline. 'Except he wasn't shot on the same day,' she said. 'The question is, who knew that Lord Ravensbourne had received that death notice?'

Jonathan's quick brain didn't miss a beat. 'You mean he was shot by someone who wanted to take advantage of it. Someone who knew the police would look for the authors of the death notice.'

My employer smiled the feline smile that spread across her face and narrowed her eyes. 'Precisely. You seem to have found us an asset, Marjorie. Young man, if you help us and keep quiet until the investigation is concluded, I believe we could work together in future. You get your story and plenty of information about future cases. We get your silence and inside knowledge about the *Daily Post*.'

He grinned and held out his hand. 'It's a deal. Pleasure doing business with you, Mrs Jameson.'

'Now, you'd better both find out what's happening. Mr Field, you may use the information about the death threat, but not the means by which you uncovered it. Is that understood?'

Chapter 30

We emerged into the newsroom. The men sat around the long table, chief reporter Nicolas Cooper at one end and chief sub-editor Henry Beeching at the other. Mr Beeching was attempting to bring calm. I slipped into the seat beside him and drew out my notebook and pencil, while Jonathan quietly pulled up a chair at the far end.

Mr Beeching nodded gravely at me. 'Take minutes, Miss Swallow. Listen to me, everyone. In Charles Maltby's absence, I'll be acting editor. I know everyone's had a shock, but we still have a newspaper to get off stone today.

'The spoof front pages are made up, ready to go at six. I will oversee the tributes to Lord Ravensbourne on page two and three of the final; page four and five will be dedicated to His Lordship's life and achievements. Cooper will write the front page lead, which will go to press last to enable us to include the latest information.

'The early pages are already made up, and the sport can go next. Is that ready, Tonhill?'

A burly man with rolled-up sleeves and a red face nodded. 'Almost, Mr Beeching. I just need to check the headlines.'

'Get it done and sent down. How are we getting on with four and five?'

Nicolas Cooper sought out Jonathan. 'I put Field onto it,' he said. 'It's just a clippings job, so it should be within his capabilities. Finished yet, have you? Or did you get detained in the pub?' He gave a nasty smile.

'I didn't go out for lunch,' said Jonathan, brightly. 'I was in Mr Maltby's office. Do you want to know why the police arrested him and Mr Pyke, or would you rather I went back to the clippings?'

'What the hell were you doing in the editor's office?' demanded Mr Cooper, which seemed to be rather missing the point.

'Tell us what you know, lad,' said Mr Beeching, leaning forward over the table.

Jonathan leaned back in his chair. 'I was looking for a clipping about Lord Ravensbourne's marriage. I thought Mr Maltby might have a folder of cuttings that I couldn't find. I knew it was urgent,' he said solemnly, although I could hear a hint of mischief in his voice. 'I went to see if it was on his desk. And I found a galley proof of the death notice that was sent to Lord Ravensbourne, along with a hand-written draft in Mr Maltby and Mr Pyke's writing.'

General excitement broke out around the room.

'Quiet,' called Mr Beeching. 'How did the police get involved?'

He glanced at me, but kept his word. 'The inspector arrived in the office just after I'd found it, so of course I had to show him. Then Mr Maltby and Mr Pyke came back from lunch, and he arrested them on suspicion of conspiracy to murder.'

The reporters were fizzing with excitement, but Mr Beeching's face was grave. He called for silence again.

'Marjorie, shut the door to the corridor. Make sure there

are no boys listening at it.'

I did as he said.

'As I'm sure you all know,' Mr Beeching said heavily, 'in England, a man is innocent until proven guilty. Not a word of what Field has just said goes outside this room. Is that understood?'

'But surely...' Mr Cooper, the chief reporter, was looking rather wan. I supposed Jonathan had taken the wind out of his sails.

'Quiet, man.' The chief sub-editor looked around the table, catching every reporter's eye. 'If it turns out that two of our own journalists are behind this crime, you can be sure we will not spare the details. But at present, two men have been arrested in connection with this foul murder. We will not name them, unless the police do so. We will not report speculation about why they have been arrested. I hope that is clear. We will continue to prepare a newspaper in tribute to our late proprietor, and announce his untimely death.'

There were murmurings of discontent, but no-one had the nerve to say anything out loud.

'Field?'

Jonathan had been looking rather deflated. He glanced up. 'Yes, sir?'

'You will take over the writing of the front page lead. Cooper, complete the tribute pages to Lord Ravensbourne.'

'What?' Cooper leapt to his feet. 'He's a junior reporter. He can't be trusted with the biggest story this newspaper has ever had.' He clenched his thin jaw and looked daggers at Jonathan, who sat as if dazed, a smile spreading across his face. 'You've lost it, Beeching. I'm not standing for this.'

'I don't think you have much choice, Cooper.' Beatrice's

clear voice rang out from the door. She looked composed, her jet-black jacket and skirt emphasising the paleness of her face. 'Mr Beeching, thank you for stepping into the breach. I will sit in on the remainder of the editorial meetings today. I want to see every page that mentions my father before it goes to press. I have spoken to our solicitor, and he has confirmed what I already knew: Lord Ravensbourne wished me to take up the reins of Ravensbourne Amalgamated Publications on his death.'

She walked to the head of the table and motioned for Nicolas Cooper to step aside. She sat in his chair and glanced around the room.

'And that is what I intend to do. Miss Swallow, you will act as my secretary. I shall work from the *Bugle* office, until my father's rooms become available again. I will write a leader about my father's death, and Miss Ponsett will write the second leader, about the Representation of the People amendment bill.

'Mr Beeching, you can move into the editor's office. The sub-editors should be called up from the canteen, before we run out of bacon. I'm sure they are enjoying working from there, but I think it would be better if they work with the reporters in this room, until the police have finished with the fifth floor.'

She looked up at the chief reporter, who seemed uncertain what to do without a chair. 'Perhaps you could organise the furniture, Cooper, so that the two teams can work alongside each other.' She smiled. 'In fact, I may decide to keep this arrangement, as it will allow for better team working.'

The men muttered in mutiny, but Mr Beeching was watching in admiration.

'You heard the lady,' he said. 'Get on with it. Send a boy down for the subs. Bring Miss Waddon the galley proofs of the tributes to her father that we have ready made-up. And Field, come into the editor's office with me and we can discuss with Miss Waddon how we're going to write that front page story.'

It was a coup. Enough to make me wonder whether Beatrice and Henry Beeching had consulted each other about it before the meeting. And if so, how long ago they had started to plan it.

Chapter 31

Somehow, the newspaper was assembled and put to bed. Miraculously, Henry Beeching had prevented news of Lord Ravensbourne's murder from spreading beyond the *Daily Post*. The spoof with the India story had worked.

Early editions of the other newspapers included bare paragraphs stating that police were investigating the suspicious death of a man at the *Daily Post*, and that two men had been arrested. They made as much of the scant police information as they could, but Lord Ravensbourne's name was not mentioned.

Mrs Jameson and I went home to Bedford Square at ten for a late supper. While we were eating cold game pie, a boy brought to the door a copy of the *Daily Post* with a blaring headline: 'Lord Ravensbourne murdered in his office.'

'Miss Waddon thought you would want to see it,' said the boy, before Graham led him away to be fed buns in the kitchen.

We spread the newspaper out on the dining table. The front page photograph was rather flattering: clearly taken in his younger days, it showed Lord Ravensbourne in riding clothes, holding the head of a fine black stallion, like the country gentleman he wasn't. The story underneath was a mishmash of what Jonathan and I had discovered, and what Nicolas Cooper had got out of me earlier in the day. I groaned as I read it.

'The dreadful discovery was made by Lord Ravensbourne's secretary, Miss Marjorie Swallow, 25, from Catford in south London.

'"He was sitting at his desk with a bullet wound through his head," she told the *Post*. "I was shocked and distressed by the dreadful scene of carnage."'

Mrs Jameson snorted. 'Did you really say that?'

I cringed, remembering how the reporter had put words into my mouth. 'Not exactly.'

We read on. 'Only Miss Swallow's patriotic experience as a nurse during the Great War prevented her from fainting dead away at the scene. She used her training to confirm death, then fled from the room and locked away its horrors before calling the police.

'"It was very upsetting. But I have seen bullet wounds before," said the brave secretary, a pretty brunette with a shapely figure. "Lord Ravensbourne was always very kind to me." She then broke down and was unable to speak to us further.'

'Oh, goodness.' Why did they have to comment on my appearance?

'Lord Ravensbourne is survived by two children from his first marriage, Theodore, now Lord Ravensbourne (23), and Miss Beatrice Waddon (24), his second wife Lady Ravensbourne (35, formerly Miss Annabel Quick) and their children Sylvia (5) and David (3). The new Lord Ravensbourne said: "Father's death is a great shock to us all. It's hard to believe he is dead. He was such a towering figure, he seemed to be immortal."'

I'd heard what Theodore had told Jonathan Field. He'd said the old man was such a devil that he'd expected him to live forever. Mr Beeching had re-written it for public consumption.

The final line of the report gave terse news about the investigation: 'The police have arrested two men, who are assisting them with their inquiries into Lord Ravensbourne's tragic demise.' A second story down page gave details of the death notice that had been sent to Lord Ravensbourne over a week ago. 'Sinister prank that foretold death,' the headline read. 'Did the author know what was to come?'

Mr Beeching had kept his word. The story didn't mention that the editor and chief leader writer had produced the death notice, or that they were currently under arrest.

Graham appeared at the dining room door. 'Inspector Carfax for you, Mrs Jameson. Shall I ask him to return in the morning?'

We exchanged apprehensive glances.

'Show him into the office,' said Mrs Jameson. 'Give him a drink and tell him we shall attend him presently.'

Chapter 32

When we joined him, Inspector Carfax was pacing in front of the bookshelves, whisky in hand, his mouth pursed in a whistle.

'You have an eclectic collection, Mrs Jameson,' he observed.

Back copies of *The Lancet*, the *British Medical Journal* and the *New England Journal of Medicine* took up several shelves on one wall. The remainder contained past editions of the *Criminal Law Casebook*, modern herbals and medical dictionaries, books on poison and gunshot wounds, and a selection of penny dreadful true crime publications.

'I also have novels by Katherine Mansfield, Virginia Woolf and F Scott Fitzgerald, if you wish to borrow some bedtime reading,' said Mrs Jameson. 'Or is Agatha Christie more your sort of thing?'

'Busman's holiday,' he said. 'I prefer PG Wodehouse.' He set down his drink. 'I apologise for disturbing you so late. I should like to know your thoughts about the likelihood of Charles Maltby, who admits to having written and printed the death notice, having murdered his employer.'

She gestured to the chairs, and we all sat down. 'My feminine intuition, you mean?'

He sighed, put down the glass and stretched out his legs.

'Maltby was playing billiards with Pyke until one. The doorman at the Press Club confirms that, for what it's worth. He then says he walked home to Pimlico, because he had a lot to think about, returning to the bosom of his wife and family at about half past two. All within the medic's window of possibility for time of death.'

'How unfortunate that he decided to walk,' murmured Mrs Jameson. 'So very difficult to check an alibi without witnesses.'

'Indeed. Mrs Jameson, I'll be straight with you. I don't believe that rabbit of a man walked into Lord Ravensbourne's office with a pistol, pointed it at his employer's head and shot him dead, then coolly strolled home. I know Scotland Yard values your experience. I want to know what you think.'

She smiled. 'I think you should test his alibi,' she said. 'I take it you have confirmed his arrival home with his wife?'

He nodded moodily. 'Not that one can rely on wives,' he said. 'But she says half-past two. She got up when he arrived back, to check on their children.'

'And have you had a constable walk the distance from Fleet Street to Pimlico, to see how long it takes?'

'It took my man an hour and twelve minutes, but he's six foot two, so he walks fast.'

'You're all so tall,' I interrupted. I saw Mrs Jameson's face flicker with annoyance. She hated it when I made banal comments. But the inspector grinned.

'Our height requirement is two inches taller than the Metropolitan police,' he said. 'Tallest constabulary in the country. Sergeant Voles won an Olympic medal, you know.'

'Really?' I was fascinated. 'Whatever for?'

'Tug of War. The City of London team beat Sweden and the United States. More importantly, we beat the Metropolitan police team.'

'This is all very charming,' said Mrs Jameson impatiently. 'But irrelevant. I am tired, Inspector Carfax. Tell me why, exactly, you do not regard Mr Maltby as a suspect.'

He sighed. 'He's just not the type,' he admitted. 'He's too timid. He even says that the death notice wasn't his idea. He says he thought it was a family joke.'

'I suppose he blamed Reginald Pyke, Lord Ravensbourne's brother-in-law,' I said. 'He hates Lord Ravensbourne. And he is more the type, don't you think?'

'Is that what your female intuition tells you?' asked Mrs Jameson, her tone scornful. I winced.

But Inspector Carfax rubbed his long face and turned his gaze on me. 'I agree, Miss Swallow. Surly fellow. And his alibi is feeble. He was with Maltby until one, then took a cab back to his rooms in Islington and slept like a baby until the morning. We're looking for the cab driver and talking to his landlady. Until such time as he's proven innocent, I'm assuming he had a hand in it. He admits to the death notice business; but he says it wasn't his idea. Just a prank, he claims.'

He paused. 'There is one person of interest we have been unable to locate, Miss Swallow. I believe you have met him. William Mead, a known communist. Several of the printers said he had threatened to kill Lord Ravensbourne. They said you overheard the conversation.'

I shivered. 'I did. He pretended to point a gun at Mr Quinn, the head printer, and said something like: "Bullet in the brain, goodbye Lord Ravensbourne".'

Inspector Carfax grunted. 'Well, Mr Mead left his work without authorisation before midnight last night. He was supposed to be working the night shift. He hasn't been in at all today. I sent a couple of policemen to his home in Whitechapel, but he hasn't been there either – or so his family say.'

He knocked out his pipe in the ashtray and rose. 'Thank you for your time, Mrs Jameson. If anything comes to you, do let me know.' He picked up his briefcase. 'Do return those papers to me tomorrow, won't you? Did you find anything of interest in them, Miss Swallow?'

I started guiltily. I'd almost forgotten Lord Ravensbourne's notes, which Mrs Jameson had abstracted from the inspector's desk that morning.

'Nothing yet,' I admitted.

After he'd gone, I slipped down the back stairs to the kitchen. Graham and Frankie were each drinking a bottle of beer and reading our discarded copy of the *Daily Post*.

Frankie looked up and chortled. 'At least it says you're pretty.'

'They say that about any young woman,' I pointed out. 'It's hardly a compliment. My mother is going to be mortified.'

'I'm sure she'll understand that these newspaper folk have their own way of putting things,' said Graham. But he looked indignant on my behalf. 'Can I get you anything, Marjorie? Warm milk?' He knew I hated beer.

'Thank you. That'd be nice.' Not that I'd need help sleeping – it was as much as I could do to keep my eyes open. I settled into the chair by the fire. 'Frankie, do you know a chap called Bill Mead? Works as a printer on the *Daily Post*, lives in Whitechapel. He's involved in trades unions and stuff.'

'Stuff?' She looked up and raised her eyebrows. 'You mean communism, I suppose. I've heard of him, all right. Don't know him, mind.'

'He's gone missing,' I explained. 'And he threatened to kill

Lord Ravensbourne last week. The police want to talk to him.'

She swigged her beer. 'I bet they do.'

I sipped at my malted milk. 'Come on, Frankie. Help me out. I think he could be dangerous. He said Lord Ravensbourne could expect the same end as the Romanovs.'

She yawned. 'After seeing those dirty pictures the bloke kept by his bed, I agree with Bill. Don't you, Marge? I bet the police wouldn't have wanted to talk to Lord blooming Ravensbourne if that secretary had reported him for groping her.'

I had an uncomfortable feeling she was right. 'But this is murder, Frankie. If Bill Mead's going around shooting people, we have to find him. And if it wasn't him, we need to know his alibi.'

She gave me a long, steady stare. 'I don't like handing blokes over to the police,' she said. 'I'll see if anyone knows anything. But I'm not making any promises.'

Graham gave an apologetic cough. 'My sister still lives in Whitechapel. Her husband works on the docks, and he's a union man. Not a communist, mind, but he hears things. Maybe I could have a word with her.'

Frankie gave him an unfriendly look. 'Remember, Graham. Whitechapel people don't like narks.'

Chapter 33

Frankie drove Mrs Jameson and me to Fleet Street the next morning, dropping me a block away so we could arrive separately. I was glad of the ride; the weather had not improved and my throat felt scratchy from the fog. I hoped I wasn't coming down with a cold. The middle of a murder investigation was no time to get poorly.

I arrived at nine. The newsroom was noisy and thronged with people; the reporters and sub-editors crowding in around hastily erected trestle tables. Mr Cooper's typewriter clacked and reporters shouted into telephones, struggling to make themselves heard above the clamour.

Henry Beeching looked comfortable in the editor's office, his door open and a steady stream of reporters going in and out. He raised a hand in greeting as I crossed to the relative quiet of the Hive.

Inside, however, the bees were not working in harmony. 'We need to finalise the next issue of the *Bugle* today,' Belinda Ponsett was insisting. 'It's so important, with the vote on Friday.'

Beatrice, pale and composed in her mourning black, nodded to me as I came in. Mrs Jameson was already there, sitting at the desk allocated to us. 'You do what you think best,

Belinda, but you know the subscription numbers. We're lucky to sell twelve hundred copies a month. The *Post* prints over a million each day, and employs eight hundred people. I have to prioritise that.'

Belinda looked to be on the verge of tears. 'You won't risk everything we've built up for that Tory rag, will you?'

Beatrice's cold gaze betrayed the singlemindedness that had characterised her father. 'That Tory rag pays our rent and funds the *Bugle*. And anyway,' she gave a brief smile, 'it's my Tory rag, now.' She turned to my employer. 'Mrs Jameson, do you have any progress to report? I understand from Inspector Carfax that my uncle has been released from custody.'

I stopped in my tracks. Mrs Jameson looked startled.

'That was not the expectation I had last night,' she said slowly. 'Inspector Carfax told me he suspected your uncle. What has he told you?'

Beatrice sighed impatiently. 'Really, I do think you should be reporting to me, rather than the other way around. The inspector telephoned me this morning to say that Uncle Reggie has been released from Cloak Lane police station, because his alibi was confirmed. His taxi-driver came forward to speak to the police.'

'I see.' Mrs Jameson stared into space, tapping her index finger on her chin. I slipped out to the kitchen to make tea. I knew better than to interrupt her when she was thinking.

As I waited for the kettle to boil, Jonathan Field came in and grabbed two cups.

'Did you see my story?' he asked, eagerly. 'My first front page lead. I'm on my way, Miss Swallow.'

I grunted. 'I saw what you said about me.'

He had the decency to look abashed. 'Cooper had written

that already, and Mr Beeching said to keep it in. But it was complimentary, wasn't it?'

'If you say so.' I looked at the cups in his hand. 'Don't tell me you're making tea for someone else? What's brought that on?'

He rolled his eyes. 'I'm looking after someone for Mr Beeching. This woman's come in, making a fuss about wanting to see Mr Pyke. She says he should be either here or at home. Mr Beeching doesn't like to tell her he's in a police cell.'

I frowned. 'But he isn't. He was released this morning, Miss Waddon says.' I poured tea into the cups and added milk and sugar. 'Where is she? Maybe I should go and talk to her.'

The woman was sitting in the corner of the office, a felt hat jammed down on her yellowish hair, clutching a handbag on her lap. I pulled up a chair next to her and handed her the cup and saucer.

'I brought you a cuppa. I'm Miss Swallow, secretary to Miss Waddon. Can I help you?'

The woman took it gratefully. 'Thanks, Miss. I'm parched. I've been all over looking for Reg… Mr Pyke.' She was in her thirties, cheaply but fashionably dressed in thin fabrics cut to the latest styles. The *Daily Post* would have described her figure as shapely. 'I'm Mrs Angerstein. He has lodgings with me, in Islington. Has done for years.'

'You know he was taken into police custody yesterday?' I asked.

'All a lot of nonsense. That's what I told the policeman when he came around last night. They should have asked me first, shouldn't they?'

'You mean… you told them what time he got home on Monday night?' I wasn't sure how that would exonerate Mr Pyke from shooting Lord Ravensbourne before he arrived home.

She nodded her head vigorously. 'He got back at twenty past one. I'd been waiting up for him, in case he wanted any supper.' She coloured. 'He sometimes likes a chop when he gets in. And a natter.'

'I see...' I mused. 'And you can be quite sure that he didn't leave the house again after returning home?'

'Quite sure,' she said, setting her chin defiantly. 'I rang the police station just after seven this morning. I wanted to talk to the man in charge, not the constable who came round last night. But they said they'd found the cabbie who picked Reg up from his club Monday night. So, they'd already let him go.

'The question is, Miss, where is he now? When he wasn't back by eight, I thought I'd better check at the police station, but he'd long gone. Then I thought I'd come here. I was worried about him, see. He's not a well man, between you and me. Liverish. But that reporter says he hasn't come here, either.'

'Wait here a second,' I said. 'Perhaps he went to stay with his family. I'll ask Miss Waddon.'

But Beatrice had not seen her uncle. 'I don't see why he would have come to Gordon Square,' she said. 'Or Regent's Park. He doesn't get on with Annabel at all. Calls her a gold-digger. I suppose he might have gone to see Theo, although I don't suppose he'd get a warm welcome at seven in the morning.'

Mrs Jameson was on her feet. 'I don't like this,' she said. 'We need to find Mr Pyke. Marjorie, call Frankie and get her to bring the car over. Let's see if we can locate him.'

Chapter 34

We dropped Mr Pyke's landlady off on the way, just in case he had returned home to Islington, and persuaded her to stay in to wait for him. Then Frankie drove to the Albany apartments, in a courtyard just off Piccadilly.

The portico to the handsome three-storey apartment block was guarded by a green-liveried porter, who was extremely disapproving when Mrs Jameson and I approached. No, he could not say whether the young Lord Ravensbourne was at home. No, he would not let us in to find out. No, he could not say whether Lord Ravensbourne had any visitors that morning.

Eventually Mrs Jameson resorted to a truly outrageous bribe in order to have him convey a message to Theodore. As soon as he was away from his post, an exquisitely pretty young woman in evening dress and a big mink coat tiptoed down the stairs, with her ivory strapped shoes in her hand.

'Wait!' I spun around and followed her across the courtyard, catching her as she paused to slip on her shoes. 'I recognise you from the illustrated papers. You're Lord Northington's daughter, aren't you?'

She looked at me with defiance. 'What if I am?'

'I work for Beatrice Waddon, Theodore's sister. We need to

know if his uncle is with him. Reginald Pyke.'

'And what makes you think I would know anything about that?' she huffed, looking down her aristocratic nose.

I took a deep breath. 'Theodore told me about you, Lady Victoria. He said you'd been out with him on Monday night. And he said you'd stayed over in his set.' Which she had clearly just done again, despite it being very much against the rules.

She drew herself up and faced me. 'I have no idea what you're talking about.'

'Oh, please,' I begged. 'I just need to know if Mr Pyke came to see him this morning. If he's still there now.'

Lady Victoria gave me a cool gaze. 'Of course not. If you really knew Dora, you'd know there's absolutely no point in disturbing him before midday at the earliest. Now, get out of my way. I need a taxi.'

She flounced out to Piccadilly, just as the porter returned.

'Lord Ravensbourne has not risen yet,' he announced. 'He has no guests and does not wish to receive any. Will that be all, ladies?'

We returned to the Lagonda and Frankie drove us back along Piccadilly. 'Where now, Mrs J?'

'We may as well call in to see Lady Ravensbourne. Turn left onto Regent's Street and up to the Park.'

Lady Ravensbourne and her two small children occupied a charming villa on the outer circle of Regent's Park. The creamy stucco pillars were well set back from the road, half-hidden behind trees. The butler conveyed Mrs Jameson's condolences and request to see Lady Ravensbourne.

The former Annabel Quick was a steady-eyed woman in her thirties with sleek chestnut hair. Her mourning dress of black crepe de chine was well-cut and tasteful. She showed no signs of excessive grief, or of inappropriate levity. I glanced around the drawing room. It too was decorated with good taste, from the heather tweed sofas and armchairs to the pleated silk lampshades and vases of carnations on the mantelpiece. I was rather impressed. I'd expected something flashier from what I'd heard of Lord Ravensbourne's second wife.

She rose to greet us and accepted our condolences with grace. Mrs Jameson stated our mission, explaining that she was a friend of Beatrice Waddon who was anxious about her uncle's safety.

'I'm afraid Mr Pyke rarely comes here,' said Lady Ravensbourne. She thought for a moment. 'He was with us at Christmas,' she said. 'We had a family party in Hertfordshire on Christmas Day, but he left the next morning. I don't believe I have seen him since.'

She looked at me with curiosity. 'I understand you worked as my late husband's secretary, Miss Swallow. May I ask if you were happy in your employment?'

I was a little taken aback. 'I'd only been there a week, Lady Ravensbourne. I had no cause for complaint.'

Her eyes rested on me a moment longer. 'I'm glad to hear it. Well, do let me know if there is anything else.'

We took the hint and departed. I thought again of Miss Pringle, and the photograph. Had Lady Ravensbourne known how her husband behaved to his female staff? But of course, I thought. She had been his secretary herself. She must know exactly what he had been like.

'Cloak Lane police station,' Mrs Jameson told Frankie. 'We'd better go back to the place where he was last seen.'

Frankie consulted her London atlas. 'Down by the river,' she announced. 'Just north of Southwark Bridge, near Cannon

Street railway station. The traffic will be horrible.'

We made a sharp exit from Regent's Park, navigated our way through the familiar territory of Bloomsbury, purred slowly along Chancery Lane which was indeed clogged with omnibuses and taxi-cabs, before skirting around St Paul's Cathedral and across the Mansion House junction.

Cloak Lane police station was a plain red-brick building with stone cladding on the ground floor, grubby with soot. The entrance was on a corner, beneath a portico bearing the City of London arms. As we started up the steps, the door burst open, and Sergeant Voles almost knocked us back down them.

'Mind where you're going,' he growled.

'Are you all right, Sergeant Voles?' asked Mrs Jameson. 'You seem in a rush.'

He straightened his helmet, which had been knocked sideways in our encounter.

'It's you,' he stated, looking us up and down with suspicion.

'We're looking for Reginald Pyke,' said Mrs Jameson. 'I understand he was held here overnight and released this morning. But he hasn't been seen since.'

He rubbed his big face, and his eyes were troubled. 'I know. But I think we might have found him.'

Chapter 35

Evil-smelling fog swirled up from the river. We darted across busy Upper Thames Street into an alley that ran between tall wharves and fur merchants on one side, and a looming brick warehouse on the other. The stink of decay rose to meet us.

I wrapped my scarf around my nose and mouth, my chest tightening as Frankie and I ran down to Old Queenhithe on Sergeant Voles' heels. Queenhithe was famous as the most ancient of London's docks, a shallow square basin cut out of the river wall, although it was barely used nowadays. Across the river, the tall chimneys of the gasworks belched dark smoke, intensifying the gloom.

I peered over the river wall. The tide was receding, galloping down to Tower Bridge with its cargo of barges and flotsam, veiled in an unhealthy yellow haze. Two lighters moored in Queenhithe swayed slowly at anchor, settling on their flat bases as the water drained away.

Someone stood on the foreshore beside a rotting wooden piling, where the silt of the river met the water. There was a muddy bundle at his feet. Sergeant Voles hailed him, and he looked up, peering through the murk, and waved an arm.

'Down 'ere, Mister.'

The sergeant gave Frankie and me a severe look. 'Stay up on

the wharf,' he warned. 'I don't want you getting swallowed up by that mud. I've seen it happen. You lose your footing, and the tide'll take you before you know it.'

I needed no persuasion to stay on dry land as Sergeant Voles climbed over the wall and descended the wooden ladder, slippery with green weed, that led down to the sloping shore of the dock.

'Is that him?' asked Frankie, her voice low. 'Pyke?'

'Can't tell from here.' The run from the police station had winded me. I leaned on the wall, closed my eyes for a moment against the stinging fog. When I opened them again, Sergeant Voles and the other man were carrying the bundle up the slope to drier land. The man returned to one of the lighters, wading through water to his knees.

'It's a body, all right,' said Frankie, unnecessarily. 'Drowned, I suppose. They'll have to winch the poor blighter up.'

'No. I've called the River Police at Wapping to send a boat.' Inspector Carfax had arrived, accompanied by Mrs Jameson. 'The sergeant can stay with the body until they arrive.' He too climbed over the wall and descended into the gloom. His footsteps filled with water, erasing themselves as he walked across the strand.

Mrs Jameson's face was sombre. 'The station had a lighter-man call in ten minutes ago,' she said. 'He saw the body rolling in the tide, caught by a piling. His mate stayed with it, while he went for the police.'

Inspector Carfax straightened up from his examination of the body, his face grim. He climbed back up the ladder, then wiped his hands fastidiously on his handkerchief, looking with distaste at the grime on his fingers. His shoes were caked in mud and the bottom of his trousers were splashed and wet.

'Mr Pyke?' Mrs Jameson asked.

'We'll need family to confirm his identity,' he said, shortly. 'But I'd say so.' He stared across the river for a moment. 'I don't like to ask Miss Waddon. It's not a job for a lady. I suppose the brother will have to do. I'd better send someone to wake him.'

I had an incongruous vision of Theodore climbing down the ladder in his pearl-grey suit and calfskin shoes, mauve rosebud in his buttonhole. But I supposed the identification would take place at the mortuary.

'Drowned, do you think?' Mrs Jameson asked. 'Was he pushed?'

The inspector sighed. 'You know I can't tell you that. The doctor will perform a post-mortem examination.' He glanced down at the beach. 'But I should say the man was dead when he went into the water.'

'You mean on account of the weight of the body and the volume of fluid in the lungs?'

He hunched his shoulders, plunging his hands into his mackintosh pockets. 'Not really. On account of the bullet hole in the back of his skull.'

Chapter 36

Mrs Jameson sat in the corner of Inspector Carfax's office, poring over the tide tables. One of the constables had brought in a big brown teapot, and I warmed my hands around a cup of strong tea.

'High tide was just before six this morning,' Mrs Jameson observed. 'It would have turned by seven and begun to recede, I suppose. Inspector Carfax, is Queenhithe Dock completely full of water at high tide?'

'Almost. There's a sixteen-foot tidal reach, and it drops about three feet an hour.' He looked at his watch. 'Eleven o'clock. Another hour and a half until low tide.' He struck a match and puffed his pipe alight, increasing the murkiness of the room.

'The River Police will know for sure, but I'd guess the water was still pretty high when his body went in. We know it can't have been before seven, when we released him. He may not have gone in at Queenhithe, of course, but given the proximity to the police station I'd say he probably did. Southwark Bridge is downstream, and the tide was going out, so he can't have gone in there. Blackfriars is a possibility, but it's further away.

'The killer probably thought the tide would take the body out to the estuary. But there are lots of obstructions in this stretch of the river. Centuries of old pilings and landing-stages, covered up when the tide's high. He got caught behind one, so unfortunately for the killer, we found him as soon as the tide dropped.'

Unfortunately for the police, no-one had watched Reginald Pyke leave the police station that morning. Several constables had been dispatched to knock door-to-door around the local streets, in the hope that someone from the warehouses and wharves might have seen him.

'Like they'd tell the rozzers,' Frankie had said, scornfully. Mrs Jameson had suggested she go and ask the lightermen and dock workers whether they had any information herself. She'd taken to the task with enthusiasm. I was glad to sit in the nice warm police station, although Inspector Carfax's pipe smoke meant the air was almost as hazy inside as out.

'What did Reginald Pyke tell you, while he was in custody?' Mrs Jameson asked. 'He must have known something about Lord Ravensbourne's death, even if he didn't realise it himself. Something that the killer decided he should not be allowed to spread around.'

Inspector Carfax sighed. 'That's the dashed silly thing. He hardly said anything. He said it was common knowledge that he didn't get on with Ravensbourne, but he'd worked with him for twelve years, so he was hardly likely to bump him off now.'

Mrs Jameson inclined her head. 'Perhaps you should send someone to Mr Pyke's home in Islington. His landlady was worried about him. It sounds as if they had a rather close relationship.'

The inspector puffed on his pipe. 'Thanks for the tip. It might be worth searching Pyke's rooms, I suppose. He admitted he wrote that death notice, but was adamant it was only a joke. Said someone had left a note on his desk suggesting it, but he didn't know who. He says he had nothing to do with the printing of it and left that to Maltby.'

'A note?' asked Mrs Jameson.

The inspector sighed. 'But of course he says he burned it, if it ever existed.'

'Has Mr Maltby been released yet?' I asked. 'I mean, he can't have killed Mr Pyke if he was still in custody.'

Inspector Carfax set down his pipe and rose to his feet. 'That is rather a point,' he admitted. 'His alibi for Monday night is firming up, too. He stopped on his walk home, had a cup of tea at the stand on Westminster Bridge. The man there remembers him. I shall go and see to it now.'

'Could we see him safely home?' asked Mrs Jameson. 'I would hate for you to lose another witness, after all.'

Inspector Carfax looked as if he'd like to give a pointed reply to that, but thought better of it. He left the room. I sneezed as the cold air whirled in through the open door.

Mrs Jameson looked at me sharply. 'Are you all right, Marjorie?'

'Actually,' I admitted, 'I feel a bit below par. I seem to be coming down with a cold.'

'Dear me, how inconvenient. Well, keep yourself well wrapped up. It's this wretched fog, I suppose. We should have stayed in Nice,' Mrs Jameson said. 'No-one gets sick on the Riviera.'

I thought with longing of our previous year's trip to the sparkling Côte d'Azur, the warmth and the colour and light. It did indeed seem a very long way from London in February.

Frankie barged through the door, eyes bright. 'Someone

was waiting for him,' she said. 'Pyke. I found a man in the Seafarer's Mission who slept in the doorway of that church down College Hill last night.' I shivered, imagining how grim it would have been to try to sleep in the cold and damp air.

'He was awake early and saw a bloke leaving the police station on the corner. Tall, he said, with a trilby hat and a big raincoat. He didn't look like a rozzer, so our man thought he'd see if he could cadge a few coins to get himself something to eat.' She grinned at me. 'This was over bacon and eggs in the Mission, by the way. I stood him a full breakfast.

'Anyway, my informant was just approaching when some other fellow came round the corner and greeted him. The tall bloke seemed surprised to see him. Said he didn't recognise him at first. Then they went off together, down towards the river. He asked them for a penny, but they ignored him.'

'Excellent work,' Mrs Jameson said. 'Was he able to describe the second man?'

Frankie shrugged. 'He was scruffy, in working men's clothes with a flat cap pulled down over his eyes. Red bandana round his neck, worn down boots. That was all he could tell me.'

'Did he have a red scar on his face?' I asked.

'He didn't get much of a look at his face.' She frowned. 'You're thinking of Bill Mead, aren't you?'

Inspector Carfax returned to the room.

'What's that about Bill Mead? If you know something, young lady, you must tell the police. He's a person of interest in this inquiry.'

Frankie shrugged. 'You'd be better off trying to find the bloke that met Mr Pyke at seven this morning.' She rattled off the description she'd given us. 'You could ask again at the Mission, but my informant reckoned there was nobody else around.'

The inspector looked at her with admiration. 'I'll do that, Miss. Thank you. If it wasn't for the rules, I'd offer you a job.'

She grinned. 'Not blooming likely. But ta anyway.'

'What's happening with Mr Maltby?' Mrs Jameson asked.

'The desk sergeant is returning his possessions now. He's free to go,' said Inspector Carfax.

Chapter 37

Poor Charles Maltby looked miserable after his night in the cells. His nose was red, his shirt rumpled and his usually neat hair had lost its precise parting. He looked like a dispirited travelling salesman at the end of a very long week.

'Kind of you to offer, Mrs Jameson.' He climbed into the back of the Lagonda after her, sniffing. 'Did Miss Waddon send you?'

We had told him Mrs Jameson was a friend of Beatrice and was working with her on the *Bugle*, I remembered. All this undercover stuff was difficult to keep straight when different people knew different things.

'She's very concerned about you,' Mrs Jameson said smoothly, not answering the question. 'And, of course, she has been very occupied with taking over her father's reins.'

He seemed to accept this. 'Who's in my office?' he asked, glumly. 'Tell me it's not Nicolas Cooper.'

'Mr Beeching is acting editor,' I reassured him. 'He and Miss Waddon are keeping things running smoothly. I'm Miss Waddon's secretary, now.'

He ruminated over this for a moment.

'I'd better get back there. Henry will be making himself comfortable in my chair. But I must get some sleep, first. I feel rotten. Have they released Reggie yet?'

We exchanged glances. Inspector Carfax had clearly not seen fit to inform him of his fellow-inmate's demise.

'Earlier this morning, I believe,' Mrs Jameson said. 'Now, Mr Maltby. Tell me more about this death notice. Miss Waddon was surprised to learn that you were involved with such a prank.'

He wrung his hands. 'I wouldn't have got involved with the death threat, if I had thought it was anything but a silly joke. I assumed that Miss Waddon knew about it.'

'What do you mean?' Mrs Jameson asked, sharply. 'Why would she have known about it?'

'Because of the n-note,' he said, miserably. 'But Reggie says he burnt it.'

'Go back to the start, Mr Maltby. Tell me about this note, and when you received it.'

It had begun two weeks ago. Lord Ravensbourne had been in a particularly foul mood.

'We all got the sharp side of his tongue that day,' Mr Maltby said. 'I heard him bawling at Miss Waddon about the finances of the *Women's Bugle*, then Reggie got it in the neck for writing a leader exactly as Lord Ravensbourne had asked, only he'd changed his mind. It was my turn next, and I'm sure every reporter in the building heard His Lordship tell me what he thought of me.'

'That must have been very humiliating,' Mrs Jameson said, kindly.

'Nothing I'm not used to. Anyway, I went out to lunch with Reg, and when we got back there was a typewritten note on his desk, on *Women's Bugle* headed notepaper. It said something like, 'never mind, one day we'll print his obituary. He can't live long in that state of apoplexy.' Then it went on to say we should show him how we'd cover his death, so he'd remember that he wasn't immortal.'

Mrs Jameson frowned. 'And you thought it had come from Miss Waddon?'

It certainly didn't sound like something Beatrice would write. For all her clear-sightedness about her father, she had been protective of him and didn't like it when people mocked him.

'Well, it was the *Bugle* notepaper, you see. And he's her uncle, after all. I thought it was a family joke. I thought she must have heard Reggie getting a hard time and sent it to commiserate. I know it was silly, but we egged each other on. We wrote it between us, and I ran off the proof early one morning, before the printers were in.'

So that was one mystery solved. But Miss Waddon was not the only person with access to *Women's Bugle* headed notepaper.

'This is me. You can drop me on the corner.' Charles Maltby climbed out on Warwick Street and unlocked the door of a comfortable-looking end of terrace house.

Frankie leaned over from the front seat. 'Where do you want to go, Mrs Jameson – back to Fleet Street? We could call in at Bedford Square. It's not too far out of the way.'

'Maybe I could get a sweater,' I said, shivering. 'It was a bit chilly down by the river.'

'All right, then. Take us to at Bedford Square. It's coffee time, anyway. Let's see what Mrs Smithson has for us today.'

Graham brought our mid-morning refreshments. I drank my coffee gratefully and took a delicious-looking chocolate éclair. After one bite I decided I wasn't that hungry. I was never ill; my mother said I had the constitution of an ox, and ate like one too. This wasn't like me.

Mrs Jameson paced around the detective agency office. 'Marjorie, do you think Beatrice Waddon sent the typewritten note that Mr Pyke received?'

'Beatrice can't type,' I said. 'She said that Belinda Ponsett was the only one of them who could. And if you ask me, Belinda was far more likely to have sent that note.'

Mrs Jameson beamed. 'Exactly. The person who sent it did not wish to create the death notice themselves – perhaps for fear of upsetting Miss Waddon. Or,' her look darkened, 'to ensure that, when Lord Ravensbourne met his death, the finger of suspicion pointed at the men who did create it.'

I went to my bedroom to fetch my woollen sweater but was caught by a hacking cough half-way up.

'Marjorie, are you ill?' Graham paused on his way down the stairs, his kind face creased with concern.

'I'm all right. Bit of a cold, that's all. I didn't sleep well,' I admitted.

'You should be in your bed,' he said, disapprovingly.

'I need another jersey, then I'll be warm enough.'

'You stay right there. I'll fetch it.'

He was back in a moment, and I struggled into the jersey, which barely fitted under my cardigan jacket. I looked as if I'd been stuffed, but at least it was warm.

'You were asking about young Bill Mead, yesterday,' said Graham. 'I made some inquiries of my own this morning, through my sister. I don't hold with this communism business, you know. Whatever Frankie says.'

'Go on, Graham. What have you heard?'

'Mead was due at a meeting on Monday night. My brother-in-law was down at Tobacco Wharf and heard that the union men were planning to talk to a man from Russia. The Soviet Union, or whatever they call themselves these days. They plan to go on strike, all together, at the end of the month.'

'Monday night? What time?' Was this where Bill had disappeared to when George Quinn, the head printer, said he couldn't find him?

Graham rolled his eyes. 'Midnight. All very secret. A pub near Fleet Street, that the print union uses for their meetings. Although it's not that blooming secret, seeing as half of the dock workers know about it.' He helped me to my feet. 'Are you sure you're all right, Marjorie? I don't want you catching your death.'

I hurried back down the stairs. 'Don't worry about me, Graham. Thanks for your help.'

Mindful of Frankie's disapproval, I said nothing about Graham's revelations about Bill Mead until I was safely back at the *Daily Post*. She dropped me on the corner of Whitefriars Street just after one o'clock, before taking Mrs Jameson down to the main entrance. Reporters and sub-editors were streaming out of the lobby to cross the street for lunch in the Cheshire Cheese.

The only reporter left on the fourth floor was Jonathan Field. He grabbed his hat from the stand and pulled on his overcoat.

'Hello, Miss Swallow. I've had a tip that the police have found a body up in Queenhithe, with a bullet in its head. I'm going up there now. Did you get rid of that woman who wanted Mr Pyke?'

'I… yes.' I supposed I should wait until the police had formally identified the body before telling him more.

'Right you are. I'll be off, then.' He grinned. 'Mr Beeching's sending me on all the best jobs now. This is what I joined Fleet Street for.'

'Wait a second.' I put a hand on Jonathan's arm. 'Do you know where the printers have their union meetings? A pub near Fleet Street?'

He shot me a surprised look. 'Why? You're not thinking of

joining?'

I smiled. 'Perhaps I should. But no, I'm looking for Bill Mead. There was a meeting on Monday night. Midnight, on the night that Lord Ravensbourne was shot.'

'Hang on a second. I've written about them before.' He flipped through his notebook. 'The Old Red Lion. Red Lion Court, up towards Fetter Lane. I'd better get going. Let me know what you find out.'

Another line of inquiry to follow up. My head ached. If I told Mrs Jameson, she'd probably send me around to the pub to see what I could uncover. I really didn't feel up to it. I remembered Inspector Carfax's words. Bill Mead was a person of interest, and I should tell him if I knew anything.

I picked up a telephone, asked to be put through to Cloak Lane police station, and told him what I knew about the meeting. No doubt the printers would get wind of it soon enough, but I didn't have the energy for anything else.

In the *Bugle* office, Mrs Jameson was taking advantage of the absence of Beatrice, who was lunching with Henry Beeching, to interrogate Belinda Ponsett. Belinda wasn't holding up too well. Her mousy hair had escaped its black ribbon and had gone frizzy in the fog. There were huge shadows under her eyes, and she had bitten down her fingernails. She looked as if she hadn't slept for days. All the work of the *Bugle* had fallen to her since Lord Ravensbourne's death.

'Is this the only typewriter in the *Bugle* office?' Mrs Jameson asked, indicating the machine on Belinda's desk. 'Because it is perfectly possible to tell when a particular machine has been used for a message. All machines have their idiosyncrasies. A slightly raised or lowered letter, a key that has become worn through over-use or damaged. Very distinctive, and I believe typewriter identification has already been used as evidence in court on blackmail and poison pen letter cases.'

'I don't understand,' said Belinda, who was indeed looking bewildered. 'Of course it's the only typewriter we have. I'd like to get one for home, but they're expensive.'

'And you are the only person to use it?'

'Well, yes. Beatrice doesn't type. But why would I be sending notes to Mr Pyke? His office is right there. I could walk over to talk to him in less time than it would take to type a message. And I don't have anything to talk to him about. I don't work for the *Post*, thankfully.' She curled her lip.

'What about the death notice?' asked Mrs Jameson. 'Did you communicate with Mr Pyke about that? Mr Maltby seems to think that someone from this office did. Mr Pyke received a type-written note, on *Women's Bugle* notepaper, which proposed that he write an obituary of Lord Ravensbourne. And only one person in this office can type.'

'That's ridiculous,' protested Belinda, her face glowing pink. 'Do you really think that Mr Pyke would take orders from me to write a death notice? I had nothing to do with it.'

'Is that true, Belinda?'

Beatrice had entered the office silently. She stood in the centre of the room, staring at her friend with cold eyes.

Belinda held her gaze for a moment, then her own blue eyes filled with tears. 'You know it is,' she said. 'I wouldn't do anything to hurt you, Bea. I could see how much it upset you.'

I felt in my pocket for a handkerchief, but mine was already used. Mrs Jameson passed over one of hers; fine cambric precisely ironed with her initials embroidered in the corner.

Beatrice drew herself up to her full height. 'Mrs Jameson, I have not been completely honest with you. I have withheld information, because I could not truly believe that Miss Ponsett was involved in my father's death. I have tried to find an alternative explanation in my mind. I tried to persuade myself I had been dreaming, or misremembered. But it seems my trust was misplaced.'

'Bea!' Belinda scrambled up from the sofa, scattering papers. 'Stop this – it's horrible!'

'Where had you been, when I heard you letting yourself back into the flat at two o'clock in the morning on the night my father died, Belinda? You needn't pretend. I woke when I heard the door open, even though you tried to be quiet. You went to the kitchen, then used the bathroom before returning to your room.'

Belinda froze and let fall the papers she had been clutching. Her round pink face was a picture of guilt, like a child caught with their hand in the biscuit tin.

'I... I couldn't sleep. I went for a short walk.'

'I don't believe you.' Beatrice's voice was full of contempt. 'You went for a walk, at two o'clock in the morning? And it just so happens that my father was shot dead that very night?'

Mrs Jameson sat very still. I held my breath. Was this the answer we'd been looking for all along?

The colour drained from her face and Belinda slumped back into the sofa.

'I was trying to help,' she said. 'Trying to save our magazine. The *Women's Bugle*. And now... it seems like I shouldn't have bothered. You care nothing for it.'

'You shot my father?' Beatrice gazed at her friend in horror. 'To save your wretched magazine?'

'No!' protested Belinda. 'I came here to talk to him. I knew he sat up late. I thought I'd have it out with him. Tell him how important the *Bugle* is, how much it means to you.' She wiped away the tears that were running down her face. 'Because… because I care for you, Bea. You know that. And for the life we have together.'

Beatrice turned away, but not before I could glimpse the disgust in her expression. 'We do not have a life together,' she said.

'Belinda.' Mrs Jameson sat by her and gripped her hands. 'This is important. What happened? What did you see when you arrived at the office?'

Belinda was staring at Beatrice, her lips parted and her eyes wet. She seemed in a daze.

'Belinda!' Mrs Jameson's voice cut through the air. 'Tell me. What happened?'

Belinda turned, her pale face reflecting hopelessness. 'I came up in the private lift from the alley,' she said. 'I borrowed Bea's key. I came straight into Lord Ravensbourne's office.' She closed her eyes and swallowed. 'He was already dead.'

'What time?' She didn't answer, and Mrs Jameson gave her a little shake.

'About one, I suppose.'

'And you are sure of that? You could see he was dead?'

Belinda looked at me then. 'Marjorie, did you know Lord Ravensbourne was dead when you arrived at the office?'

I nodded, recalling in my mind the small round hole in the centre of his forehead, ringed in dark crimson.

'Immediately.' I returned her gaze. 'But I called the police. Why didn't you?'

She wrung her hands. 'Because I knew this would happen, of course. I knew someone would suspect me, because of what Lord Ravensbourne said that day.' She switched her gaze to

Beatrice. 'I just didn't think it would be you, Bea. I thought you'd have more faith.'

The door opened.

'Go away,' shouted Beatrice.

Theodore stood in the doorway, face pale as his parchment-yellow shirt.

'Bea, old thing,' he said, swaying slightly. 'Completely beastly morning. I don't suppose you have any brandy?'

'I'm busy,' she snapped. 'Go and tend to your hangover elsewhere.'

He staggered to a chair and sat down. 'Not hungover. More bad news, I'm afraid. Uncle Reggie. They've just fished him out of the Thames.'

Chapter 39

'What on earth do you mean?' Beatrice spun around to look at him.

Theodore shook his head, tears in his eyes. 'The wretched police made me go and look at his body. Most ghastly thing I've ever seen. Poor old Uncle Reg. I say, are you sure you don't have brandy?' He began to pull open drawers at random. He seemed far more upset by his uncle's death than that of his father.

'In the sideboard, Marjorie.' Beatrice indicated the cupboard beneath the window. 'I'll have one too.' She didn't offer any to Mrs Jameson, or Belinda, who was still hunched on the sofa.

I retrieved the bottle and poured a couple of glasses for the siblings. I wouldn't have minded one myself. My cough had subsided, but my chest still hurt, and my throat was sore.

He took a sip. 'A policeman bashed on my door at I don't know what time this morning. He told me they'd released Uncle Reg at seven, but a couple of hours later they found a body in the river, and needed me to identify him. Next of kin and all that. So they dragged me off to a horrible place in Wapping.' He shuddered. 'Terribly grim. And they had poor Uncle Reggie all laid out on a trolley under a sheet, you know. Dead.'

Mrs Jameson flashed me a warning glance to tell me to keep quiet. No need to let them know we'd already seen Reginald Pyke's body in the Thames mud.

'Theo, that's horrible. I'm so sorry.' Beatrice crossed the room and embraced him awkwardly, the first sign of affection I'd seen between the siblings. 'You must be so upset.'

'He'd been shot,' said Theodore, his voice shaky. 'Like Pater. A bullet in his head. When they told me he'd been found in the river, I supposed he'd drowned. I don't know, fallen off a bridge or something.'

'Shot?' echoed Beatrice. She turned her gaze on Belinda.

'Well, you can't blame me for that!' exclaimed Belinda. 'I was with you all morning.'

'Whose blaming anyone for anything?' asked Theodore, looking bewildered. 'I say, Bea, what's going on?'

She shrugged and turned away, her jaw clamped shut.

Theodore turned to Belinda Ponsett. 'Have you been upsetting my sister? Pater was right about you, wasn't he? You just hang on her, like some sort of horrible leech. Don't you think it's time you left our family alone?'

A smart rap on the door made us all jump. The drama was interrupted by Inspector Carfax, who stood in the doorway with a grave expression.

'Miss Waddon, I'm afraid I will have to ask you all to wait outside. Information has come to light which means I need to search this office.' I supposed he was following up Reginald Pyke's evidence about the typewritten note.

Beatrice stood. 'But you can't. It's my office – I'm working here. I forbid it.' She folded her arms.

'I hope this will not inconvenience you for long, Miss Waddon, but it is necessary. I have a search warrant.' He held out a sheet of paper, which she ignored.

'No,' called Belinda. 'We have a magazine to get out next week, Inspector. It's out of the question. And there are sensitive documents here, regarding the women's franchise bill.' She jumped to her feet and clasped her hands, standing in front of her desk.

He looked her up and down, his face impassive. 'I'm sure there are, Miss Ponsett. But unless they relate to criminal activity, they are not of interest to me or my officers.'

'I say, is this really necessary?' asked Theodore. 'We've had some bad news, you know. It's a bit much, turfing the girls out of their room. I've had a rotten morning all round.'

Inspector Carfax inclined his head. 'Indeed, Lord Ravensbourne, and I am most sorry for your family's loss. However, I assure you this is necessary. I would advise you to co-operate. I don't want to have to resort to force.'

Mrs Jameson rose and put her hand on Beatrice's arm. 'I think it would be best to allow Inspector Carfax to carry out his search, Miss Waddon.'

We trooped out into the newsroom. Most of the reporters had returned from lunch, and they watched with interest as a dozen policemen trudged into the *Bugle* offices.

Henry Beeching emerged from the editor's office. 'What's going on?'

Beatrice sighed. 'It's terribly inconvenient. The police say they need to carry out a search.'

Mr Beeching ushered her into his room. 'Come in here.' He waited for the rest of us to follow.

Theodore glanced at his watch. 'Actually, I'd better dash. I was supposed to meet Taffy Morgan at White's half an hour ago for a spot of luncheon. Not that I can imagine eating. But I suppose another brandy wouldn't go amiss. Steady the nerves and all that.' He loped across the floor to the lift.

'What's up with him?' asked Mr Beeching. 'He doesn't seem his usual self.'

'I'm afraid we have had more bad news,' said Mrs Jameson, gravely. 'Mr Pyke and Mr Maltby were released from custody this morning. Mr Maltby is at home, but Mr Pyke has been found dead.'

'Reggie? Good Lord.'

Beatrice sighed. 'Poor Theo. He looked on Uncle Reggie almost as a father, especially after Mother died. This will hit him hard.'

Belinda Ponsett hovered just inside the office by the door, uncertain whether she was invited in or not. I stood the other side of the doorway, absorbing her admission that she had returned to the offices on Monday night and seen Lord Ravensbourne dead in his chair. Could Belinda, with her round schoolgirl face and giggle, really have shot Lord Ravensbourne? I tried to remember the timeline, pinned to the wall of the *Bugle* office now being turned over by the City of London police.

The crime was unlikely to have been committed after half-past one, according to the doctor's report, giving a mere ninety minute window of opportunity for the murder to take place. I cudgelled my tired brain into action.

Beatrice and I had taken a taxi back to Bloomsbury together after midnight. She had been dropped off first, in Gordon Square, and had put her head around Belinda's bedroom door to say goodnight. That must have been at about twenty past midnight. No doubt Beatrice would have taken time to get ready for bed and drop off to sleep. Perhaps the earliest time at which Belinda could have left the house was a quarter to one. And she returned at two o'clock, which left – if she had indeed walked, as she'd claimed – one hour for the journey and fifteen minutes in the *Post* building. Fifteen minutes to take the private lift up to the flat and do whatever she had done there. Gasp in shock at a dead body – or shoot a man dead.

Inspector Carfax opened the door. 'Miss Waddon and Miss Ponsett, will you please accompany me?'

'What is it?' Belinda was jumpy as a cat.

Mrs Jameson rose. 'Might I accompany the young ladies, Inspector?'

He looked at Beatrice with raised eyebrows. She heaved herself out of her chair. The vitality that had been her hallmark seemed to have drained away during the day's travails.

'If you wish, Mrs Jameson,' she said. 'I have nothing to hide.' She glanced at Belinda, as if she could no longer speak for her friend.

I trailed behind them into the *Bugle* office, hoping I wouldn't be noticed. A policeman shut the door behind me and stood stolidly in front of it. Two others were busily unpinning our timeline and lists of suspects from the wall next to the map and putting them into cardboard boxes.

'Those are mine,' said Mrs Jameson, sharply.

Inspector Carfax glanced at her. 'They contain information related to a murder investigation. They will be returned to you in due course.'

Both editors' desks had been cleared, papers and contact sheets and pot-plants heaped onto the floor. Two policemen stood guard over Belinda Ponsett's desk. Her typewriter had been removed and boxed up, her clutter of papers placed into cardboard folders and even the photograph of herself and Beatrice in the quadrangle at Girton College had been removed.

One item lay on the empty desktop, wrapped in a pale pink lace-edged handkerchief.

'Is that your handkerchief, Miss Ponsett?'

She nodded, puzzled. 'It looks like it.'

Inspector Carfax pulled on a pair of white cotton gloves and delicately unwrapped the object. It was a silver-barrelled revolver with a smooth wooden handle, small enough to fit into a pocket. It looked similar to the guns that had been advertised as suitable for women to carry for self-defence, until the law had been tightened a few years ago.

'And is this your gun, Miss Ponsett?'

She stared at the object in horror. Her mouth dropped open, but she said nothing.

'Good God,' muttered Beatrice, turning her face away.

'Please answer the question, Miss Ponsett. Is this your gun, and do you have a firearm licence, as required by the Firearms Act of 1920?'

'No! No, of course not. I don't have a gun. Horrible things.'

'How do you account for this gun being found in your desk drawer, wrapped in your handkerchief?'

'I can't,' said Belinda, blankly. 'I've never seen it before.'

'Inspector Carfax,' interjected Mrs Jameson, 'I believe Miss Ponsett requires legal representation, if you are to question her further. Is she to be arrested? Have you issued a caution?'

The inspector looked as if he would like to throw Mrs Jameson out of the room, if not the window. 'Kindly keep silent. I know my business.' He flared his nostrils as he turned back to Miss Ponsett.

'Belinda Ponsett, I am arresting you on suspicion of murder. You do not have to say anything unless you wish to do so, but anything you do say will be taken down and may be given in evidence against you.'

Belinda took two staggering paces across the room towards Beatrice, arms outstretched in supplication. Then she toppled forward as if someone had cut her feet from underneath her.

Chapter 40

'Catch her,' called Inspector Carfax. Two policemen darted forward just before Belinda hit the floor, breaking her fall with practised ease. I wondered whether policemen were specially trained to catch fainting females.

'Lay her down.'

The men turned her onto her back, her unruly hair spreading across the floorboards. Her black skirt had hitched up to reveal a pair of chubby knees and the top of her woollen stockings.

Inspector Carfax leaned over her supine body, twitched her skirt down to decency, then straightened and sighed. 'I suppose we'd better call a doctor.'

I hurried forward. 'Let me help. I have some nursing experience.' Her face was parchment-white to her lips. Her pulse was slow but steady, however, and her shallow breaths came regularly. Her wide forehead was clammy with perspiration.

'I think she's just fainted.' I crouched beside her. 'Belinda? Can you hear me?' I unfastened her black necktie and loosened the collar of her blouse.

She blinked, and her staring eyes focused on me. 'What...?' She tried to struggle upright.

'Don't try to get up. You fainted, that's all. Stay still,' I told her.

Inspector Carfax brought over a chair, and I lifted her legs onto it. 'You need to get the blood back to your head.'

'She'll have plenty of time to recover at the police station,' said the inspector. 'And to come up with an explanation for that firearm.'

He wrapped the revolver again and placed it in a cardboard box. 'Sergeant Voles, send this to the ballistics department. They can tell us if it fired the bullet that killed Lord Ravensbourne, or Mr Pyke.'

The sergeant took the box.

'Miss Ponsett should see a doctor before she goes anywhere,' said Mrs Jameson. 'I won't have you hauling her off to a cell before she's been checked over by a physician. Miss Waddon, is there a family doctor you can call?'

Beatrice sat rigid on the chair behind her desk, looking resolutely towards the window.

'I do not wish to be further involved in this matter,' she said, stiffly. 'I assume Miss Ponsett can be attended by a doctor at the police station.' She glanced towards her former friend, and I was shocked by the hardness of her expression. 'The sooner she can be removed from my office, the better.'

Miss Ponsett squeezed her eyes and mouth tightly shut, as if in great pain. She rolled onto her side. It was like watching a wounded animal. Whether or not she was guilty of what she'd been charged with, this was distressing.

Somehow, she gathered herself, clambering onto the chair. 'I am quite all right now,' she said. Her voice shook, but her attempt to regain some dignity was touching. With trembling hands, she gathered her hair together and twisted it into a bun.

'Marjorie, call my doctor and ask him to come here at once,' said Mrs Jameson. 'Inspector Carfax, surely you do not wish to take a woman into custody when she is patently unwell and needs medical attention? We must find a quiet place for her to sit and recover.'

'Mr Pyke's office,' I suggested. The former broom cupboard had stood empty since Mr Pyke himself had been arrested the previous afternoon.

Inspector Carfax sighed. 'All right. Constable, you go with them and wait outside. I don't want any tricks.'

Mrs Jameson and I each took an arm and helped Belinda out of her chair. A crowd of reporters had accumulated outside the *Bugle* office door and fell back as we emerged.

'What's happening, Miss Swallow? Is it something to do with Reginald Pyke's death?' asked Jonathan Field, back from his trip to Cloak Lane.

'Please make way.' Mrs Jameson sent her basilisk stare around the crowd, quickly clearing a path. 'Miss Ponsett is unwell and needs to rest quietly.' Henry Beeching hovered behind the reporters. 'Mr Beeching, perhaps you would see if Miss Waddon requires any help?'

We settled Belinda in Mr Pyke's cupboard, with a police constable standing officiously outside the door, and I telephoned our regular doctor. I wondered why Mrs Jameson was so solicitous of Belinda Ponsett. The discovery of the gun, coming on top of her revelation about her midnight trip to the *Daily Post* offices, was surely damning evidence. And she was clearly implicated in the death notice sent to Lord Ravensbourne.

But I knew better than to question my employer's methods. I resorted to my usual role in the office and went to make a pot of tea.

When I returned, Mrs Jameson was questioning Belinda

with quiet urgency. What route did she take to Fleet Street, and did she see anyone on the way? What time had she arrived at the office, and had she encountered any staff on her way in or out of the building?

'I don't know.' Belinda was hiccupping sobs into a pink handkerchief.

'My dear, I will act for you. But I need your help. I think you may be in less danger in police custody than you would be here.' Mrs Jameson kept her voice low. 'Ah, Marjorie. There you are. Quickly, take down these notes.'

I passed a teacup to Belinda. She sipped the hot sweetened liquid. It seemed to calm her down a little.

'I promise you,' she said, 'I never saw that gun before in my life.'

'I know. Marjorie, write this down. Miss Ponsett left Gordon Square at one o'clock and arrived here shortly after half past one. You are sure of that, Miss Ponsett?'

She blew her nose and nodded. 'I dressed after Beatrice had said goodnight, and waited until almost one before I left. I walked through Russell Square, then across Lincoln's Inn Fields to Chancery Lane. The half-hour struck at St Dunstan's just as I turned into Fleet Street.' She shivered. 'I took the private entrance from Hanging Sword Alley up to Lord Ravensbourne's flat.'

Mrs Jameson tapped her chin rapidly. 'Where was the elevator when you arrived? Street level, or did you have to wait for it to come down?'

'I think... yes. The lift was there already. I was nervous, and warm from walking so fast. I'd expected to wait a moment, to have time to cool down. But when I went into the vestibule, the lift car was at ground floor level. I took it up and went through the lobby – the light was on in his office – and saw him straight away. He was already dead.' Her nostrils began to quiver again, and she dabbed at her eyes. 'I went straight back down and ran home. I didn't see anyone...'

She stopped short, and her hand flew to her mouth.

Mrs Jameson didn't miss it. 'Who did you see, Belinda?'

'It was further up Fleet Street, on my way home. I saw Mr Mead. But he was heading the other way, down Fleet Street towards the *Post*. I supposed he was going home, or back to the night shift. He said he'd been at a meeting.'

'At half past one in the morning?' Mrs Jameson looked sceptical.

'It's true,' I said. 'There was a midnight meeting of the print unions with some of the dockers, in the Red Lion pub. Belinda, did you tell him what you'd seen?'

She nodded quickly. 'I was in a bit of a state. He asked what was wrong, and I told him.'

No wonder he'd decided to lie low, I thought. He must have known he'd be a suspect, after his threats to shoot Lord Ravensbourne. I thought uneasily of the 'phone call I'd made to Inspector Carfax. If Bill Mead had been at the meeting until he met Belinda on Fleet Street, then he couldn't have killed Lord Ravensbourne. My head ached. It was all such a muddle.

Dr Francis, a kindly man with white hair and a reassuring smile, put his head around the door. 'You called, Mrs Jameson?'

Ten minutes later, he'd given Belinda a clean bill of health and Inspector Carfax came to escort her from the premises.

'Courage, Miss Ponsett,' said Mrs Jameson. 'Think of the suffragettes. You have nothing to fear. I shall be working for you. I will speak to my solicitor at once and he will go to the police station to ensure you are correctly treated.'

Belinda managed to raise her head and walk steadily across the room, a policeman on either side. The reporters watched in silence. In the editor's office, Henry Beeching and Beatrice Waddon paused for a moment, then resumed their business.

Chapter 41

We retreated back into Mr Pyke's cupboard. Mrs Jameson sat behind the desk and took a clean sheet of paper from the stack. She started to scribble down a new timeline.

'Marjorie, which way did you and Miss Waddon exit the building after leaving Lord Ravensbourne at midnight?'

I thought back. 'We came through the editorial offices. I picked up my coat and hat, then we went down to the main entrance.'

Mrs Jameson's mouth stretched into her cat-like smile, and I saw the implication immediately. 'Lord Ravensbourne and I used his lift to get up to his office after lunch. I don't think anybody used it during the afternoon or evening. So, if it was at ground level when Belinda Ponsett arrived, someone had used it in the interim.'

She nodded her approval. 'Precisely. The killer exited the building that way, after shooting Lord Ravensbourne.'

I hunched into the other chair. 'But the gun? Surely that suggests Belinda was the killer?'

Mrs Jameson expelled air noisily from her nostrils. 'On the contrary, it was a crude attempt to frame her. As soon as the gun was produced, I knew Belinda was innocent. Although it is unfortunate, to say the least, that she did not admit before today to her visit to Lord Ravensbourne's office.'

'Or call the police when she found him dead,' I said feelingly. I remembered my own shock at encountering the body, the horror of those glazed eyes. If Belinda had called the police, I would have been spared that. I felt I had seen enough violently dead bodies to last me a lifetime.

Mrs Jameson ignored my interjection. 'If she had been the killer, she would have disposed of the gun somewhere less obvious than her own desk drawer. She'd have dumped it on the way back home, thrown it into the river. You cannot imagine she would have killed Lord Ravensbourne, gone down to the *Bugle* offices, wrapped the gun in her handkerchief and put it in her desk – all while taking the risk of being seen by the editorial night shift – then gone back to Lord Ravensbourne's office and taken his private lift to the street?'

It did sound unfeasible. 'But what about Mr Pyke? Maybe she needed to keep the gun for him. Perhaps he knew something that she didn't want him to tell anyone.'

Mrs Jameson smiled. 'Except she cannot have killed Mr Pyke, because she was with Miss Waddon all morning. I believe you are correct that the killer feared Mr Pyke knew something incriminating. But I very much doubt that killer was Miss Ponsett.'

She gestured around Mr Pyke's cupboard. 'It was clever of you to suggest this room. See if you can find out what inconvenient fact Mr Pyke knew, while I arrange for my solicitor to attend Miss Ponsett at Cloak Lane police station.'

She left, and I scanned the room methodically. What can't you see? Mrs Jameson had taught me to ask. What isn't there, that ought to be?

The big desk dominated the tiny room. The green leather

desk top had a stack of clean paper on a worn leather blotter, a tortoise-shell pen tray containing a cheap fountain pen and spare nibs, and a pot of blue ink. The electric lamp with green glass shade threw a pool of light on the desk.

It was tidy; no half-empty cups or ground-out cigarettes in the ashtray. I supposed the cleaners would have been around early in the morning.

There was no spike, I realised. Nowhere for the leader writer to file discarded versions of his columns. A narrow metal filing cabinet had been squeezed into the corner. Presumably that was where he kept his papers. I sighed, imagining how long it would take me to go through them.

I scanned the rest of the room. His furled umbrella still hung from the back of the second chair. A wastepaper bin sat in the corner by the door, empty of papers.

I squeezed behind the desk and opened the top drawer. A half-used box of safety matches, three boxes of Craven A cigarettes, a stray boiled sweet that had accumulated a coat of fluff, and a couple of pencils with the leads broken.

In the drawer below that, a stack of headed writing paper and envelopes; a set of raffle tickets from a long-past bazaar; a pile of cards bearing invitations to dinner with various politicians and to government functions. I supposed a leader writer must be courted by political parties hoping to win him over to their causes.

'Hullo. Is the coast clear? Why have they marched the busy bee off to clink?'

It was Jonathan Field, eager to know the latest.

I supposed the police would make an announcement soon enough. 'Come in. They found a gun, and they've arrested her for Lord Ravensbourne's murder. But Mrs Jameson is convinced she's innocent.'

'Whew.' He whistled. 'What are you looking for?'

I sighed. 'I don't know. That's the trouble. But we think that Reginald Pyke must have known something about whoever killed Lord Ravensbourne. I'm trying to find out what that might have been.'

He pulled open the top drawer of the filing cabinet. 'Sounds like you could do with some help. Shall we see what we can find?'

We spent an hour going through papers. Mr Pyke had kept all the previous columns he had written, including those that Lord Ravensbourne had discarded. I guessed that His Lordship changed his mind about the leader so often that previously discarded columns might have been pressed back into use later. We paid particular attention to the leaders written in the past month, but found nothing of note.

The final leader Mr Pyke had begun writing – but left unfinished – was his tribute to Lord Ravensbourne, written on the day of his death. It was dutiful rather than generous, listing his achievements and acknowledging his influence on the newspaper industry. There was also a copy of the 'spoof' leader, which linked to the early edition's front page about Lord Curzon's comments on the situation in India. The leader made much of the decision of the new Labour prime minister to act as his own foreign secretary.

'Anyone who knows India will regret that Lord Curzon, with his unparalleled knowledge and experience of the sub-continent, is no longer the steady hand at the helm of the Foreign Office,' it read. 'We are reliably informed that matters in King Charles Street are in complete disarray.

'The role of Foreign Secretary cannot be conducted from

the corner of the Prime Minister's desk. If Mr MacDonald does not trust any of his colleagues in the role, perhaps he should ask Lord Curzon to step into the breach.'

Something about the piece nagged at my attention. I set it to one side, hoping it would come back to me.

'Anything?' I asked Jonathan.

He shook his head. 'There's a stack of old cuttings about Lord Ravensbourne in an envelope here. Do you want to take a look?'

I turned them over. Yellow and brittle with age, the oldest recorded Lord Ravensbourne's wedding to Miss Virginia Pyke in 1899. Young Arthur Waddon was resplendent in morning dress, with a broad grin and a tall, delicate-looking young woman in a gauzy veil on his arm. She looked slightly stunned. I read the text beneath the photograph. Reginald Pyke had been Arthur Waddon's best man.

The next clipping, dated one year later, celebrated Arthur Waddon's takeover of the *Daily Post*. There was a photograph of him at his desk, cheroot clamped between his teeth and a copy of the newspaper in his hand, looking triumphant. And in 1904, the same photograph was used to record that the *Daily Post* had become the first newspaper on Fleet Street to sell over a million copies each day.

Nothing for a decade, then a death notice. Virginia Waddon had died at home, after a long illness. She was mourned by her husband Arthur Waddon, the newspaper proprietor, and her children Beatrice (14) and Theodore (13). No mention of her brother Reginald, although he had perhaps cared for her more than her husband.

Next in the pile, a clipping dated February 1916 showed Lord Ravensbourne in top hat and tails, emerging from

Buckingham Palace with his new wife Annabel. His piratical grin was this time celebrating his ennoblement for services to public morale during the War. He had wasted little time mourning for his dead wife.

'How sad,' I said. 'Mr Pyke kept all these clippings about Lord Ravensbourne's career. And Lord Ravensbourne barely seemed to notice him, except when he wanted to give him orders.'

'They used to be friends,' said Jonathan. 'That's what the older reporters say, anyway.'

The remaining cuttings recorded the births of the two younger children, Theo's going up to Oxford, Beatrice's magazine launch. I gathered them together to put them back in their envelope.

A name jumped out at me from a headline on the back of one of the early cuttings.

'Artist Julian Jameson dead in tragic accident,' it read.

Chapter 42

There was a photograph, a head-and-shoulders shot of a handsome man with curling dark hair, a neat beard, and roguish eyes. Julian Jameson, the symbolist painter who had been fashionable – notorious – at the turn of the century. Who had died twenty years ago, leaving a wealthy widow. Mrs Jameson, my employer.

She had never told me the circumstances of her husband's death. Only in recent months had I discovered that he'd been a famous artist, and that he'd treated her with great cruelty. I held the brittle piece of paper between my fingers. It seemed wrong, to snoop on Mrs Jameson's past when she had never discussed it with me.

But curiosity won. I read down the column of text. 'The death has been announced of the painter Julian Jameson, whose paintings of mythological subjects have been exhibited at the Royal Academy. Mr Jameson, who had made his home in Rome for many years, died on Tuesday when a gun he had been cleaning went off unexpectedly, causing fatal injuries.

'In a statement, the Italian police confirmed the manner of death, which took place at the artist's apartment on Via Giulia, and said it was not thought to be suspicious.

'Mr Jameson's widow Iris, the subject of several of his

paintings and an American citizen, is being supported by the American consul, Mr Henry Caldwell. He told Associated Press: "Mrs Jameson is very distressed by the tragic accident that has befallen her husband. She thanks the public for their condolences and asks for privacy."

'Mr Jameson's only child, a boy, died of fever at the age of four earlier this year.'

Jonathan was reading over my shoulder. 'Is that your Mrs Jameson?' he asked. 'And hang on a minute.' He frowned. 'Henry Caldwell – he was the American ambassador to London, wasn't he? Wasn't Daisy Caldwell his niece?'

When we had investigated the death of the American ambassador's niece Daisy the previous year, Mrs Jameson had told me she owed a great debt of gratitude to Mr Caldwell. This support, I supposed, was what she had been referring to.

'She was.' I re-read the article. 'Poor Mrs Jameson. What an awful thing to happen. So soon after her son's death, too.'

'There you are, Marjorie.' I jumped as if stung by a wasp, and tried to shove the clipping back into its envelope. Mrs Jameson strode across the room and took it from me. She read it, face impassive, and gave a sharp nod. Then she turned it over to read the article about the *Daily Post* reaching its circulation milestone. She folded it and returned it to the envelope.

'Have you found anything that sheds light on why someone would wish to shoot Mr Pyke?' she asked. Clearly, we were not going to discuss the fatal shooting of Mr Jameson in 1904.

'I don't think so,' I admitted. 'We found those cuttings about Lord Ravensbourne's life. But I couldn't see anything in them. Although…' I picked up the spoof leader, about India and Lord Curzon. It was still nagging at me. 'I don't know. I feel like I'm missing something. But this is just about who's in charge at the Foreign Office.'

She took it from me and read it, eyes narrowed. 'I see.' She put the spoof on the table and looked around the sparsely furnished room. 'Perhaps I shall make a call on an acquaintance there. It might confirm my current theory. If you're finished, Mr Field?'

He jumped to his feet. 'Of course, Mrs Jameson. I was just trying to help.'

She waited until he had gone, then handed me back the envelope of cuttings.

'I do not wish anyone else to see this. Or to be reminded of it myself. Do you understand?'

Over the eighteen months we had worked together, I had grown to greatly admire Mrs Jameson, to trust her judgement and strive to earn her praise. She had introduced me to people and places I would never have seen if I had stayed in Catford. She had taught me well, paid me generously, shared her experience of the world. But I was not foolish enough to forget that she was my employer. We were not, and would never be, friends.

'Of course, Mrs Jameson. I'm sorry. My curiosity got the better of me when I saw the name.'

She gave a brief smile, a compression of her lips to acknowledge my apology. 'I have trained you to be curious, Marjorie. I cannot complain if that is what you have become. Now, we have one more suspect to follow up. Time for you to pay a call on Mrs Butcher.'

Chapter 43

I took a taxi-cab south of the river to Kennington, as Mrs Jameson had called Frankie to take her home to Bedford Square.

Mary and Tom Butcher had the ground floor of a neat terraced house on Bonnington Square, yellow London brick with an archway over the front door to the street. When I arrived, Mary was on her hands and knees scrubbing the red tiles of the porch, her hair tied up in a scarf.

She looked up at me and sat back on her heels.

'Hello, Miss Swallow. This is a surprise.'

'I'm sorry to disturb your work, Mrs Butcher. I wanted to bring you these. To say congratulations and see how you were getting on.' I held up a bunch of early daffodils. It had been all I could think of, to explain my unexpected visit.

She eyed them suspiciously and got to her feet. 'Come in, then. Tom's out fetching some furniture from his parents' place. We're still getting straight.'

Half-unpacked boxes stood around the kitchen, although there was crockery on the shelves and yellow checked curtains hung in the window over the sink.

Mary ran the tap and filled a tall glass for the flowers. 'Thank you.' She set them on the table and turned dark unsmiling eyes on me. 'What's this about, then? I read about you finding Lord Ravensbourne's body. I can't say I'm sorry he's dead.'

I needed to show she could trust me, to regain the brief camaraderie we'd had at work. 'I don't think anyone's sorry, except for Miss Waddon. He was…' I hesitated. 'He was very unpleasant. A difficult man.'

'He was a brute,' she said, forcefully.

'He was,' I agreed. 'We're better off without him.'

She sighed and filled the kettle. 'Come on, then. I'll make a pot of tea, and you can tell me all about it. Did he try it on with you? Don't tell me you were the one that shot him? They do say you should suspect the person who finds the body.' She laughed and pulled out a chair for me. 'Call me Mary. I'm still not used to Mrs Butcher.'

I laughed along with her. 'I was tempted, and it was less than a week. How did you stand it, Mary? You were there for – what – six months?'

'Six months of hell, Marjorie. I'd have left sooner, but I was looking after my mother. My salary was all we had. The pay was better than any other job I'd have got. But then the union got the printers a raise, and Tom said it was enough that we could get married, find a place of our own, and Mum could live with us. She's staying with her sister this week, to give us a bit of privacy, like. Tom's been waiting for me, see.'

She blushed, dimples in her pink cheeks as she smiled. She looked so happy to be finally married, and free. I hated the thought of what I was going to say next.

'Mary, I found a photograph of you, in Lord Ravensbourne's drawer.'

She stood stock still, her face frozen.

'I think you know the one I mean.'

She swallowed and made an attempt to speak, but stopped. She kept her eyes fixed on the table, her hands bunching up the dishcloth she'd been using to dry the teacups.

She cleared her throat. 'Where is it?'

It was in my handbag, but I didn't think I would tell her that.

'At home. The police were searching the office, you see. I didn't think you'd want them to see it. Mary, does Tom know what Lord Ravensbourne did to you?'

She looked up, lashes wet. 'Why, are you going to tell him? Blackmail, is that it?' She threw the dishcloth to the floor. 'Well, you won't get a penny from me. I've no secrets from Tom.' She glared at me. 'Blooming cheek of it, coming here with flowers. I knew there was something.'

Oh, heavens. 'Of course I don't want money. I just wanted to tell you.' This was all getting rather awkward. 'What with Lord Ravensbourne's death… it would make rather a strong motive, you see. If Mr Butcher had known about it.'

'Motive?'

'Well. For murder.'

She laughed, then stopped and gave me a strange look. 'You're serious. Are you working for the police, or something?'

I decided it was time to come clean. 'I'm a private detective, Mary. I was brought in by Miss Waddon, to investigate the death notice sent to Lord Ravensbourne. And now I'm trying to find out who killed him.'

'Good heavens.' She sat down, ignoring the kettle that was whistling away in the background. I took it off the hob and filled the teapot.

'So you were pretending, all the time? Right from the interview.'

'I'm afraid so.' I set a cup of tea in front of her. 'I wanted to find out who had sent the death notice. I thought I could only do so if people didn't suspect me.'

She laughed again. 'You should have asked me, then. That was Mr Pyke and Mr Maltby. Pair of idiots, messing around like schoolkids. I bet they're pleased he's dead.'

I stared at her, my turn to be surprised. 'You're right, I should have.'

'I slipped it onto his desk for them. And I was jolly glad when I saw how much it rattled him,' she said. 'He hated anyone taking the mickey out of him. He pretended not to care, but it hurt. I could see that.' Her tone was full of venom.

I remembered his tearful fury in St Bride's, and could well believe it.

'Mary, I hate to ask this. But the police might want to talk to you eventually, and they'll ask.' Once they'd discovered Belinda was not their murderer. 'Where were you at midnight on Monday?'

She stared at me again. 'I was here, at home in my bed. And jolly pleased not to have to be hanging around Fleet Street till all hours.'

'Alone? Or was Tom here?'

I saw confusion on her face. A moment of uncertainty, calculation.

'He had a meeting,' she said, reluctantly. 'Something to do with the union. I told him, it sounded dodgy. But he said it was important, some Russian bloke coming to talk to them all at the Red Lion pub.' She took a sip of tea. 'I expect that Bill Mead was there. He can vouch for Tom, can't he?'

Chapter 44

By the time I finally got back to Bedford Square, I was exhausted. I went to report to Mrs Jameson, but Graham said she had gone out to dine with a friend.

'We'll have supper in the kitchen,' he said. 'Come down when you're ready.'

I was looking forward to a cosy cup of tea in the kitchen by the fire. But when I walked down the back stairs, Frankie was waiting for me, her stance belligerent as a boxer and her face flushed with fury.

'Bill Mead's been pinched by the police,' she said accusingly, as soon as I pushed through the door.

'What?'

'Bill. You told them where to find him, didn't you? You betrayed him.' Her fists were clenched, and she looked as if she might take a swing at me.

'Don't be silly. I didn't know where he was,' I said, backing away.

'Well, someone told them to start looking at the Red Lion. And they found him, all right. He'd been sleeping in the attic room there.'

Oh, goodness. My call to Inspector Carfax seemed like days ago.

'Well, I didn't know he was there!' I exclaimed. 'I just knew there was a meeting there on Monday night. Anyway, Belinda Ponsett saw him after she'd seen Lord Ravensbourne dead, and they've arrested her. So, they'll let him go now, won't they?'

Frankie gave a mirthless laugh. 'You don't have a clue, do you, Marge? The police don't care whether Bill had anything to do with Lord Thingummy's death. The whole plan for the general strike is in ruins. Bill was setting it up with the dockers and the transport workers. They were meeting representatives of the miners on Monday night. Now they're all being charged with sedition. All thanks to you.' She shook her head in disbelief.

'Now then, Frankie.' To my relief, Graham came through from the butler's pantry carrying a couple of bottles of beer. 'What's all this about? That's no way to talk to Miss Marjorie.'

'She told the police about Bill's meeting,' said Frankie. 'She's nothing better than a copper's nark.'

That hurt. Frankie and I had been through fire together in the course of Mrs Jameson's investigations, and although we disagreed about politics, we'd become close as sisters.

'Calm down,' snapped Graham. 'Don't say things you'll regret.' He sat at the table, hands on his knees. 'And you'll have me to contend with, too, Francesca. I told Marjorie about the meeting. My sister had heard about it from her husband. It wasn't the best-kept secret in London, was it?'

Frankie turned on Graham. 'She didn't have to tell the blooming police, though, did she?'

'I jolly well did,' I exclaimed. 'Bill Mead had been missing since Lord Ravensbourne's murder. And he'd talked about putting a bullet in his head just a day or two earlier. What was I supposed to do?'

She shrugged. 'You should have sent him a message. I'd have taken it.'

I stared at her in disbelief. 'When I asked you about Bill Mead, you said you didn't know him. And now you know all about the meeting and were prepared to take messages to him?'

'I know people that know him. That's all.' She kicked the table. 'But there was a lot of work went into that meeting. Setting it up and all.'

'I bet there was,' said Graham. 'Bringing some communist trouble-maker over from Russia, from what I hear. Spreading trouble, setting up honest men to lose their jobs.'

I collapsed in a chair by the fire and wished they would stop shouting. Bedford Square was my sanctuary from the world, the place I felt safest. Graham and Frankie were my best friends; Mrs Jameson the best employer I'd ever had. We felt like a family; the comfortable family that I'd had before the War, which had fractured and fallen silent after my brother's death.

Nothing seemed to be going right with this case. I thought of poor Belinda Ponsett, locked in a cell and wondering if Beatrice would ever believe her innocence. Reginald Pyke, eaten up with envy of his former friend, and now lying cold in a mortuary. Mary Butcher, accusing me of blackmail.

And here we all were, fighting like cats in a sack.

'Stop it,' I muttered. 'Stop it, stop it. Please.' Tears began to trickle down my face, and I felt weary to the bone.

Mrs Smithson came in and opened the oven to remove a handsome fruit cake.

'What's all the to-do?' she asked. 'Miss Marjorie, whatever's the matter? It's not like you to be down-hearted.'

I wiped my eyes. 'I'm just very tired,' I said. 'My head hurts. I think I'll go and lie down.'

Graham and Frankie stopped arguing.

'Have a glass of milk and a bit of cake,' Mrs Smithson said. 'I'll cut you a slice as soon as it's cooled. That'll set you right.'

I shook my head. 'I don't want to eat anything,' I said. 'Sorry. It looks lovely, but I'm not hungry.'

Mrs Smithson and Graham exchanged a worried glance.

'You're poorly,' said Graham. 'We should call Dr Francis.'

'No need.' I hauled myself up, then climbed the stairs to my little bedroom under the eaves at the top of the house. I crawled under the covers, pausing only to kick off my shoes, and closed my eyes.

Chapter 45

It was quiet when I woke. All I could hear was the purring of Sooty and her kittens, curled up on my feet. I was thirsty and hot, and my head felt rather muzzy.

I sat up and lit the lamp, then drank a glass of water and checked the alarm clock. It was eleven o'clock. I groaned, remembering I was still wearing my day dress. I supposed I'd better get changed into my pyjamas, hang up my crumpled dress and see what I could do about the creases in the morning.

Once I was out of bed, I realised I was hungry. I hadn't felt like eating much at lunchtime, and I'd gone to bed without supper. I remembered the cake that Mrs Smithson had made – a big Dundee cake, plump with raisins and orange peel, topped with toasted golden almonds. Before I got undressed, I'd go down and have a slice, maybe with a cup of warm milk.

I pulled on my shoes and tiptoed down the back stairs. All was quiet in the kitchen. The big gas range radiated warmth, the scrubbed deal table gleamed white in the moonlight, the fire was banked up, so the embers glowed softly. One of the kittens had accompanied me downstairs and curled up before it, giving an enormous yawn that showed its little pink tongue. I bent to scratch behind its soft ears.

The cake was in a tin on the pantry shelf, every bit as

magnificent as I'd remembered. I cut myself a decent-sized wedge and set the milk pan on the stove top to warm.

I thought of Belinda Ponsett, locked up in Cloak Lane. I'd spent the night in a police cell in France the previous autumn, after being wrongfully accused of causing a man's death. I remembered how frightened I'd been; the cold comfort of a bare bench to sleep on and the hostility of the other women in the cell. Worse, not knowing what was going on outside, whether anyone was working to help me get free, how long I would be incarcerated and isolated from the world. Mrs Jameson was convinced that Belinda Ponsett was innocent. But if she was, then who had killed Lord Ravensbourne?

I shivered and sipped my warm milk. My handbag was still beside the chair by the fire, where I'd dropped it earlier in the evening. I picked it up and rooted through. The photograph of Mary caught my eye. I stared at it. She'd said she had no secrets from her husband. Did that mean he knew?

I imagined how I'd feel if someone I loved, my new wife, had been assaulted like that. And if Tom had been at the meeting in the Red Lion, he too had been near the *Post* offices on the night of Lord Ravensbourne's death.

As Mrs Jameson often said, no-one knows if they are capable of murder until the circumstances arise. I thought with unease of the newspaper cutting about Julian Jameson's accidental shooting.

And there, neatly folded in the side pocket of my handbag, was the pile of notes from Lord Ravensbourne's desk. His final critique of his last edition of the *Daily Post*. I'd read through them before and hadn't seen anything of any import. But now I spread them on the table again.

Criticisms of headlines, pithy rejections of photographs

– especially photographs of women over the age of thirty. Shrewd comments about what 'the man on the promenade at Blackpool' might think about various news stories.

And one note that didn't seem attached to a news story or cutting: 'Call the Foreign Office'. Was it an instruction to investigate the situation in India, perhaps? Reginald Pyke's leader came back to me, the words about Lord Curzon and the Foreign Office needing a steady hand on the tiller.

But Lord Ravensbourne wasn't interested in overseas news. He liked stories about murders, or aeroplanes breaking speed records, or film stars getting divorced. The sort of thing he imagined the man on the promenade at Blackpool reading with relish over his morning tea and toast. It was Mr Pyke who argued for the *Daily Post* to give more prominence to world affairs. So why did Lord Ravensbourne think someone needed to call the Foreign Office?

I thought again. The leader that Mr Pyke had written referred to 'matters in King Charles Street' being in disarray, according to 'reliable sources'. Which reliable sources? The stack of invitations in his desk had included several to receptions at the Foreign Office. Who had sent them?

My head started to fill with wild possibilities. Had Reginald Pyke uncovered some sort of plot? Perhaps it was something to do with the situation in India, and he'd told Lord Ravensbourne about it. Or, more likely, something to do with Russia. There were Russian refugees all over London, former aristocrats who had fled their country estates in a scramble to escape the fate of the Romanovs. And now there were Soviet agents, like the one who met Bill Mead and Tom Butcher in the Red Lion, infiltrating British society.

What if someone – someone connected to a communist plot

– had shot Lord Ravensbourne, and then later Mr Pyke? Could it have been the Soviet agent who'd been conveniently nearby in Fleet Street?

I shook my head. It seemed fantastical. But there was something in it, I felt sure. Something that might lead to the discovery of whoever killed the two men – both shot through the head like the Tsar of Russia.

Who else might be at risk? If Mr Pyke had a contact at the Foreign Office, he might be next. I imagined a Soviet assassin creeping from the Red Lion pub, making his way through the foggy streets with a gun in his pocket, heading for Westminster. I couldn't call the Foreign Office myself and say that someone there was in danger. Unless I knew who to call. Mr Pyke's Foreign Office contact.

I'd seen no sign that Mrs Jameson was home from her dinner yet, or I'd have consulted her. I groaned. There was only one thing to do. I had to go back to Mr Pyke's office and look again, now that I knew what I was looking for. After the dreadful row I'd had with Frankie, I didn't feel I could ask her to come with me. Also, if this was a communist plot, Frankie might think I should cover it up.

I pulled on my coat and hat, then put the papers back into my handbag, checking my purse for coins. I could take a taxi-cab to Fleet Street, search the office for the name of Mr Pyke's contact. If I found something, I could call the police so they could warn him.

I scribbled a quick note in case anyone found my empty bed and worried about me. Then I wrapped a scarf around my nose and mouth, let myself out of the kitchen door and stepped up into the foggy night.

Chapter 46

The night watchman at Whitefriars Street barely raised his head from his copy of the *Racing Post* as I went through to the lift, telling him I had to check on some papers for the morning.

The presses roared in the basement, churning out hundreds of thousands of copies of the *Daily Post*. Outside, vans stood ready to whisk them to the railway stations for distribution to every corner of Britain, so that men on the promenade at Blackpool, Brighton, Skegness and Southend could read them with their tea and toast in the morning.

Only a couple of night shift men were left in the newsroom, drinking tea and playing cards as they kept an eye on the newswires. They were too intent on their game to take any notice of me. I went into Reginald Pyke's office, lit the green-shaded lamp and shut the door firmly behind me. I set the note from Lord Ravensbourne in the middle of the table, next to the draft of the spoof editorial about Curzon and India. Then I pulled out the drawer in which Mr Pyke had kept all his invitations and extracted those which referred to events at the Foreign Office.

They were mostly for evening receptions: drinks parties to celebrate visits from overseas dignitaries or newly appointed diplomats. The stiff white invitation cards had the gilded royal crest at the top and RSVP at the bottom, but no individual's name. 'The Foreign Secretary requests the pleasure of the company of Mr Reginald Pyke at…' was the format.

However, one card had a pencil scribble on the back.

'Hope you can make this one, Reggie. I wouldn't mind a quiet word,' said the note. My antenna twitched. That must be Mr Pyke's contact. The signature beneath the note was hard to read: George? Gerald? But there must be hundreds of people working at the Foreign Office. How could I find out who sent the invitations?

The door opened.

'Marjorie, whatever are you doing tucked away in Uncle Reggie's cupboard?'

The incongruous figure of Theodore Waddon lounged in the doorway, wearing black tie and tails. His bow tie was skew-whiff and the white gardenia in his buttonhole drooped a little. He pulled off his pale kid gloves.

'Frightful night to be out. I've been to the opera. It was ghastly – nobody I knew there at all, so I had to listen to the caterwauling alone. Completely wasted evening. You're not still working, dear girl? You look like you've slept in that frock.' He twitched his tie straight.

I blushed, knowing that I had done just that. 'I remembered something in your father's notes. I was trying to understand it,' I said.

He pulled out the second chair and extracted a gold case from his jacket pocket. 'Care to smoke? I know what you fashionable females are like. No? Don't mind if I do, I hope.' He lit a slim cigar and leaned back in his seat as fragrant smoke billowed around his head. 'Bliss. There's something so deliciously decadent about setting fire to a two-sovereign

Cuban cigarillo, don'tcha think? Rolled on the thighs of dusky maidens, what?'

I tried not to cough. At least the cigar had a pleasant smell, unlike the rough tobacco the reporters made their roll-up cigarettes from. For a moment I had a flash of memory, opening the door to Lord Ravensbourne's room and finding him dead. I frowned. What had brought that back?

'Actually,' I said, 'you might be able to help me. You work at the Foreign Office, don't you?'

He laughed. 'Well, I'm supposed to. Never really got the hang of this work business. But go on. Try me.'

'Do you know who this would be?' I showed him the scribbled note on the back of the card. 'It's an invitation to an event at the Foreign Office, three weeks ago. Whoever it is says they want to talk to Mr Pyke privately. I can't read the signature. George, do you think, or Gerald?'

Theodore held out his hand and I passed it to him. He scrutinised it. 'No idea. Dreadful scrawl, ain't it? Why do you want to know?'

I tried to explain. 'I think Mr Pyke knew something connected to your father's death. And I wondered if it was to do with the Foreign Office, because of the note Lord Ravensbourne left. Here.' I showed him. '"Call the Foreign Office." But your father never cared about foreign news stories. That was more Mr Pyke's interest. I wanted to find out who he knew at the Foreign Office, and why it was important.'

Theo tossed the invitation back onto the desk. 'Not sure I follow you, Marjorie. All going a bit over my head, I'm afraid. But I'll tell you what. You help me out, and I'll ask around at the FO tomorrow. It shouldn't be too hard to find out who puts together the guest list for those dreary receptions they try to drag one along to.'

I beamed. 'Would you really? That would be so helpful. Thank you, Mr Waddon.'

He laughed, tapping ash into Mr Pyke's ashtray. 'It's Lord Ravensbourne now, don'tcha know? But you can still call me Dora. Not that you ever do, I notice. Why is that, eh?' He leaned across the desk and picked up my hand, idly circling the ink smudges on my fingers.

I felt my colour mount and hastily withdrew my hand from his caress. 'It wouldn't be proper,' I said.

His smile was teasing. 'Proper? Good God, I hope not. I've never tried to be proper, and I don't mean to start now. All right, then.' He reached into his other pocket and pulled out a sheaf of paper. 'I've promised to help you out tomorrow. Now you can return the favour. Remember those scavenger hunts?'

I groaned. I wasn't sure I was up to thinking of more clues tonight.

'How many do you need? I can work on them in the morning, when I've had some sleep,' I offered.

He looked at his watch. 'Too late, my girl. They'll have set off already. I was hoping to find my sister or someone, but you'll do nicely, if you have a decent coat to put over that frightful frock. Vicky's let me down – she claims to have the 'flu or something dreary. I'll drive, but I need someone to help me work out the clues and get the loot.'

He pointed to the first one. 'Come on, Marjorie.'

'But I can't…' I stopped and read it. 'An inverted pyramid from César's Palace. I mean, that one's quite obvious, isn't it?'

'Is it? I told you, I'm a chap of limited intellect. That's why I need Vicky, only she's missing in action. What is it, then? Something to do with the pyramids? Wait! Cleopatra's

Needle!'

I sighed and scribbled the shape on my notepad. 'Look. An inverted pyramid – a cocktail glass. And from The Ritz cocktail bar. César Ritz was the founder of The Ritz hotel. You could get one of those quite easily, I should think.'

He jumped up with surprising energy. 'Come on, then. Your carriage awaits, Cinderella. I'm taking you to The Ritz.'

Chapter 47

'Oh, no.' I tried to protest, but he held out my coat and hustled me into it.

'Don't be a drag, Marjorie. We'll have a quick glass of champers, you can help me work out the next clue, and then I'll drop you home. And tomorrow I'll find out who the mysterious Gerald or George is, and what he wanted with Uncle Reggie.'

I hesitated. But it would be lovely to go back to The Ritz. When I first began working for Mrs Jameson, she was living at the hotel while she hunted for a house to lease. I had got to know the staff well. Indeed, our butler Graham had worked at The Ritz, and had been tempted away by Mrs Jameson when she bought the house in Bedford Square.

'All right,' I said. 'Just one drink.'

Outside I was rendered speechless by the beauty of the sports car that sat by the kerb, hemmed in by newspaper vans.

'Like the motor, do you?' Theodore patted the gleaming black paintwork of the brand spanking new Bentley. 'She's called Betsey. Does a ton if you push her. Hop in, then.'

I stepped onto the running board and squeezed into the passenger side. The red leather racing-style seat fitted snugly around me. The hood was up, but it was going to be a chilly ride.

'Here.' Theodore reached between the seats and pulled out a dark, divinely soft fur throw. 'Wrap yourself up in that. Vicky won't mind. It's a foul night.'

I cocooned myself in Lady Victoria's mink, while Theodore pulled on thick sheepskin gloves, pressed the starting motor button, blasted his horn to clear a path through the vans, and purred up Whitefriars Street.

We drove through the heart of London, the streets busy even on a cold February night, along Strand to Trafalgar Square, catching a glimpse of Nelson looming through the fog, high on his column. Then up Haymarket, past the Theatre Royal and across Piccadilly Circus where the illuminated advertising signs glittered.

Theodore drove recklessly, expecting everyone else to get out of his way. The policeman at Piccadilly Circus gave us a particularly hard stare as we shot across the junction. Then we were sailing along Piccadilly, past Hatchards, Fortnum and Mason and the Royal Academy, before he pulled up with a squeal of brakes in front of The Ritz.

He killed the engine and jumped out of Betsey. 'Keep an eye on her, will you?' he asked the green-uniformed porter, who'd immediately sprung to attention.

I grinned at the boy's look of surprise as he recognised me. 'Evening, sir. Evening, Miss Swallow.'

'Good evening, Charley. Lord Ravensbourne and I are having a quick drink. Is Frank behind the bar tonight?'

It was Theodore's turn to look surprised as we strolled down the thick floral carpet. 'They know you here?'

I smiled, relishing the feeling. 'They certainly do.'

The cosy Rivoli Bar was darkly glamorous with smoked

glass and red lacquer like a Chinese box. I led the way to the onyx-clad bar.

'Miss Swallow! How wonderful to see you back. Will you have your usual?' Frank the barman had become a great friend during Mrs Jameson's stay at the hotel. He reached for the silver cocktail shaker. I quailed for a moment. But perhaps a French 75 was exactly what I needed to perk me up.

'Thank you, I will.'

'Same for me, old chap,' said Theodore. He pulled out a chair for me at one of the little tables. 'I say, Marjorie. You're a dark horse, ain't you? First name terms with the barman at the Rivoli, and he knows your favourite cocktail. Do you live a double life?'

I remembered he still thought I was an ordinary secretary. 'My previous employer stayed at The Ritz when she first arrived in London,' I explained. 'So I was here quite a lot.'

He gave me a sidelong glance. 'What a very dull explanation. I shall continue to believe you are an international woman of mystery, travelling the world solving crimes and staying in the best hotels. A secret agent going undercover, what?'

I laughed, although this was a bit too close to the truth for comfort.

'As you prefer. Now, talking of solving mysteries, what's the second clue on your list?'

He showed me. An acorn from a grim stone oak grown in the City of London.

'There must be hundreds of oak trees in the London parks,' I said.

'Ah, but they're not in the City.' Theodore shook his head gloomily. 'I've been caught out that way before. Anything that says City of London means it has to be in the square mile. And grim stone must mean some specific oak, or they wouldn't have put it.'

I mulled this over. It was a quirk of London's history that the various districts had grown up independently, only merging together as they grew. The City of Westminster, where Parliament sat, was quite distinct from the City of London, which even today was a separate body with its own Lord Mayor, run by its own corporation. That's why the City police was separate from the wider London Metropolitan force.

'I can't think of any big parks in the City,' I said. 'I suppose there must be some oak trees around, although I don't know where.' The City of London was the business district. Apart from the newspapers of Fleet Street, it was mostly devoted to banks, insurance companies, lawyers and stockbrokers. It wasn't known for leafy squares or recreation parks.

'Your drinks, My Lord.' Frank delivered the cocktails to our table. 'Will there be anything else?'

I gave my most winning smile. 'I shall need to borrow this glass for a while. When I've finished my lovely cocktail, of course. Is that all right, Frank? We're on a scavenger hunt. Lord Ravensbourne is very keen on them.'

I took a sip, the bubbles from the champagne tickling my nose. The warmth from the gin and the sharpness of lemon filled my mouth. Delicious, and exactly what I'd needed. I began to feel a bit brighter.

Frank gave a doubtful look at Theodore, who was tackling his French 75 with enthusiasm, then glanced towards the door. 'Of course, Miss Swallow. Whatever you like.'

I followed Frank's gaze. The hotel manager, Mr Peterson, stood in the doorway to the bar with Charley, who was pointing our way. Mr Peterson glided over to our table, adjusting the cuffs of his immaculate evening suit.

'Good evening, Lord Ravensbourne.' He didn't look pleased to see him. 'May I have a word regarding your account?'

'Business after pleasure,' said Theodore. His easy smile almost covered the irritation in his tone. 'I'll call by the desk when I've finished my drink.'

'I would prefer to speak to you right away, sir. My staff have orders not to serve you further until the account is settled,' said Mr Peterson, firmly.

'Oh, really, what a lot of rot,' Theodore protested. He shifted uneasily. 'Come on, old chap. It'll all be sorted out this week.'

But Mr Peterson wasn't going anywhere. With a sigh of irritation, Theodore got to his feet. 'Shan't be a tick, Marjorie. You can work out that clue, while you're waiting.' He handed me the sheaf of paper.

'Oh dear,' I murmured.

'Sorry about that, Marjorie. He's skipped out on his bill too many times,' confided Frank. 'What are you doing with him, anyway? You're not in his usual crowd.'

I yawned and turned to the list of clues. 'It's work. Well, sort of. I have to help him solve this clue, then he's going to drop me back at Bedford Square. We're investigating his father's death. He's helping me find something out.'

Frank glanced at the list of clues. 'Anything I can help you with?' When Mrs Jameson was staying at The Ritz, Frank and I had enjoyed doing puzzles together when he was off duty. He liked word games and riddles in the newspapers. I explained about the acorn and the City of London.

He grinned. 'It's obvious, isn't it? The Corporation of London owns the forest up in Essex. I grew up near there, in

Chingford. There are plenty of oaks in Epping Forest.'

'Oh, well done.' I frowned. 'But what's this business about a grim stone?'

Frank looked very pleased with himself. 'Grimston's Oak. It's famous. Named after Robert Grimston, a cricketer who lived locally. It's very old, they say, hundreds of years. It's near the Cuckoo Pits, north of Connaught Water. Anyone around there knows it.'

'Oh.' I scribbled his words down.

'You're not going there now, are you?' Frank looked alarmed. 'It's not a good idea to go up there in the dark.'

I smiled. 'Don't worry, I won't. Lord Ravensbourne will drop me home after this.'

'So long as he does.' Frank returned to his station behind the bar, and before long Theodore was back, all smiles again.

'Nothing a little inheritance can't sort out, what! Now, how're you getting on with that clue, Marjorie?'

I explained about Epping Forest and the Grimston Oak. I should have told him that Frank had worked it out. But I wanted Theodore to be impressed with my airy display of knowledge.

He was. 'I say, good show. Clever old stick, aren't you?' He swallowed down the rest of his cocktail. 'Now, drink up. I'd better drop you home, before I head up to Epping. I've a long drive ahead.'

Chapter 48

I snuggled into the fur wrap, the glow from my cocktail warming my stomach. The engine purred as Theo drove north up Bond Street, past high-end jewellers and fancy florists. I could get used to this, I thought. Zipping around London in a Bentley, wrapped in mink and nipping into The Ritz for late-night cocktails.

I yawned, the motion of the road and the effects of the gin conspiring to make me sleepy as Theodore swung into Burlington Gardens, past the back entrance to his home in the Albany buildings and towards Regent Street. It had been a very long day.

'Have a nap,' suggested Theodore. 'You look exhausted. I'll have you home in a tick.'

I closed my eyes and drifted off.

When I awoke with a start, it was to darkness, except for the headlights sweeping the empty road ahead.

'Where are we?' I looked around in panic. We had left the fog behind, and stars glittered diamond-bright in an onyx-black sky. A waning moon illuminated hedgerows either side of the road and bare fields beyond. My neck felt stiff, and my feet were freezing. 'Why didn't you drop me off?'

'It seemed a shame to wake you,' said Theodore, carelessly.

'You don't mind, do you? We're almost there.'

I said nothing for a moment. I did mind, very much, but there didn't seem to be anything I could do about it. The road was deserted, and I could see no signs of houses. We must have been driving for ages.

'Why don't you pick an acorn from any old tree and tell them it's from the Grimston Oak?' I asked. 'There must be some oaks in these hedgerows.' I just wanted to get home.

He gave me a shocked glance. 'Couldn't do that, dear girl. Cheating. One should never cheat in a game when there's nothing to lose but one's reputation.'

My own reputation was not going to be enhanced by spending half the night alone in a motor car with the new Lord Ravensbourne, especially given his father's record with secretaries. I remembered with unease Theodore's hand on mine in the office. I'd been stupid to agree to go for drinks with him. I supposed I'd been too caught up with the glamour to think properly.

'Where are we?' I asked again.

'Lord knows. We've just passed a place called Woodford Green, if that means anything to you. Dashed long drive, isn't it?'

He was smoking a slim and fragrant cigarillo. Again, the smell triggered something in my memory. The moment when I'd opened the door to the late Lord Ravensbourne's office and found his body.

I stared at the cigar for a moment, then pressed my eyes closed to think. The late Lord Ravensbourne had been sitting in the chair at his desk, a glass of brandy at his elbow and his scribbled notes in front of him, a half-smoked cheroot in the ashtray. The smell of cigar smoke had lingered in the cold air, mingling with the stench of blood.

Lord Ravensbourne's cheroots did not smell fragrant like Theodore's cigarillos. They were pungent, eye-watering. I tried hard to remember. The window had been open when we left; closed when I returned. And the smell… the smell of tobacco smoke in the morning had been pleasant, not harsh.

Someone who smoked fragrant tobacco had been in Lord Ravensbourne's office after Beatrice and I had left for the night.

I opened my eyes onto the dark road ahead and thought very hard indeed. Had Theodore been in Lord Ravensbourne's office that night? If so, I was in trouble. Real trouble.

'Perhaps you could pull over next time we come to a village,' I said, lightly. 'I ought to find a public telephone box to call home, or they'll worry.' I tried a self-deprecating laugh. 'Sorry to be a nuisance.'

He glanced at me. 'We'll be there soon.'

He drove on, a long, straight road flanked now by woodland. A few isolated gates indicated the presence of houses, but there were no lights showing at this time of night. A petrol garage flashed past, and I called out again.

'I say! What about that?'

He said nothing, but kept driving. I scrutinised his profile. There was little sign of the aimless idiot about him now. His jaw was set, his eyes fixed on the road, his mouth a straight line, lips compressed.

'Where are you taking me?' I asked, trying to keep my voice steady.

'Ranger's Road is the closest we can get to the oak.' He flashed me a grin, quite unlike his usual pleasantly vacant smile. The grin of a wolf leading Red Riding Hood deeper into the forest. 'Why, do you have somewhere else to be?'

A lodge stood at a crossroads just ahead, a gas lamp illuminating the sign outside: Warren Hill House.

'Stop, please,' I called. 'I want to get out.' He was driving much too fast for me to make a jump for it.

I wound down the window, dug in my handbag for my purse, and dropped it into the road as Theodore wrenched the wheel around and pulled the car sharp left. Someone would find it and see my name in my pocket book. But would they find it in time?

Ranger's Road was so narrow that twigs from the trees tapped against the hood on the Bentley. Theodore roared along, swung left again and pulled into a lay-by.

'This'll do.'

My mouth was dry. I tried to remember the basics of my jiu-jitsu self-defence. If only I'd kept up my practice, as Frankie had urged. If only Frankie herself was here now, not miles away asleep in Bloomsbury.

'Get out, Marjorie. We walk from here.'

I did as he said, wondering how quickly I could run back to Warren Hill House for help. He was tall, he'd outpace me. If only I hadn't been wearing my ridiculous heeled shoes, if only I'd had my sensible lace-up boots. He switched off the headlamps and I was engulfed by blackness, my eyes struggling to penetrate the dark.

I backed away from Theodore and stumbled into a puddle of freezing water that engulfed my feet. I staggered to regain my balance.

When I looked up again, my eyes beginning to accustom themselves to the dark, Theodore was pointing a small handgun straight at me.

Chapter 49

'Please put that down, Mr Waddon.'

'I think we should use proper titles, don't you? As we've reached the formal stage of the evening. You can call me Lord Ravensbourne.'

I held his cool gaze. 'Do you really work at the Foreign Office, Lord Ravensbourne?'

He laughed. 'Oh, you're still worrying about that, are you? Well, I did say I'd help you find out. Gerald, who sent that invitation to poor Uncle Reggie, is the senior civil servant in the India department. I'm supposed to be working for him. I did go in once, a month or so ago. Didn't care for it much, so I left at lunchtime. Never got around to going back.'

I licked my lips. 'Well, I don't suppose that matters, then. Would you mind not pointing the gun at me?'

He ignored my request. 'I didn't think anyone would mind me cutting the job, but Gerald told Reggie. They were old school pals; Reggie more or less got me the berth after Oxford. Anyway, Uncle Reg let something slip to Pater. My father was terribly boring about that sort of thing. There was all this nonsense about stopping my allowance and cutting me off without a bean if I didn't go back, which would have been tiresome.'

'You shot your father for your inheritance?' I tried to keep my voice calm. The longer he talked, the better my chances of finding a moment to escape.

'Well, not straight away. I had to do a bit of scene-setting, don'tcha know?'

'The death notice?'

He laughed. 'That was Vicky's idea. Clever girl, Lady Victoria. And terribly loyal. She rather fancies being Lady Ravensbourne one day. It was a useful distraction, and I liked the idea of rattling the old man before delivering the coup de grâce. And he was rattled, hey? You saw him that day.'

I shivered. Theodore's light tone was so at odds with the darkness of what he was saying.

'He was worried, yes. And sad.' I remembered him in St Bride's church. 'He was sorry that people didn't respect him. I think he felt unloved.'

'Ha!' Theodore's handsome face crumpled for a moment, and I wasn't sure whether he was laughing or crying. 'As if anyone could love him, after the way he'd treated us. And our mother.' He looked at me with the eyes of a small boy still grieving.

'I was at my ghastly boarding school when Mamma died, you know. Pater didn't even come to get me himself – he sent Uncle Reggie. And he sent me straight back after the funeral.'

All this time I had my eye on the gun. His hand was dropping, and I was calculating whether I could dive for it and disarm him without getting hurt.

'Pater thought I was little better than an imbecile. Although, you see, I'm not quite as intellectually challenged as everyone thinks. I discovered it can be rather useful, being thought an idiot.

'A bullet through the brain was the least my father deserved. And I did enjoy seeing him frightened at the last.'

With these words, he snapped to attention again and raised the gun until it was pointing at my head.

'Now, Miss Swallow, if you could just pick that up, we're ready to go hunting. Lots of acorns in this woodland, I should think.' He grinned at me, teeth flashing white. 'That' was a shovel propped up against the side of the Bentley. 'Go on. You don't expect me to carry it, do you? I'm not an agricultural labourer.'

I picked it up. It was heavy. The rough wooden handle snagged on my gloves and the iron blade was encrusted with dried mud.

'After you, Miss Swallow.' He gestured towards a narrow path, an opening among the dark trees and bushes.

'I'd be more comfortable if you weren't pointing the gun at me,' I said. My teeth had begun to chatter.

He sighed. 'Well, we'd all be more comfortable if you hadn't gone snooping around and making unfortunate enquiries, Miss Swallow. I shall be an absolute wreck tomorrow, and Lord Beaverbrook is holding a masked ball for his daughter's birthday. Now, come along and don't be tiresome.'

Mouth dry, I walked along the path, carrying the spade awkwardly before me. Could I use it as a weapon? Turn suddenly, swing it at his head? But he was too close; I could hear his breath right behind me. He brushed something cold – the gun? – against my cheek.

'Don't do anything rash, will you? I'm a much better shot than my father.'

After a few minutes we emerged into a clearing. The half-moon rose above the tree-tops, casting an eerie light.

'What do you think? Are those acorns underfoot, Miss Swallow?'

I said nothing, catching my breath.

'Well, you can check while you dig, I suppose. Perhaps I could plant one with you. Would you like to be marked by an oak tree? Very English. I think I'd prefer something a bit more exotic, myself. A pomegranate tree, perhaps, or a fig.' He paused. 'Go on, then. Start digging. I'd help you, but I can't risk getting mud on these trousers. There won't be time to have them cleaned before tomorrow's party.'

I was shivering so hard I could barely grip the shovel. I stuck the blade into the soft leaf mould. Oak leaves, wet and dark, disintegrating into mulch. I had to keep him talking. Sooner or later, he'd let his guard down.

'I understand why you didn't like your father,' I began, turning over a spade full of mulch.

'Nobody liked Pater,' he exclaimed. 'The world is a much happier place without him. That nice Mr Beeching gets to be editor, Bea gets to run the company as she was born to do, and I can enjoy a peaceful life.'

'But I don't understand why you killed Reginald Pyke,' I continued. 'I thought you liked him.'

'Ah, well. That was rather sad, I admit. But Uncle Reggie knew about the Foreign Office business, and Pater's threats. It was only a matter of time before he realised I'd sent him that note suggesting the death notice. It took me ages, typing the thing out, you know. I don't know how you girls manage it. Anyway, I didn't want him blabbing about any of it to the rozzers. He's terribly indiscreet.

'I paid a taxi driver to tell them he'd taken Reggie straight from the Press Club to his home. Then it was just a matter of hanging around the police station until they let him go. He was surprised to see me in the gardener's old clothes, but I told him I'd been sleuthing around and found something down by the river. He was curious as a cat, of course.' Theodore chuckled, then gave me a sharp look. 'He didn't feel a thing, you know. Didn't even see the gun. I was very careful.'

His coldness terrified me. If he'd cold-bloodedly shot his favourite uncle to save his own skin, there was no way I would be able to talk him out of killing me. I remembered how genuinely upset he had seemed after viewing Reginald Pyke's body. Had it all been an act, or had he been shocked to be confronted with the results of his actions?

'And then you pushed him into the river,' I said. 'And planted the gun in Miss Ponsett's desk, so the police would blame her for the murders.'

He shrugged. 'Bea will thank me for it one day. Ponsett is such a pill, don't you think?' He inspected my shallow hole. 'Can you hurry up a bit? We don't have all night. Well, you do, I suppose. But I'd like to get to bed before dawn.'

'Did you plan to kill me tonight?' I asked, my voice breaking. Sweat was cold on my forehead and neck. The hard ground beneath the leaf mould was heavy to shift and my arms ached from the weight of the spade.

'You, dear girl? No, not at all. I don't do this for fun. That'd be rather gruesome, don'tcha think? I went to rootle through Uncle Reggie's office to see if he'd hung onto anything incriminating. And there you were, laying all the cards out on the table and asking me what they meant.

'Well, I had to do something, didn't I? You'd have worked it out, you or that female who's been hanging around the office with you. Mrs Jameson. Not, after all, one of Bea's suffragettes, but a private detective.

'Luckily, I had the list of clues in my pocket. Vicky and I wrote them last night for next week's hunt. I suppose we'll have to change them now. Don't want half of our gang showing up in Epping Forest and poking around in the undergrowth, hey?'

He laughed. I found myself joining in, a nervous titter. I'd started to feel rather peculiar, as if the top of my head was detaching itself from my body. I was so tired. Perhaps I should sit down for a moment and rest.

I heard, faintly and then more distinctly, the sound of a motor car in the distance. It was the first I'd heard since we stopped. Hope flared. Perhaps I could distract him, run to the road and flag it down.

But he heard it too.

'I think we'd better get this over with. Step down into the hole, Marjorie, and look towards that tree. I promise, you won't know a thing about it.'

I stared at him. No. No, this couldn't be happening. All my confidence, my belief that I would somehow be able to overpower him and escape, deserted me.

'Please,' I whispered. 'Please, Theo. Don't. I'm not ready.' That was all I could think. I wasn't ready to die.

He sighed. 'Well, you can stay there, of course. It would just make it neater. Save me from spoiling my trousers.'

'I don't want to die,' I shouted. I flung the spade at him as hard as I could and threw myself to the ground as a shot cracked above my head. I curled into a ball, rolled over, and then launched myself towards the nearest bush. If I could just get to cover, I might be able to make a run for it. But my legs were so heavy, it felt like running in a nightmare.

'Don't be tiresome.' He walked towards me, as relaxed as if I'd merely refused to make him a cup of tea. 'It'll just take longer, and I might not get a clear shot at you. Wouldn't want to have to wing you first.'

I curled under the bush, prickling myself on the spiky holly leaves. I squeezed my eyes shut and thought of my parents, Freddie, Mrs Jameson and my friends at Bedford Square. I wondered if they would ever find out what had happened to me.

A gun cracked, and a bright light flooded my brain.

Chapter 50

'You blighter! You hit me.'

I opened my eyes. Theodore was clutching his arm and staring back into the clearing. A light beam – an electric torch, I supposed – swung back and forth across the scene. Theodore's gun lay on the ground in front of me, inches from my face. I gazed at it blankly for a moment, then grabbed it.

'Marjorie?' Mrs Jameson hurried over, her pistol trained on Theodore. 'There you are, dear. Thank goodness. Are you hurt?'

I couldn't speak. I gazed up at her and shook my head.

'That's good. Inspector Carfax and Sergeant Voles will be here soon. I'd better keep this one under control, before he makes his escape. Lord Ravensbourne, step away from Marjorie. Do you have a handkerchief to bind up your arm? Let me see. There's not much bleeding, fortunately.'

'You've ruined this suit,' complained Theodore, taking a handkerchief from his trouser pocket and dabbing at the wound in his upper arm. 'I warn you, I shall expect you to pay for the damage.'

A small, slim figure hurtled across the clearing and threw herself down beside me. She had my purse in one hand.

'Marge!' Frankie grabbed my shoulders, as if she didn't

know whether to hug me or shake me. 'You blooming idiot! What were you thinking, going off on your own with him? If it hadn't been for that barman at the Ritz, you'd be a goner. He telephoned Graham to check you'd got home all right. We didn't even know you'd gone out.'

I sat up and my face crumpled. 'I'm sorry.' The tension of the past hour overcame me, and I began to cry, painful sobs that hurt my chest.

'Aw, don't do that.' She gave me a little shake, then hugged me fiercely. 'You'll set me off. I thought I'd never see you again, you daft ha'porth.'

I tried to smile. 'Even if I'm just a copper's nark?'

'Even if you're a blooming idiot who doesn't understand politics. You'll get it, one of these days.' She glared at Theodore. 'It's toffs like him you need to be worried about. Not union men like Bill Mead.'

I shut my eyes. They felt sore and gritty, as if I had sand in them, and my head ached. The cold from the earth had seeped into my joints. I felt like I might never get up again.

Another car engine sounded, approaching rapidly then stopping with a squeal of brakes.

'I say, Mrs Jameson,' said Theodore. 'Would you pass me my gun? I'd like the opportunity to take the gentleman's way out. A trial would be such a public spectacle, much as one likes to entertain the masses.'

'I don't think so. We've already seen what you are prepared to do with a gun,' she said.

'Well, likewise. On my honour, I won't hurt anyone else. I don't think prison would be very congenial, for one of my sensitivity. It's not so much the noose, you know, as the unpleasantness beforehand.' He ran a finger around his collar, where a pearl stud gleamed.

Mrs Jameson gave a bland smile. 'Nonetheless, I should prefer to see justice take its course. I understand you attended an English public school, Lord Ravensbourne. I imagine that prison will not be such an unfamiliar experience.'

His face twisted in distress, as the two policemen crashed into the clearing, shining a bright torch on proceedings.

'Is that what happened in Rome, Mrs Jameson?' Theodore murmured. 'Justice taking its course?' Then he seized the spade, swung it at Mrs Jameson and knocked the gun from her hand. He sprinted into the woods with surprising speed.

'After him, sergeant!' shouted Inspector Carfax.

Sergeant Voles crashed through the undergrowth in pursuit. It was not a long chase. He brought Theodore down in a rugby tackle. We heard him bellow a caution, then drag him back, handcuffed to his own wrist.

'Well done,' said Mrs Jameson. 'I'm sorry I gave you the trouble of a chase, Sergeant Voles. I thought I had him pinned down.'

The sergeant grinned. 'No trouble. I like a bit of exercise now and then.'

Inspector Carfax regarded her with exasperation. 'Why on earth didn't you wait for us to arrive? Did you inflict that gunshot wound, Mrs Jameson? You know I'll have to report it. You might be prosecuted.'

'She saved my life,' I said, staggering to my feet with Frankie's help. 'He was going to shoot me dead, and bury me.' I showed him the gun, and pointed to the hollow at the inspector's feet. 'He made me dig the grave myself.'

The inspector stared at me, at the hole, then at Theodore. His usually smooth hair was rumpled, his evening suit ripped and muddied. He'd lost the gardenia from his buttonhole altogether. He stared back, defiant as a small boy caught in some minor act of cruelty by a schoolmaster. For once, he had no urbane quip to offer.

'Take him to the car,' Inspector Carfax told Sergeant Voles. 'Let's get this animal locked up.'

Exhaustion claimed me. I sagged at the knees, and needed Frankie and Mrs Jameson to help me walk to the Lagonda. They wrapped me in a blanket and laid me on the back seat.

I slipped into a feverish sleep long before we arrived home to Bedford Square. I had a vague impression of Graham lifting me out of the car and carrying me into the house. My mouth was dry and hot, but I was chilled to the bone. I managed a few sips of warm milk, then slipped back into troubled dreams where I was digging and digging, knowing that if I stopped for a moment I would die.

Chapter 51

For the next few days, I floated in and out of consciousness. I was dimly aware of Dr Francis's worried face, tangled sheets soaked with sweat, a racking cough that left me gasping for breath. But mostly I slept.

I finally awoke to bright sunshine pouring in through tall windows, and screwed up my eyes against the light. I still ached, but the hot and cold feeling was gone. My mouth was dry, my lips parched.

'Marjorie? Are you awake?'

'Mum?' I opened my eyes again and struggled to sit.

'Don't try to get up.' My mother put an arm around my shoulders, plumped a pillow behind me, then raised a glass to my lips. I drank the cool water gratefully, breathing in the familiar smell of her, the comforting softness of her breast.

'Take it slowly.' Her voice was steady. 'Feeling better, now? That nice Dr Francis said the fever broke last night.' She squeezed me to her. 'You gave us all a nasty fright.'

I lay back on the heaped pillows and looked around. This wasn't my attic bedroom. And I certainly wasn't in my old room at my parents' flat over the shop. The elegant geometric-patterned paper on the walls, the black and silver silk curtains and the mirrored dressing table made that clear. I was in the best guest bedroom in Bedford Square, and the room was full of flowers.

'What day is it?' I asked. My chest still felt tight.

'Tuesday. You've been in bed since Thursday. You had that nasty influenza that's been going around, Marjorie. And I must say, it was just like you to carry on when you were getting ill, rather than tucking yourself up in bed with a hot-water bottle. I've told your Mrs Jameson, she needs to take better care of you. It's not right, expecting you to work all the hours that God sends. You'll wear yourself out, and then where will she be?'

Goodness. I tried and failed to imagine Mrs Jameson receiving a scolding.

'She sent us a telegram on Thursday afternoon, because the doctor was so worried. I've been here ever since. Mrs Jameson has been very hospitable, I must say. Lovely house, isn't it? Everyone has been so kind, especially Mr Hargreaves.'

A telegram. I could only imagine the panic that had caused. All through the War we had lived in fear of a telegram, until it finally came.

'Your father closed the shop early on Saturday, he was that worried about you. He's left Sidney in charge now – that's the new boy, he's very good. He's the grandson of Mrs Maybridge, who used to have the sweet shop next door to the haberdashers and does the cleaning rota at St George's.'

'Is Dad here now?' I asked, before I got the full history of Sidney Maybridge and his family. My father never closed the shop early. Even when the telegram had come about my brother, he'd stood stolidly behind the counter for eight hours, staring into space.

'He's just outside. But are you sure you're up to seeing

anyone? Dr Francis said you were to drink some beef tea when you woke, and he's left a bottle of cough elixir for you. Two teaspoons a day.'

'I'd like to see Dad.'

She bustled to the door. 'Come in, Dave. She's awake now. But don't go over-exciting her. I'm just popping down to the kitchen.'

My father sidled in, his white hair plastered down and his hands clasped over his ample tummy. He was in shirtsleeves with his best black waistcoat and silver watch chain.

'How're you feeling, Marjorie?'

I held out my arms and he embraced me gingerly.

'I thought I was going to lose you,' he whispered.

'Oh, Dad. I'm so sorry.' I wondered if he knew just how close he had come to losing me – and not to the 'flu. I squeezed him tight.

'Well, no point crying over spilled milk.' He took the chair next to the bed, pulled out his handkerchief and blew his nose loudly. 'I'd better be getting back to the shop, now you're on the mend.'

I took his hand. 'Thank you for coming. It means a lot.'

He squeezed my fingers. 'You're still my daughter, for all you're so grown up these days. Now, listen to me. You know that pianist chap who used to come around on Sundays?'

My heart contracted. 'Freddie.' Both my parents had been upset when I refused his proposal at Christmas. I knew how much they liked him.

'Nice young man, even if he doesn't have a steady trade. Well, he's been calling here every day since you've been sick. He brought those flowers.' Dad pointed to the bouquet on the dressing table. Pink roses, my favourites. 'He wants to see you, before he goes. But only if you're well enough.' Another trumpet into his handkerchief.

'Before he goes where?'

'America. His band has been asked to go and play in New York, then all over the country. A big tour, he says. He'll be gone for the best part of a year.' Dad squeezed my hand again.

'I see.' Freddie had always wanted to go to New York, to visit the jazz clubs of Harlem, and to travel to New Orleans and hear the marching bands. But a year seemed like a very long time. 'Thanks, Dad. Tell him I'd like to see him, too.'

A smart rap on the door, and Mrs Jameson put her head around.

'There you are. Sorry to disturb. Your mother said you were looking a bit brighter today.'

My father jumped to his feet as if the chair had delivered an electric shock to his bottom.

'I'm just on my way, Mrs Jameson. Thank you for all you've done for Marjorie. I need to be getting back. Much obliged.' He sidled out the door.

Mrs Jameson sat in the newly vacated chair and patted my hand.

'It's a relief to see you sitting up again. Inspector Carfax will be pleased. He needs to take your statement. Thankfully my evidence was sufficient to keep Ravensbourne locked up over the weekend. But he wants to talk to you as soon as you are well enough.'

I nodded, although the thought of giving a statement was daunting. Wednesday night felt like an age ago. Had it really happened? It seemed like a dream – the car, The Ritz, the forest. And the digging, the endless digging, in the woods.

'Theodore Waddon shot his father,' I said, dragging my mind

back to his casual confession. 'And Mr Pyke. Uncle Reggie. Because of the Foreign Office.'

'I know. By the time you left on Wednesday night, I was certain that Theodore was the murderer. I just needed to piece together enough evidence for the police.' She gave me a severe look. 'I hadn't expected you to take him for cocktails and head off to Epping Forest on a midnight jaunt.'

'I'm sorry,' I said. 'I wasn't thinking properly.' I supposed I'd been getting sick already, and it had muddled my brain. It was hard to explain now why it had felt like a good idea.

My mother came back in with a bowl of broth on a tray, steaming hot and smelling savoury. My stomach rumbled appreciatively.

'Now then, Mrs Jameson, I'm going to have to ask you to let Marjorie be. She needs to get her strength up. I'm sure you understand.' Mum stood over my employer.

'Of course.' Mrs Jameson knew when to make a graceful retreat. 'Just let me know if I can help with anything, Mrs Swallow.'

Chapter 53

Jonathan Field, now a senior reporter at the *Daily Post*, forged a path through the crowded, noisy bar. Journalists roared stories and jokes at each other as waiters darted between them. Someone was banging away on the piano with more enthusiasm than skill; a parrot was squawking in the corner. Underfoot the floor was strewn with sawdust.

'Are you sure this is the right place?' called Mrs Jameson, although she was laughing at the chaos.

'You bet, Mrs Jameson. We have a private room upstairs,' shouted Jonathan. 'We couldn't let you leave Fleet Street without experiencing the Old Cheshire Cheese.'

We filed up the stairs into a dark wood-panelled room where gas lamps glowed against the mahogany, illuminating framed prints of caricatured politicians and sportsmen. A fire crackled invitingly and the long wooden tables were set with venerable silver and crisp white napkins.

Henry Beeching rose from a seat at the far end of the central table.

'I'm so pleased you could join us, Mrs Jameson. Hello, Marjorie. Have a seat. Welcome to the best chop-house in London.'

The Old Cheshire Cheese, he explained, had been serving

ale and chops to journalists since the seventeenth century, and little about the place had changed during that time.

'Charles Dickens wrote about the Cheshire Cheese and dined here often, as did Samuel Johnson, who lived just around the corner. Your countryman, Mark Twain, came here whenever he was in London, Mrs Jameson.

'Miss Waddon apologises that she is unable to join us. She has much to do to stabilise the situation across Ravensbourne Amalgamated Publications, as I'm sure you will understand. The shareholders have demanded an extraordinary general meeting.'

'I quite understand,' said Mrs Jameson. 'Please send her my regards.' Beatrice Waddon had kept relations with Bedford Square to the bare minimum since her brother had been charged with the murder of her father and uncle, and with attempting to kill me. She had, perhaps surprisingly, settled our bill promptly.

We sat around the long table, Mrs Jameson next to Henry Beeching, who had been officially confirmed in his role as editor-in-chief of the *Daily Post* and *Sunday Post* titles. Charles Maltby, although still nominally editor of the *Daily Post*, had been on sick leave since his arrest and release. He too had been stricken with 'flu, and his recovery had been much slower than mine. Mr Beeching had proposed we join him at this dinner, supposedly to celebrate the life of the late Lord Ravensbourne but in reality to mark the passing of the newspaper group into a new era.

Belinda Ponsett waved at me from her seat the other side of Jonathan. She looked much happier; the pinch of constant anxiety had lifted from her brow and she'd had her hair cut in a becoming shingled style. Although she remained editor of the *Women's Bugle*, she no longer lived with Beatrice in Gordon Square. Beatrice had, rather decently, set up a trust to run the *Bugle* as an independent publication, and taken out a lease for separate offices. Belinda's salary as editor was sufficient for her to rent a pleasant room in a shared house in Mecklenburgh Square. Frankie told me she'd taken Belinda to the Caravanserai Club, where she'd been rather a hit.

'Can't believe you didn't realise,' Frankie had told me, scornfully. 'She'd been in love with Beatrice Waddon since the day they met, but Beatrice hated the whole idea. Poor Belinda needed some serious cheering up.'

Looking around the room, I could see Mary Butcher at the printers' table. Tom had a protective arm around her slim shoulders. I was glad I had finally burned the photograph of her. Bill Mead, not surprisingly, turned his back as soon as he saw me. He'd been released for lack of evidence, although he was unlikely to forgive me for tipping the police off about his hiding place. He and the other printers were chatting away with Frankie, who had elected to sit with them rather than at the top table.

The waiters poured claret and set down plates of lamb chops, glistening and golden, with buttery mashed potato and creamed spinach. My mouth watered. I'd regained my appetite in the weeks since my illness, and was completely in agreement with the doctor's instructions to build up my strength.

'Mrs Jameson, I know we can't report anything until the trial. But just between us, how did you know Theodore Waddon was the murderer? Completely off-the-record, of course.'

My employer laughed. Jonathan was never off-duty.

'It was simply a matter of piecing together the elements in a methodical way, beginning as always with motive and opportunity,' she said. 'Who benefited from Lord Ravensbourne's death? That was always my starting point. His employees were quite likely to have played a trick on him, as Mr Maltby and Mr Pyke did with the death notice. But murder is a serious business, and none of the staff was likely to benefit materially from his death.

'Belinda Ponsett had much to lose, and at one time I considered her a suspect. But when someone tried to frame her by planting a gun, I knew she was innocent.' She smiled at the young woman. 'Beatrice, Theodore and Lady Ravensbourne were joint beneficiaries of the will, and stood to inherit millions. Miss Waddon and Lady Ravensbourne lacked opportunity, as Miss Waddon took a taxi home with Marjorie and Lady Ravensbourne was at home with her children and servants.

'But Theodore had by his own account been driving around London all night, with only his thrill-seeking girlfriend for company. A young woman, as anyone who reads the newspapers will know, whose family has a noble title but empty coffers. Lady Victoria had plenty of incentive to collude with Theodore Waddon.'

She took a sip of wine. 'I had dinner with a friend at the Foreign Office, who told me that Theodore had walked out of his job on the first day, which I assumed had jeopardised his inheritance. He was also the most likely person to have met his uncle from the police station. And he planted that gun in Belinda's desk, right under my nose.'

Jonathan shook his head in admiration. 'Inspector Carfax said it must have been female intuition.'

'No such thing,' said Mrs Jameson, crisply. 'If the inspector improved his powers of observation, and used logic and the principle of Occam's razor, he would not have to rely on intuition, female or otherwise.'

He frowned and took out his notebook. 'Sorry, whose razor? Is that a police term?'

Mrs Jameson, always delighted to know more than anyone else in the room, shook her head. 'Look it up, young man. Look it up.'

The chops were followed by sponge pudding spotted with plump raisins and half-drowned with custard. Just as I thought I'd burst, the waiters brought around the savoury course: the Cheshire Cheese's famously pungent cheese on toast.

'I'll have that if you can't manage it,' said Jonathan, who had disposed of his in two bites.

'No, you won't. I'm under strict instructions to put on weight,' I told him. But after a nibble, I had to admit defeat. 'Go on, then. Take it.'

Freddie Gillespie had left for America with the All Stars Jazz Orchestra two weeks ago. I'd been sad to see him go, but a tiny bit relieved as well. We'd made each other no promises; he'd not repeated his proposal of marriage. He had adventures ahead of him, and so did I. Perhaps we'd meet again when he was home.

After the speeches, during which Henry Beeching tactfully managed to praise the late Lord Ravensbourne's business acumen without mentioning his son's murderous tendencies, the tables were pushed to the side of the room. One of the reporters began to thump a popular tune out of the old piano, and the printers sang along.

'Care to dance?' asked Jonathan, holding out a hand. I usually loved dancing but shook my head. The previous week, he had asked me to go to the pictures with him. I liked Jonathan, and I liked going to the pictures, but was in no hurry to get into an understanding with another man.

'I'm too full of dinner,' I told him, laughing. He turned to Belinda Ponsett instead and whirled her onto the floor.

Mrs Jameson came and stood beside me, her eyes resting on Jonathan. 'You do know that plenty of women carry on working after they marry, don't you? Especially these days.'

I glanced at her. I wasn't going to take advice on matters of the heart from my employer, especially after what I'd learned about her late husband's death.

'My mother, for a start,' I said. Mrs Jameson, like many rich women, was apt to forget that most working women had little choice in the matter. 'And lots of women remain single, too. Especially these days.'

'There you are, then,' she said. 'And now that I've had the pleasure of meeting Mrs Swallow, I can see where you get your grit. I like her very much.' She grinned. 'Even if she did like to make sure I knew who was in charge of your wellbeing.'

'Perhaps,' I ventured, 'we could leave that to me, now?'

'Perhaps. If you promise to take better care of yourself, and fewer risks with your safety. I can't be there to rescue you every time.'

I smiled demurely. I'd promised that before. I didn't seek out risk, but it was an inevitable part of working as a detective. I wasn't going to turn down opportunities or stay meekly at home. I would go back to my jiu-jitsu training, so I was better prepared to deal with the unexpected.

'I'll take care of myself, I promise.'

'That's good. There's a stack of letters from clients in the office. It's time we got back to work.'

Back to work. I felt the familiar tingle of excitement. I couldn't wait.

***

Enjoyed Death On Fleet Street? Get the prequel novella free.

So how did a nice girl like Marjorie Swallow end up working for a lady detective? And what happened during her interview for the job, in the Palm Court at the Ritz Hotel?

Subscribers to my Readers Club can download a free novella, *Murder At The Ritz*, which answers these questions and more! Readers Club members get a monthly newsletter with news about my books, events, exclusive short stories, recommendations and special offers. Sign up at my website, annasayburnlane.com.

I loved writing *Death On Fleet Street*. If you enjoyed reading it, I would be so grateful if you left a quick review to let me know. I read all my reviews, and they make a huge difference in helping other readers find new books to enjoy.

Historical note

When I started work as a journalist on local newspapers in the early 1990s, almost all the British newspapers had already left Fleet Street. Digital printing had overtaken the inky-fingered printers and we no longer used 'hot metal' linotype machines or compositors. But the romance of Fleet Street still had an allure.

Fleet Street was the home of British newspapers. The first print shops in London were set up in the street from around 1500, serving the many lawyers' chambers. The first daily newspaper, the *Daily Courant*, was established in 1702, with offices above a Fleet Street public house. The link between journalists and the British pub goes back a long way! Before long, the nascent newspaper business was headquartered in the street of ink.

Fleet Street was in its heyday in the early years of the twentieth century, with dozens of newspaper offices (and pubs). The 'media barons' Lord Northcliffe and Lord Beaverbrook set up mass-circulation popular daily newspapers, including the *Daily Mail* and the *Daily Express*. Just about every household in Britain took a daily paper, and competition between them was fierce.

Most newspapers printed several editions a day, and if they wanted to protect an exclusive story so that their rivals couldn't get it, they would print a 'spoof' first edition, holding back the exclusive until the first edition had been printed and left on the newspaper trains for the regions. The London final would then carry the real story, 'scooping' the opposition.

I made good use of the British Newspaper Archive for my research, and many of the news stories discussed in the *Daily Post* are taken from real newspaper reports of the time. These include worries about the rising price of sugar, trouble in India, the bill to extend the franchise, the trial of 'Brilliant' Chang on drugs charges and the death of the poor lady who jumped off Westminster Cathedral tower.

Lord Beaverbrook's daughter Janet Aitken Kidd published a memoir, *The Beaverbrook Girl*, which gave lots of juicy details about her father. Beaverbrook, I hasten to add, wasn't anything like as unpleasant as my fictional Lord Ravensbourne, but I borrowed details from his life. He had a flat at the top of the Daily Express offices and frequently enjoined his staff to write for 'the man on the Rhyl Promenade'. Janet enjoyed a glamorous social life, including the occasional scavenger hunt around London.

I imagined the Daily Post building at the corner of Whitefriars Street and Fleet Street, where the real Hanging Sword Alley runs through the buildings to Salisbury Square. On my last visit, the entire block was a building site for an enormous new Salisbury Square development, and sadly the alley seems to have been swallowed up. It gained its sinister name from the sign hung up to advertise a fencing and sword fighting school!

There are many books about Fleet Street by former journalists. Arthur Christiansen's *Headlines All My Life* and Robert Edwards' *Goodbye Fleet Street* gave vivid impressions of working under the media moguls in Fleet Street's heyday.

Edwards described Beaverbrook as 'kind, brutal, considerate, selfish, honest, eccentric and a bit mad, but utterly sane in his judgement of newspapers.'

Best of all was my visit to the St Bride Foundation just off Fleet Street, which has a printing workshop where former Fleet Street printers tell tall tales of the old days. St Brides Church with its distinctive spire still stands next door, an oasis among the noise of the city. The church spire was the inspiration for the first tiered wedding cake.

If you'd like to find out more about the research behind my novels, look out for my Substack blog *The Stories Behind the Story*.

Acknowledgements

Thank you to Mick and Barry, former Fleet Street printers and now stalwarts at the St Bride Institute. Sorry I couldn't get your story about the pub piano into the book.

Thanks to the staff at the British Library, who did their best to help me locate the books I needed despite the difficulties caused by the cyber attack on the library.

Thank you to my fantastic editor Alison Jack and terrific cover designer Donna Rogers. You're the cat's pyjamas.

Thanks to my ace beta reader team: Christina, Rosalie, Radhika, Madeleine, Jean, Emma, Michelle, Cynthia, Candice, Victoria, Deborah and Dana.

About the Author

Anna Sayburn Lane is a novelist and journalist who writes historical mysteries and contemporary thrillers.

Anna studied English and History at university, then began her career as a reporter on a south London newspaper, later moving into medical journalism.

She published her first novel, the literary thriller *Unlawful Things*, in 2018, followed by *The Peacock Room* in 2020, *The Crimson Thread* in 2021 and *Folly Ditch* in 2022. *Unlawful Things* was shortlisted for the Virago New Crime Writer award and picked as a Crime in the Spotlight choice by the Bloody Scotland crime writing festival.

She later switched to writing historical murder mysteries set in 1920s London. *Blackmail In Bloomsbury* is the first in the series, featuring apprentice detective Marjorie Swallow. It is followed by *The Soho Jazz Murders, Death At Chelsea, The Riviera Mystery* and *Death On Fleet Street.* More to come!

Anna lives between London and the Kent coast.

You can connect with me on:

🌐 https://annasayburnlane.com

Subscribe to my newsletter:

✉ https://annasayburnlane.com/signup

Also by Anna Sayburn Lane

Step back into the roaring twenties with classic detective novels set in the jazz age. *The Riviera Mystery* is the fourth in the series featuring plucky apprentice detective Marjorie Swallow.

Blackmail In Bloomsbury (book 1)
Everyone at the party had a secret. Someone killed to keep theirs...

When a bohemian party ends in murder, there's no shortage of suspects. Half of Bloomsbury wanted Mrs Norris dead – but who wielded the knife?

Was it the handsome but troubled artist? The vivacious young actress? Or the aristocratic lady novelist? Marjorie and Mrs Jameson must find the true killer to save an innocent man from the noose. From the garden squares of Bloomsbury to the seedy backstreets of Soho, they navigate the glamour and peril of Jazz Age London in a thrilling story of secrets and lies.

The first in the 1920s Murder Mystery series, *Blackmail in Bloomsbury* will delight fans of Agatha Christie and classic crime.

The Soho Jazz Murders (book 2)
It's January 1923 and London feels dreary after the excitement of Christmas. So Marjorie is excited about meeting the American Ambassador's niece, a genuine 1920s flapper with a love of jazz, dancing and fun.

But their night out at Soho's infamous Harlequin Club comes to a tragic end. Soon Marjorie is working undercover as a dance hostess in the club to unmask the drugs gangs that threaten the West End. It's a perilous occupation - and there are more deaths to come.

The Soho Jazz Murders is the second in the 1920s murder mystery series, featuring the irresistible apprentice detective Marjorie Swallow.

Death At Chelsea (book 3)
Detective duo Mrs Jameson and Marjorie Swallow are called to investigate when a famous gardener suspects that someone is sabotaging her priceless lilies, ahead of the 1923 Chelsea Flower Show.

But soon it's not just the flowers that are dying. Rival gardeners, intrepid plant hunters and King George V himself are caught up in a poisonous bouquet with its roots deep in the mountains of Tibet.

The third in the Marjorie Swallow 1920s Murder Mystery series takes readers to grand country houses, dodgy pubs serving Covent Garden flower market and – of course – all the glamour of Chelsea.

The Riviera Mystery (book 4)

A September trip to the French Riviera sounds just the ticket for apprentice sleuth Marjorie Swallow. But when she steps aboard the famous Blue Train to the Mediterranean coast, she discovers this won't be an ordinary vacation.

Surrounded by diamond merchants, film stars and artists, Marjorie is swept off her feet by the beauty of the Côte d'Azur – and by one artist in particular. However, romance goes on hold when she's caught up in the aftermath of a death at a glamorous party.

Soon she's asking herself exactly who she can trust, as her investigations lead her down a twisting road of money, passion, art and murder.